THE
SEMBLANT

BOB GOODWIN

The Semblant

© Bob Goodwin 2022

ISBN (Paperback) - 978-0-6481533-8-2
ISBN (eBook) - 978-0-6481533-9-9

Cover design by Spiffing Covers

www.spiffingcovers.com

PUBLISHER
Bob Goodwin AUSTRALIA

I dedicate this novel to the 2022 Covid-19 vaccination team at Longreach & Central West Region of Queensland Australia. A more supportive, inclusive, and professional body of friends does not exist

Chapter 1

The First Discovery

It was eight in the evening, on Saturday the twenty-ninth of March, when fifty-three-year-old Madonna Knight knocked loudly on door number seventeen. Madonna was both the owner and manager of the Knight's Rest Motel at Ipswich, west of Brisbane. Her offsider and husband, Charlie, stood behind her slurping beer from a stubby, while swaying slightly from side to side.

'He's got the *do not disturb* on the bloody door,' he drawled.

'It's been hanging there for a day and a half,' said Madonna.

'Well, he might be a busy man. Wants a bit of peace and quiet, love.'

'He still owes us for today.' She knocked louder.

'Shit then… that's not fuckin' right.' Charlie, wearing only a pair of shorts and thongs, staggered forward and slapped the door with an open hand. 'Buster, you owe us some cash. Come on! Get your lazy arse out here.' He went to slap again but Madonna grabbed his arm.

'Let's just go in, shall we?' She showed Charlie the key.

'Well yeah,' he slurred. 'We're the fuckin' ones in charge.' He moved aside using the wall to keep himself upright. 'Yeah, this guy can get stuffed. Shitbag penny pincher.'

The lock clicked and Madonna entered. Charlie, using the door for support, followed.

The layout was standard cheap motel design - a double bed facing a wall-mounted television over a bench with a small built-in fridge below; an air-conditioner high on a wall near the bed; a wardrobe on the opposite side, and a small bathroom tucked away at the end of the room.

'Bloody cold in here,' said Charlie, giving a shrug before emptying the last of his beer.

Madonna flicked on the fluorescent light. It flickered for several seconds showing flashing images of a man sitting on top of the bed leaning against several pillows. He was caked with makeup. Most prominent were his bright red and smiling lips. The man had short black hair which was brushed back neatly. His eyes were wide open and he was wearing a frock with a yellow daisy pattern. His image illuminated on and off multiple times as the light flashed.

'Holy mother of God!' yelled Charlie, falling back against the open door, which flew back knocking out the door stopper, and allowed the handle to punch a round hole into the plasterboard.

'Hello there!' shouted Madonna.

The light stopped flashing and the couple stared at the man who was completely still. The top sheet and quilt were neatly folded over his waist, covering his legs and forearms.

'Sir!' she called out while taking some cautious steps forward.

'I think you mean, madam,' said Charlie with a chuckle, followed by a long loud burp. He rubbed his round belly while keeping an eye on the motionless person on the bed. 'Holy shit! Be careful there, love.'

Madonna stood next to the bed with a slight lean. 'I think he's dead.'

'Get his wallet,' said Charlie. 'Take what he or she owes us.'

'Really, Charlie! Is that all you can offer here?'

'Please your bloody self, woman. I'm getting a beer from his fridge. The damn poof can pay for that too.' He opened the fridge, grabbed a bottle and twisted the cap off.

Madonna took hold of an edge of the folded quilt and lifted. She squealed, dropped it, and bolted to the door, bumping her husband's shoulder on the way. Charlie wobbled, staggered, and fell to the floor, somehow managing to keep his beer upright.

*   *   *

Three detectives and one forensic officer, all wearing gloves and shoe coverings, inspected the scene. The officer was taking photos of everything, while the detectives looked at the ten severed thumbs and fingers from each hand, all lined up neatly on the bottom sheet adjacent to their respective hands. All the digits had been cut through at each joint, and the twenty-eight pieces were lined up like in readiness for reassembly. In a gap between his legs was a shrivelled, detached penis. Underneath the man was a small plastic backed sheet that had soaked up some of the blood-stained ooze.

In the bathroom it was a different story. The shower cubicle door had been removed and was propped out of the way against a wall. Every available towel was blood stained. The tiles on the walls of the shower and elsewhere were smeared and speckled with blood. On the shower floor were just a few remaining bloody streaks, forming arcs towards the drain where some thick clots hung, partially clogging the outlet. On the mirror, written in blood were the words – *NEVER HOLD ME AGAIN– DADDY.*

Chapter 2

Harmony – Part 1

On Friday morning, the eleventh of April, Harmony Magenta Lake sat across from Robert Williams, her psychologist. She was taking her time to respond to his last question.

'On a scale of one to ten.' Williams had asked. 'Ten being the absolute most important thing for you in your life – how would you rate this *urgent* need you have to get laid?' He reclined back in his office chair. A move that made the fifty-year-old's round belly become more prominent.

Harmony looked upwards as she thought about her life, her parents, her younger brothers, her job as assistant manager at Loretta's Fashion House. She moved her head side to side, brushed a hand through her blonde locks, pursed her lips, and pondered a little more. She thought of her friends – particularly her very best friend Crystal Whitlock, with whom she entrusted every secret. She thought back to her most recent boyfriend, Martin Jorgensen, who dumped her after she refused to let him ejaculate into her mouth – and that was now nearly six months ago.

'I'd say it's now reached a nine point nine out of ten. Well, at least... you know... it's six months since I last did it. That's pretty pitiful, right? Especially for someone of my age in their sexual prime.'

'What about your father's recent heart surgery? How does that rate?'

'Oh yeah. That's just dad. I care about that 'n all... probably about a four out of ten.'

'And your intentions to commence studies towards a Bachelor of Design in fashion, and desires to ultimately setup your own business?'

Harmony nodded. 'Yeah, I want that for sure… one day… who knows. Could be a six on your scale. But how can I even concentrate on studying or anything much else when my mind is so distracted… when my body is full of needs. Do you understand? Do you understand women's needs, Robert?' asked the nineteen-year-old.

Williams did his best to take a deep breath without making it too obvious, then redirected the question.

'I see many women here. I try to reframe some of their concerns and help them see alternatives. Help them see the priorities in their lives. You were referred to me by your GP who was of the opinion that you had some serious anxiety issues and some vague suicidal thoughts…'

'Well,' interrupted Harmony emphatically. 'If I don't get laid sometime soon, I'm sure I'll just fucking die!'

'I see, but that probability seems unlikely.'

'Huh… to you maybe.'

'Harmony, this is our third session. To be honest, I think there is little more I can offer you. I think the Valium prescribed by your doctor is unnecessary. It also seems you have set some personal goals which, no doubt, you will achieve in due course, and I would expect that any related anxieties would then subside… at least in the short term. It may be worthwhile sometime in the future that you start to look at the bigger picture, but that is something for you to consider down the track.'

Harmony sat forward, nodding slowly. Her eyes widened. 'I get it. I so, soooo get it. Thank you, Robert.'

The psychologist tilted his head to the side. 'What is it that you get, exactly?' He leaned forward too, copying her body language.

'I should go out and actively pursue my goals. Get laid.' She shifted her gaze upward. 'Find a nice horny guy and sort out my anxiety… the Tribal Moon… that's it.'

'What's the Tribal Moon?'

'Only the best nightclub in the city. The best place to pick up or get picked up. Thank you. You're the best. I gotta call Crystal.'

Robert Williams let himself fall backwards into the chair. 'Glad to be of service,' he sighed. 'You can show yourself out.'

Harmony was up and gone in a moment.

'God give me strength,' mumbled Robert with a glance up and a raise of his hands. 'Or at least send me a bottle of scotch.'

Chapter 3

The Tribal Moon

On Friday evening, the eleventh of April, Bentley Hopkin-Jones sat alone at a small table in a corner of the Tribal Moon Nightclub sipping a Bloody Mary. Since he had arrived, he had been studying two young women on the dance floor. The pair would dance for around fifteen minutes then take a margarita break, check out guys around the club, chat and giggle, finish their drinks then head back to the floor – plus or minus a bathroom break. Bentley thought of having both at the same time, but this would add a layer of complication that, for now, he was not prepared to deal with. A past failure at such a task, despite being many years ago, was still vivid in his mind.

The "Tribal" was set down some stairs off Edward Street in Brisbane City. The unassuming narrow doorway gave little indication of the large space below that boasted four bars, two dance floors, twenty private booths and a capacity for five-hundred guests. Tonight though, and for the past two weeks, the numbers were down to around three hundred, thanks to a tragic incident on the evening of Friday the twenty-eighth of March.

The club was constructed like a scene from a Mad Max movie with rusted metal beams and poles seemingly haphazardly stuck over the ceiling and walls, heavy rope netting dangling here and there, pieces of weirdly welded machinery mounted on walls, some of these machines pouring out fog into the masses below. There was heavy metal mesh around the four bars making them look like alcoholic fortresses. Beams of light danced in synchronicity to the music, changing colour and transforming the scene from the look of a hot desert to the appearance of the ice-cold Antarctic.

Gerry "Bones" Bonering was head of security — a no-nonsense, mountain of a man with a sarcastic, dry sense of humour. Generally, Bones would sit in his office scanning the bank of security monitors. Occasionally, depending on staffing numbers, he would have an offsider. Bones would leave every hour or so to do his rounds. He'd pull up some of the bouncers who were being overly friendly with the patrons, and grab hold of any customers, male or female, who looked likely to cause a scene. His preferred approach was to grab their jaw with one hand and twist them around to see his face and wag a large finger in front of their eyes. Words were rarely required. Even at sixty-two years of age, he had lost little of his fitness and strength over the past fifteen years working at the nightclub.

Bones strolled through groups of club patrons parting them like a shark through baitfish. For the third time he looked down at Bentley as he passed. The guy had been sitting on his own for over three hours, getting up only twice and returning both times with more Bloody Mary's. He had watched him on the monitor. His only engagement with others thus far had been to move some young people along who wanted to sit with him. Surprisingly, no one, not even some burly young men, hung around to argue the point.

Bentley was more than just handsome. His face was contoured to perfection with slightly raised cheeks, full, but not exaggerated lips, and an angular jawline decorated with fashionable stubble. His wide eyes were a deep, rich metallic blue. His jet-black hair was short on the sides with a small, brushed back wave at the front.

Bones stopped and towered over the seated Bentley. He noticed the black t-shirt under the dark denim jacket – something he regarded as a lazy dressing habit. 'You waitin' on someone?' growled Bones in his usual gravelly voice. Bentley's eyes widened. He nodded and smiled broadly, then raised his drink.

'A simple yes or no would suffice,' added Bones as he competed with the thumping bass of the dance music. 'This table seats four. You can wait elsewhere and allow others to use it.'

Bentley stood and gestured with his fingers for Bones to come closer. The big security chief was never one to ask twice or respond to such directions, but he couldn't help himself and felt compelled to comply. He lowered his head allowing Bentley's mouth to come within millimetres of his ear.

There were muffled whispers, interspersed with some clicks and pops, and some deep breathing sounds. Bones could feel the hot air from Bentley's mouth. After a few seconds the security boss stood and walked away continuing his rounds.

Minutes later he was back in his room checking the monitors. He looked at Bentley, recalling the encounter, but not any of the words that the guy had whispered in his ear. There had been times lately when he had questioned his own sanity – like finding his car keys in the fridge, making a coffee only to find another already half drunk, and time after time walking into the supermarket without any shopping bags. Maybe this was another sign, forgetting what a guy had said after just a few minutes. He gave a shrug and a deep sigh and told himself it was all okay, no big deal. Anyway, now he felt okay about the guy who had been sitting for hours and not sharing his table. Whatever had been said to him was enough to settle any seeds of annoyance. Bones shifted his attention to other patrons and other screens.

The young blonde and brunette needed a break. They stopped dancing and headed to one of the caged bars.

'You got your ID lady,' said the barman to Crystal.

'Every fucking time!' Crystal Whitlock flashed her ID. 'How do you think I even got in here?'

'Sorry. You look way younger than nineteen. You come to me for your next round we'll be all good.'

'This is a good thing, you know,' said Harmony.

'Is it?'

'Guys go for younger girls… and some girls like the young ones too. I know you're happy for either.'

'Well, nothing's happened yet… for either of us.'

'These are for you, ladies,' said the barman. 'Compliments of the lonely guy over there, sitting on his own.'

Bentley watched the barman speak to the girls, then tip his head in his direction. The barman pushed over two margaritas. The girls turned their heads as one and made eye contact. Bentley smiled back, displaying a perfect set of white teeth. A light beam settled momentarily across his face lighting him up.

'Oh my God!' gasped Harmony, the blonde and taller of the pair. She put a hand on her chest.

'Why haven't we seen him before now?' giggled Crystal, her companion.

'I thought you were hoping for a girl tonight?'

'This guy could change my mind,' gushed Crystal.

Bentley remained motionless, wide-eyed, and holding a fixed teethy smile, locked onto Harmony.

'I need to meet him.' With her drink in one hand, she headed towards the stranger.

'Go! Go! Get over there girl,' gurgled Crystal. 'This is your chance to sort out those silly anxieties. If you need more company, give us a wave.'

Harmony never heard her friend's words. In fact, she could hear nothing, not the music, not the crowd, not the clinking of bottles and glasses. She felt like she was gliding across the floor, drawn like a moth to a flame. As she closed in, her man rose slowly to his feet. Bentley's eyes widened further, now strangely filling out his eye sockets to nearly double their size. Harmony stopped in front of his face. He kissed her on the lips, his warm tongue quickly caressing her lower lip. They sat. Bentley's eyes returned to their previous size. The couple sipped their drinks, saying nothing.

In the security room, Bones nodded when he saw the slim lady in the body-hugging sequin miniskirt sit with his whisperer friend. For a fleeting second, he felt himself smile. He shook his head. 'He's no friend! Get a grip Bonehead!' he chastised himself loudly. 'Good grief, man!' He still had no recollection of any conversation following his asking the guy to move elsewhere.

Back at the table, Harmony was entranced by her man. She glided her hand inside his jacket as they kissed. Her fingers wandered over his t-shirt. There was a tight six-pack, firm pectorals – his nipples were large and erect. She wanted this man she didn't know and had yet to even speak to. It felt both irrational and inevitable at the same time.

Crystal looked warmly over at her friend, wondering if she should head over and join them. As Harmony nuzzled into Bentley's neck, Crystal smiled then raised her glass to the handsome man who now stared back at her while his neck was kissed and sucked by her best friend. She thought she noticed his neck become longer and shook herself, disengaging eye contact before quickly glancing back. Now his eyes appeared bright red. His white teeth looked like the teeth of a lion in his open mouth. She screamed and squeezed her glass which shattered in her hand. Crystal Whitlock toppled backward off the bar stool, hitting her head hard on the concrete floor. Within a moment two bouncers were at her feet. They cleared a space and attempted to rouse her. Bones arrived. He called triple zero. The four-person table a few metres away had been vacated.

Chapter 4

The Incident

2 Weeks Earlier

On Friday evening, the twenty-eighth of March, Bones sat with Tony Rizzo in the security room drinking coffee and watching the guests via the wall of nine screens, three of which rotated through several views of the club. In size, Rizzo, a thin wiry man, was the opposite to Bones, but in ability he was at least his equal. His running and boxing workouts kept him slim and agile. Rizzo had surprised many a Tribal Moon patron who incorrectly assumed he was a pushover.

With a flick of his head to one of the top screens, Tony Rizzo pointed out a tall, tanned lady on the dance floor. 'Check out this chick in the shiny hot pink skirt.'

'Ah ha. Seen her. It's a wonder how her tits stay in,' replied Bones. The lady in question wore a short dress with a shoelace tie around the neck. Two strips of the material swept across her breasts and behind her back, leaving the inner and lower half of each breast, and her abdomen, exposed. Her long blonde hair swung in time to the beat.

'I think she's danced with nearly every available dude in the place,' added Tony.

'And there's plenty of others that probably wish they were available. She's made herself the centre of attention.' Bones looked at his companion. 'You're looking a bit keen yourself there, mate.'

'You never know,' said Rizzo with a nod and a grin.

'I'm thinking that droopy pointy nose counts you out,' said Bones in all seriousness.

'Fuck off. That's not nice.'

'The truth can be a bitch sometimes. Suck it up princess.'

Tony Rizzo just stared and shook his head. Both men refocused back on the screens. Tony slowly reached up and felt his nose.

Four young men were sitting at a table near the dance floor. They had started their drinking with beer but were now onto their second round of cocktails and contemplating some tequila shots. The group, along with many others, had been ogling and chatting, somewhat disrespectfully, about the tall scantily clad woman. Her dance style was a bit different. She writhed her body from head to foot while moving her arms in a fluid waving motion. The music pumped out Spirit Genie's upbeat song *Respect Love* – a favourite club track.

She's a callin' me, I can tell
Wanting it from me
Showin' me with those moves
Wantin' me in those grooves
Give her respect she's no ho…

'That is one real sexy dance,' said Viraj, 'I think it should be illegal.'

'I bet you wouldn't mind a bit of interracial though,' added Brian, the only one sporting a mullet. 'A bit of black shaft in that white snatch.'

'If I wasn't half pickled, I'd probably resent that remark,' laughed Viraj.

'What about you Johnny?' asked Gus, a man with untidy, straggly black hair and a round torso. 'Too hot for you to handle?'

'I think she is stunning,' said Johnny. 'Possibly the most beautiful woman I have ever seen in my life. You guys should listen to those song lyrics and show her a bit more respect.' Johnny was smiling, not taking his eyes off her, and moving his head this way and that, as other dancers obstructed his view.

'Listen to this guy,' scoffed Gus, looking around at Brian and Viraj. '*Stunning. Beautiful. More respect.* When all he wants to do is bury his face in her twat.'

'Mate, sorry to say, but she would eat you alive,' added Brian as he slapped Johnny on the back. 'And what's she gonna think of a bloke who throws up after every second drink.'

'I can't help that. I've been unwell. And at least I'm not maggoted like you ferals,' replied Johnny.

'You need staying power,' said Gus. 'Last week I hung on while Cheryl nibbled my dick for nearly fifteen minutes. Look at you. Mister Scrawny. You can't drive a six-inch nail with a tack hammer, mate. Or, in your case, a one-inch nail.' Gus laughed, rubbed his hand over his stomach then grabbed his genitals through his jeans and jerked them up and down.

'She's moving on again, guys,' said Viraj. 'She's dumped that flashy dresser guy mid song.'

'Fuck! She's heading this way boys,' exclaimed Gus.

The lady turned away from her dance partner and strolled, catwalk style, up to the table of the four young men. She scanned them all quickly. Three were already moving to their feet. She looked at the seated guy, a pale unshaven man with a rosy, red birthmark on his cheek in the shape of Tasmania. His hair was barely longer than a crew cut, and he looked the youngest, and definitely the thinnest of the four. She invited him to the dance floor with a smile and a come here finger. Johnny stood and moved around his friends.

'No fucking way! Fuck you Johnny!' yelled Brian. 'Don't worry boys she'll be back before you know it.'

Be nice to her. She deserves better
For you, forget it. She's a taken
Respect her and care for her
Love her and beware her …

In the security room the two men were still watching. 'Look at that,' said Tony Rizzo, as he shifted his attention from one monitor to another. 'Now she selects the least likely dude with the worst dress sense of anyone.'

'I've not seen her here before. Let's take a look at her ID,' said Bones. Everyone entering the Tribal Moon would be required to glance at the security camera and have their identification scanned into the database – no ID, no entry.

The lady in the hot pink dress took Johnny's hand and walked him across the dance floor to the opposite side then continued to a private booth. A moment later two guys and a girl scooted out of the private room. One guy still trying to do up his pants as he left.

The private booths at the Tribal Moon, were not entirely private. While there were no security cameras inside, there was no door on the narrow front entrance either. Half the booths had floor to ceiling walls, the others had half sized walls that you could stand and look over or into. The bouncers were under instruction to stick their head in from time to time. While sex acts and drug taking was not encouraged, all security personnel were unofficially told to turn a blind eye, providing no one was being hurt and all activities were consensual, and more or less, legal. True enough, there had been several overdoses that had required an ambulance. Bones argument was that it was better they do that here where there would be a quick response than out in a city street or park, and *touch wood,* so far no one had died. All the booths had a semi-circle of padded vinyl seating around a central low fixed table, suitable for up to seven people. Cushions of all colours and sizes were strewn around the area.

The beautiful lady pushed the young man onto the seat and leaned close to his ear. She made three pop sounds like a cork coming out of a champagne bottle, followed by a sharp click and two quick hisses like a pressure cooker releasing a burst of steam.

'Hello Medora,' said Johnny Randall. A feeling of absolute contentment and ecstasy drifted from his head, across his chest and to his groin. Medora lowered her head to his belt and undid it with her mouth, as easy as you might with your fingers. Her hand moved to his shoulder and pushed him back over some cushions. Her other hand undid his torn jeans. Johnny helped pull them down as best he could from his near horizontal position, most eager for her to continue. His boxer briefs were stretched out to their limit.

*   *   *

'Her ID says Medora Hammerstein,' said Rizzo checking an iPad. 'Age is... twenty-nine. Lives at Chermside. She's never been here before.'

'Hmm... get Joey to pop his head in there and check,' instructed Bones. 'Something about this doesn't feel quite right.'

Tony squeezed the black button on the side of a walkie talkie. 'Joey, spot check on cubicle three if you could, mate.'

On the floor, near a caged bar, Joey adjusted the small microphone dangling on a cord from an ear-piece. 'Booth three. Will do, Tony. Cheers mate.'

After twelve large steps Joey's squarish head popped around the padded entryway to booth three. He saw the woman leaning over the young guy's pelvic area. He nodded his appreciation on seeing her backside no longer covered by her skirt. Her head was moving up and down with her blonde hair stroking the young man's thighs as she moved. Joey smiled and moved away and squeezed a button on his headset. 'All good, Tony. The young dude's getting a head job. Half his luck. Cheers.'

*   *   *

Johnny looked down at Medora. Her tongue had slid out the side of her mouth. It had thinned and lengthened and was wrapped around his penis three times like a coiled spring. The tongue slid up and down on his shaft while her mouth created a wonderful vacuum on the head of his cock. Something deep in his brain told him this was odd, but something else told him this was the best feeling of his life. He was paused there, right at the intense moment of pre-ejaculation – stalled there in absolute paralysed ecstasy. The engorgement he felt bordered on pain, but a pain that somehow added to his pleasure. One thing he was sure of was that this was near double the erection he had ever had in his life.

For Johnny, time seemed to be in slow motion, and seconds felt like minutes as Medora worked her magic. Eventually she uncoiled her tongue and positioned herself over him. She lifted her G-string a little to the side and allowed him to slide into her. She clamped her pelvic muscles around him and made just three long and slow, up and down movements. Johnny exploded into her. His semen kept shooting and pulsating out of him. His testicles cramped up into his groin squeezing out everything he had.

Medora placed a hand on top of his nearly bald scalp. Her fingers spread apart, her hand stretched larger, as if made of rubber, until her grip was on his forehead, near his ears and the back of his head at the same time. She smiled through a mouth that had grown in size, with her lips protruding and growing wider with every second. Her neck became longer and thicker and took on a mottled green and black colour. The fingers on Johnny's head turned inward and shiny black claws pressed into his head as he remained swallowed up with the biggest and the last orgasm of his life.

Medora's hand spun one way and then the other in a semi-circular motion. Blood flowed into his eyes, over his ears and onto the cushions. Johnny felt the warmth of the blood flowing over him and somehow this became one with his orgasm. He was loving every moment. After only seconds the claws had cut through the scalp and bone. She removed the top of his skull. Her ever-growing, pouting open mouth descended onto the pink and grey convoluted brain tissue. Her lips extended even further engulfing the entire organ. Then she sucked. Johnny's eyes rolled up and his pupils dilated as he died with a smile fixed on his face. Medora's neck swelled and contracted as brain tissue slid through her throat. For twenty seconds she was in her own world of orgasmic delight. When she sat back up, a fine mist blew out from her mouth in a long, contented hiss. His skull was left an empty bloody shell. Medora's features slowly returned to normal. She repositioned her breasts in her dress. There was one final thing to do.

Bones and Tony Rizzo sat back, chatting about rugby, sipping more coffee and watching the monitors. 'Look, Bones,' squawked Tony. 'She's out and about again.'

Bones leaned forward. 'What's she got under her arm?'

'It's a fucking cushion. What's with that? And the dude hasn't come out yet.'

'Probably fallen asleep. Let's do a round and check ourselves,' said Bones. They both stood, straightened up their white shirts at the same time, and headed down a narrow staircase.

Bones was first into cubicle three. He flicked on a strong light from a small torch. 'Holy fuck!'

Johnny's body lay on the vinyl seat. There was one blood-soaked cushion supporting his neck and shoulders. He shone his torch around the booth and looked under the table, but Johnny's head was nowhere to be seen.

Rizzo peered in. 'Oh! Jesus! What the fuck, man?'

'Rizzo! No one enters or leaves this club. Lock the doors.' Tony Rizzo was staring. Stunned. 'Fuck, Tony. Move it. Now!'

'On it.' Rizzo finally turned and hurried away as bouncer Joey swaggered up with a quizzical look on his face. 'You, Joey, stand right here.' Bones pointed to the entryway to booth three. 'Keep onlookers away. I'm calling the cops.'

Joey glanced in. 'Fuckin' Jesus!' He covered his mouth, then stood blocking the entrance and looking outward at the crowd, some of whom were now pointing and looking in his direction.

Medora was already outside and walking briskly up Edward Street with the cushion cover containing the two parts of Johnny's head under her arm.

Chapter 5

Finding Medora

At seven o'clock on Saturday morning, the twenty-ninth of March, Detectives Jan Silverton and Clive Anderson entered the property of an old Queenslander in Rode Road, Chermside, on the north side of Brisbane. This was the address of Otto and Medora Hammerstein. Parked outside the home on the road were two police cars and six uniformed officers – just in case.

Silverton looked at the pictures once more as the pair moved along a narrow cement pathway towards the house. 'Has to be the daughter, surely. Pretty common for daughters and mums to have the same name.' She looked at the ID printout and the copy of the entry pic from the Tribal Moon.

'Yeah,' agreed Anderson. 'And she was wanting to stay off the radar. No birth registered. Not on any electoral roll. No credit card. Not even a fucking parking ticket, along with a bogus driver's license. Who gets away with that shit these days?'

The slender and younger Jan hopped up the four steps to the verandah. Four strides later she raised a black dragon door knocker and knocked three times. Clive Anderson had a hand on his Glock 22 under his jacket and stood half a step back and to the side. Jan knocked again.

The detectives heard footsteps then the sound of a large key turning the old door lock. The front door opened and before them stood an old man in a dressing gown and slippers. Anderson eased his hand a little way from his weapon.

'Can I help you both? I'm not interested in any of that religious guff. I'll tell you…' The old man paused on seeing the police badges and ID.

'Just a few minutes of your time if we could, sir,' asked Detective Silverton.

'You can take your hand off your gun, sonny.' He looked at Anderson who looked every day of his fifty-eight years, with a circle of short grey hair around a bald centre. 'I'm not a dangerous person.' The detective moved his hand completely from his jacket, coughed into his palm, nodded and gave a forced smile.

'Are you Otto Hammerstein?' asked Jan.

'I think you already know I am,' breathed Otto.

'Does Medora Hammerstein live here?'

'Is this some sort of sick prank thing?' he grumbled.

'No sir. This is her picture. Is she your daughter or some other relative?' The detective held up the A4 sheet showing the image of a blonde lady in a skimpy pink skirt. The wrinkly-faced man gasped and staggered backward. The detectives rushed in, managed to prevent his falling, and lowered him into a wicker chair in the hallway. He sucked in a few deep breaths as he slumped in the seat. The detectives squatted at either side of him.

'Can I get you a water?' asked Silverton.

He shook his head and waved a shaky hand. 'No, thank you. Let's sit in the lounge,' he puffed, some colour slowly returning to his cheeks.

Silverton lightly guided him to a recliner. The lounge was spacious and adjoined the dining room. All the furnishings looked old but in good order. The lounge sofa and two recliners were upholstered in a pale-yellow floral pattern that matched the padded dining chairs. The dining furniture was a dark polished timber with beautifully turned and sculptured legs and ornate carved sides. A shout bellowed from the front door. 'Anderson! Silverton!'

'We're fine, Geoff. Stand down. All's well,' Anderson called back.

'You guys bring a whole squadron or what?' asked Otto.

'We weren't sure what to expect. We're investigating a brutal murder,' said Silverton openly.

'That's sad, but I can't see how that has anything to do with me.'

'Sorry, I didn't mean to infer anything of the sort. However, we believe a lady who was using the name, Medora Hammerstein, may be able to assist us with our enquiries.'

'And you're telling me that the lady in the picture is the one you're looking for?'

'Yes, sir. And seeing it seemed to upset you. Do you know this person?'

'Can I see it again please?' The detective looked at him unsurely. 'It's okay. I'm sitting down now,' added Otto.

Jan Silverton moved a dining chair and parked herself next to the old man. Clive Anderson remained standing and wandered about the room checking out photos, vases and trinkets.

Jan handed the old man the photo. 'Is this your daughter?'

'It's not my daughter. We never had any children. What you're showing me here is a picture of my wife. At least this is her…' He tapped the picture lightly, 'This is her from sixty years ago.' He looked deeply into the image. 'You were such a stunner my darling. I was the luckiest man alive. She never had a dress like this one though… more's the pity I guess.' He glanced at Silverton then glided a dry scaly hand over the image. 'All the curves in the right places. What a life I had with you my beautiful Medora. Beyond forever, my darling.'

Anderson picked up a photo from the mantle shelf over the fireplace. 'Is this your wife?' he asked displaying the black and white picture of two people dressed to the nines and dancing.

'Yes, she was a great dancer,' said Otto shakily. 'Won prizes. That's her now near your elbow.'

'What? This?' The detective pointed to a ceramic urn.

'Yes, she was cremated three weeks ago.'

*   *   *

Silverton waved to the backup cops, signalling for them to leave with a nod and a thumb's up.

'What's your story, Clive? We should've known about the dead wife before we even left the office.'

'Sorry, I never thought to check the death registry. But no harm done.' Clive closed the gate behind them. 'He called me *sonny*.'

'Except, as far as detectives are concerned, we look totally incompetent,' she said strutting away and half looking back at him over her shoulder. 'It would have been a better start to have been offering the poor man our condolences right at the outset. They'd been together for over sixty years.'

'As I said, no harm done. And there's no sign of any young person living there. Mission accomplished I say. And yeah, he called me *sonny*.' Clive ran a hand over his face. 'Yeah, I still got it,' he mused.

'You infuriate me sometimes. I know it's a while since you worked CIB, but this is basic stuff.' Jan Silverton hopped in the driver's side of the silver BMW M3 sedan, slamming her door closed a little harder than she intended. Outside Clive Anderson gave a big sigh and rolled his eyes. 'Fuckin' women bosses,' he whispered under his breath before opening the car door.

They headed back towards Brisbane City, not talking for the first ten minutes.

'And it's not *mission accomplished* at all,' said Jan trying to keep a civil tone. 'He said the picture was his wife. He was absolutely certain of it.'

'The wife is sitting above the fireplace. Sorry to say, but her clubbin' days are long gone.' Clive crossed his arms.

'Don't be a fucking smartarse. Yes, she's dead. I know that. The point is, for whatever reason, someone has gone to a lot of trouble to use her name and address and make themselves look like a young version of Medora Hammerstein.'

'And so… someone does all this to get away with decapitating a young man at a nightclub, then bugger off with the dude's head inside a cushion cover? I don't get it.'

Jan glanced across at him a couple times. 'You are a real detective, right?'

'And I've been one a few years longer than you, sweetheart.'

'Then, *sweetheart*, you should know we have way more questions than answers. And we need to do some solid leg work to sort this shit out. So, let's all do our allocated jobs correctly. You dropped the ball before. I won't have that on my watch.'

Silverton was not only referring to Anderson's failure to do a thorough check on the Medora Hammerstein name, but also to other times he had been lazy in past investigations. The most recent, and most serious occasion being when he was protecting a known offender and allowed another man into the safe house to have a private chat with this protected witness, only to find that both had disappeared ten minutes later.

'I have fully explained all that, as best I was able, many times over for Christ's sake. So don't you start. Why Edwards saddled me with you is beyond me,' blurted Clive, cursing the chief inspector's decision. He peered out the window with his face pushed against the glass and mumbled a few more words. 'You're one cranky fucking bitch.'

'Who has excellent hearing,' snapped Silverton. 'And don't take this badly, but I would have much preferred to keep Davis as my partner. Unfortunately, he's reassigned to the Ipswich case, and I'm under instructions to make your transfer work.'

'You're welcome to Davis. That guy's so bent he could kiss his own arse. And I guess a poof investigating a poof murder knows whose arse to sniff for information.'

'Oh my God! You have no bloody clue. And the word is gay, Clive,' she shouted. 'Are you able to articulate it?'

'Bent, gay, homo, whatever you call it, it don't change who he's kissin'.'

She pushed a hand through her auburn hair then shook her head roughly. Her hair, in a bob style, fell back perfectly into place. There was no further chat on the drive back to their office in Roma Street, Brisbane City.

Chapter 6

The Autopsy

The headless, and naked body of Johnny Randall, lay on the stainless-steel autopsy trolley at the Eckersley Forensic and Scientific Services Centre. Dr Christopher Pendleton had just completed a Y incision, cutting deeply from each shoulder joint to the bottom of the sternum and then straight down the middle to the top of the pubic area. The layers of skin, fat and muscle were laid open in large flaps exposing the rib cage and the internal organs.

There was a knock on the glass at the top half of the door. Detective Jan Silverton caught the doctor's eye as he glanced up. He waved her in with a bloody glove. Clive Anderson followed but remained close to the exit. Silverton donned gown, mask, hairnet and gloves.

A loud cracking noise made Clive gasp. The cracks continued. Pendleton was using bone cutters to cut each rib at the sides. Once all ribs were cut, he removed the rib cage and placed it on the bare trolley behind him. The heart and lungs were now fully exposed. Anderson was studying the scuff marks on his black shoes.

'Hello, Jan. How's Edwards treating you?' asked the doctor in a soft voice that was almost a whisper. He was clad in personal protective dress including a large set of protective glasses over his own fine rimmed spectacles.

'Let's say the more time I spend out of the office the better.' Silverton finished tying her gown and joined Pendleton on the opposite side of the corpse.

'Hey there Clive,' called Pendleton across the room, getting a quick glance and a wave in reply. 'It's about time Vince lightened up,' he said to Jan. 'He'll end up in an early grave. I've told him so a thousand times.'

Johnny's neck hung over a sink which was built into the end of the autopsy trolley. Some oozing blood-stained fluid dripped into the sink making a light tapping sound. The room itself was spotless, with a massive amount of stainless steel – benches and backsplashes, cupboards and drawers, several sinks, air vents and two more cadaver trolleys, all gleaming in the well-lit room. Next to the doctor was a smaller instrument trolley with all the necessary tools laid out – two saws, several scalpels, the bone cutters, four pairs of different shaped scissors, forceps, various probes, and bevelled and angled instruments for lifting and separating tissue.

'What do you make of this, Jan?' Pendleton pointed to a thick grey and mottled pink wad of tissue hanging out of Johnny's neck. The detective took a step and leaned over the body.

'Is that the spinal cord?'

'Correct.'

'I've seen headless bodies before but not quite like that.'

'Exactly,' beamed the doctor excitedly through widened eyes. 'That's because in decapitation the neck is usually completely severed through – skin, muscles, tendons, bone and spine. You may see something resembling this with death from hanging, especially where there is a significant fall before the noose does its job, but this happened in a small private booth in a nightclub. Also, the tissue was severed with an extremely sharp tool, very neatly right down to, but not through the cord itself – this is inconsistent with hanging. And oddly, it seems this occurred on all sides of the neck simultaneously. Some sort of super sharp, serrated piano wire or something similar I would suspect. The end of the spinal cord we can see was not cut. I believe it was torn through just below the lowest part of the brain, the brain stem. Strange as it may seem, I believe this tearing away happened before the decapitation.'

'Is that even possible?'

'The blood at the crime scene was far less than you would expect from such an attack. I think he was dead before he lost his head.'

'Oh my God! She turned to her partner. 'You hear that Clive?'

'I heard. I just don't need to see, thank you. And why does it always smell so bad in here?'

'The exhaust fans are on, Clive. This body has not decomposed. I don't know what you're complaining about.'

'Chemicals mixed with a stale cherry smell. I can't stand it.'

'So, Chris, how could something like that possibly happen?' asked Jan.

'Without having the head, I can't know for sure. It reminds me a little of eating grapes. You pull a grape off the stem and a small amount of the fruit remains attached as the grape comes free. The stem being the spinal cord and the grape being the head... you see?'

'Ah ha, yeah, I get it,' nodded Silverton. 'But how?'

'Someone has gone through the skull, or less likely, up under the chin.' Pendleton shrugged. 'It's an intriguing one that's for sure. And there's more... can you notice anything else unusual?'

'Detective Silverton pointed to a dark orange and black protrusion near the stomach. 'This looks different.'

'Yes, that's the pancreas protruding from behind the stomach. Large, discoloured and cancerous.'

'And there's a large white mark on the liver and several white spots.'

'I suspect they are metastatic growths possibly from the pancreas.'

'The bowel looks a bit misshapen in places.'

'Those lesions that look a bit like cauliflower. Yes, more cancerous growths. This guy had only weeks to live. Don't know yet if he was being treated. There are no puncture wounds from injections. And there's one other thing detective, that I'm sure you've already seen.'

'Well, I've noticed his penis is very blue… and patchy looking… possibly more so than you would normally expect.'

Clive Anderson shook his head and mumbled, 'Cauliflower, grapes, cherries, patchy dicks… that's enough.' He let himself out. Chris and Jan briefly turned their heads then resumed their discussions about Johnny's body.

'Yes, the penis,' continued Pendleton. 'I've taken swabs. Semen there for sure, and other secretions that need further analysis. This guy had sexual intercourse right before, or even as, he was murdered. Very intense intercourse… there is a lot of bruising.'

'Now I have even more questions to answer.'

'And I have a lot more work to do here. I'll remove all the organs and examine them individually. I need to study the severance cuts more closely. And there's the pathology results too.'

'Let me know if anything else shows up?' The detective stepped back and began removing her protective wear.

'I'll be in touch, Jan. Nice to see you again. When you see Vince, tell him I said hi, and tell him from me not to keep skipping his blood pressure meds.'

Silverton smiled. 'Will do, Chris. Cheers.'

Chapter 7

Harmony – Part 2

Bentley Hopkins-Jones drove his white Mercedes A250 Sports down the ramp and into the underground car park of an apartment building at South Bank, alongside the Brisbane River. The vehicle glided quietly into a vacant space numbered 446.

In the passenger seat was nineteen-year-old Harmony Magenta Lake. Her gaze had been fixated on Bentley ever since he escorted her out of the Tribal Moon twenty minutes earlier. Her right hand had been rubbing his knee and thigh, and venturing to his inner thigh and over the large bulge in his chinos. Her handsome man had looked back at her several times, and while she couldn't recall his words exactly, she was sure he had told her how beautiful she was, how gorgeous her dress was, and how he had an intense desire to undress her and explore her body. This was the therapy she needed. This is exactly what her psychologist had recommended.

Bentley opened her door, smiled warmly, and took her hand. The couple took the elevator to level four. As the doors slid open, Bentley scooped her up in his arms and carried her from the lift and down a white hallway lined with attractive hanging prints of oceans, beaches and seashells. He paused at room 446, and while kissing her, unlocked the door. Harmony was slightly intrigued by his dexterity, after all, he was holding her with both arms and yet was still clever enough to unlock and open the door. Their tongues parted and he stepped into the apartment. The door closed behind them. A second later the lock clicked.

Chapter 8

Sydney

Fabian Carver did his best to avoid talking to other people. For him all occasions felt awkward, difficult and challenging. Sometimes even a simple *thank you*, would come out wrong. He'd stumble over the words, stutter it out, or drag out the *thank* to *thaaaaank,* or say it too softly to be heard, or splutter it out way too loud along with a bit of spit, and embarrass himself.

For a tall man, Fabian moved with surprisingly short, but rapid steps, head down, past the multiple food and coffee outlets, boutique shops, alcohol stores, fashion and souvenir stores. He was in a hurry to get out of Sydney Airport and away from the masses of people milling around trying to bump into him. His carry-on suitcase ran along behind him clicking away on the tiles. Only ever carry on. Checked baggage only added that extra layer of frustration and potential contact with others.

He had told himself – *go to Sydney. Get the motor-home and drive home to Brisbane. That's all Fabian Carver – you have no other Sydney business to attend to.*

He had been looking out for a suitable vehicle for some weeks, eventually finding just the one – a second hand 2021 Jayco for just under ninety grand. It was on the smaller side of motor homes, but just perfect for one person. His plan was to leave his property, rent it out, and reside for the next few years in the motor home – driving around the country and doing everything he wanted, needed, or felt compelled to do.

Soon he was in an Uber and off to the private address to do a final inspection of the vehicle. In the Uber app, he had specified "quiet preferred" in his rider preferences. Nevertheless, his driver, asked him how he was, if he liked the music being played, and what he was up to in Sydney. He successfully answered – *okay; yes*; and *nothing much* to the questions without falling into a blubbering stuttering mess.

Fabian looked at the dressing on his left wrist. As he touched it softly with his fingers, disturbing thoughts filled his mind. He recalled an evening with his father…

…Fabian had promptly left school after the last class of the day – year six science with Mrs Hartigan. He walked for thirty minutes, arriving home by three-thirty. An hour later he set about preparing dinner. As he chopped the carrots and potato, he began to feel anxious. This was not unusual but being a Friday, it was likely to be the worst day of his week. Other days his father was home by five, but tonight it could be anytime from five to midnight.

At four-forty-five he put the sausages on and prepared some gravy. By five o'clock everything was ready, but his father was not home. It was a delicate balancing act, keeping the meal in good shape the entire time so it was still at least a little appetising for his dad.

At ten o'clock Fabian fell asleep on the sofa in front of the TV. At eleven forty-five a car door slammed shut and George Carver staggered towards his low-set weatherboard home. It was his father's vomiting, just outside the front door, that woke Fabian.

'Boy,' shouted his drunk dad. He rubbed his arm roughly over his mouth. 'I need water.'

Fabian was instantly awake and immediately into panic mode. He grabbed a plastic tumbler and filled it with water and hurried to the open front door where his father stood.

George drank half of it, then tossed the tumbler to the floor and staggered into the lounge. While the furnishings were old and worn, thanks to Fabian, the lounge was at least tidy. George let out a long burp. Fabian stood near him.

'Why the fuck are you standing there? Get my fucking dinner!' George dropped onto a red leather lounge chair where the red surface was cracked and had peeled away on the arms and front of the seat.

Fabian opened the oven, took out the plate with an oven-mitt, sat it on the bench and removed the saucepan lid covering the food. The carrot and potato were shrunk, dried and stuck to the plate. The sausages were shrivelled. The oven had been too hot, and he'd fallen asleep. The gravy was in a saucepan on the stove. It was cooler than it should have been. He tipped it on the food and a thick, congealed matt floating on the top, slipped onto the plate.

Young Fabian stared at the plate and cried…

The sound of a horn and a squeal of tyres from a truck, brought Fabian back to the present. The truckie raised his middle finger to the driver of a Suziki Swift at the intersection. The Swift driver took off through the red light. His Uber driver chuckled, Fabian wiped a tear from the corner of his eye, then looked aimlessly out the window.

*   *   *

On arrival at Glebe Point Road in Glebe Sydney, Fabian was instantly reminded of the Addams Family as he looked at the home. It was a two-storey house with what looked like a tower in the middle, extending to a third floor and an attic above that. The windows were elongated and barred.

Dressed in smart casual attire and looking a bit like a Mormon doing the door-knocking rounds, Fabian Carver walked up the cement pathway to the door with his small suitcase following him.

A man, with some resemblance to Uncle Fester, greeted him after a knock on the door.

'Hello, I've come about the Jayco m… m… mmmmotor home.'

'Yes, of course. You must be Fabian,' said the bald fat man.

Fabian nodded and smiled.

'She's just over there in the driveway. Let me show you all the bells and whistles… you can leave your case here… I'm sure it will be safe.'

Fester, wearing large shorts and a faded white t-shirt with *FRIENDS* written on the top and a pic of the TV cast underneath, headed to the driveway. Fabian followed, disregarding the advice and bringing his bag along.

The vehicle was in good order just as he had been told over the phone. It had everything he needed. As he already knew, the kitchen and bathroom were small, but no big deal for one person. The air-conditioning was running perfectly. The double bed was more than adequate and there was ample storage space.

'I'll buy it,' said Fabian.

'Great. Do you want a test drive?'

'No.'

'Hmm… okay, well let's go back inside and sort out the details.'

'Let's do it here,' said Fabian as he sat at the small dining table and pulled his suitcase near to his legs.

'No worries. I'll go get the paperwork. Are you good with payment?'

'Yes.'

'I'll be baaack,' said Uncle Fester with an intentional drawl trying to sound like some version of Arnold Schwarzenegger. He dropped heavily down the two steps as he left the motor home causing it to sway.

In a moment Fabian Carver found himself back at his old home...

It was morning, and his father was still asleep, as he looked at himself in the bathroom mirror. He lightly touched his red and swollen cheek. He moved his jaw up and down. He picked up a blood-stained washer and dabbed at the base of his nose cleaning up a little ooze that remained.

A few minutes later he was doing his best to clean the dinner off the wall and pick up the pieces of the broken plate. So many times he wanted to leave, but he was now paralysed by fear and couldn't go even though he knew what was coming. Twice he had left, both times being returned by the police. He couldn't endure such a beating again.

At ten-thirty, when he heard the shower running, Fabian lay down and curled up on the sofa. All too soon the shower stopped, then he heard that song playing – "Boy of Mine". He sobbed quietly.

I love you my most special boy
More than you can ever know
I need to be with you
Time and time again
My special boy
Lay with me and be mine...

Minutes later his father emerged into the lounge just wearing his y fronts. George Carver was a short stocky man with short cut black hair. He was still in good shape. His years of excessive drinking balanced out to some extent by his construction work.

'Hello Fabian, my special boy. I'm so sorry about last night. I will make it up to you, my darling.' George walked closer and stood looking down at his son. 'Here my gorgeous boy.' George held out a folded white skirt and top with a yellow daisy pattern. 'Put these on for daddy.'

You are the one I need
To help me face the day
Being there for me
A tonic that sees me through…

'Here we are!' announced the fat man loudly. 'Just a couple of signatures… the payment… then we're all set to go. Do you have a bank cheque?'

'Huh… oh… yeah… no.'

'No bank cheque? How are we settling this today?'

'I have ca…ca…ca… cash,' said Fabian. He stood and rolled his suitcase to the double bed where he opened it and took out a vacuum sealed plastic bag. He slapped it on the table.'

'Really?' Fester looked at the wads of cash pushed up against the plastic. 'Is that eighty-nine thousand nine hundred dollars?'

'Yes. Exactly.'

'Wow! I've never seen so much cash. You didn't rob a bank or something?' he chortled.

'Certainly not.'

'I'll have to count it.'

'Of ca… ca… course.'

Fester forced himself along the narrow bench seat on one side of the table, his belly hanging partly over the top, effectively beheading Ross, Rachel and Chandler and burying the other three.

'What do you do for a crust, my friend?'

'Is that r… r… relevant?'

'No mate. Not really. Just being friendly you know. It's called conversation.' He gave a forced chuckle.

'Hmm… I was a s… ss… software engineer. Right now, I'm in between jobs.'

'Cool. Great. Interesting. I'll count now.'

'Thank you.'

Fester unzipped the plastic zip lock and pulled out the hundred-dollar bills and started counting.

Fabian drifted back once more…

As he lay kneeled on the sofa, rocking forward and back, with his father behind him, he did his best to find that special place he had created in his own mind. A sanctuary he could visit. A place where he could escape from himself and his life. The sea water was warm, and the waves washed gently over him, pushing him lightly side to side while a melodic tune filled the air. There was no one else there. Never anyone. Just himself. A strong, confident, well-spoken, and exceptionally clever person… never Fabian Wallace Carver. Anyone but him. The days were always warm and sun drenched, with the sand white and pristine. In his sanctuary he moved slowly from the water and knelt on the sand. He lifted handfuls of the white grains and put them in his mouth. The sand transformed from grittiness to melted white chocolate.

'It's exactly right,' declared Uncle Fester.

'Oh… g… g… gr… great,' stammered Fabian. Some spit flew out. He belatedly covered his mouth.

Chapter 9

Click Snap

The Magnolia Bar and Diner in inner Sydney was a social meeting and entertainment venue open to all, but hugely popular with gay men. The diner was decorated with posters of past American movie legends – Marilyn Monroe, Bette Davis, Judy Garland, Rock Hudson, Cary Grant, and many others. The diner booths were specifically designed to replicate an American diner, with vinyl bench seats – high backed and brightly coloured, each in a different colour of the rainbow. The tabletops were laminated with a multi-coloured swirling pattern.

Separate, but adjacent to the diner, was the long bar. Even in daylight, thanks to the heavy maroon curtains, it glowed with purples and reds. Vinyl covered stools with short backs lined the length of the bar. Low lounges with coffee tables and a small, raised stage, defined the carpeted area to one end of the Magnolia Bar. At the opposite end was a large video screen showing shadowed dancers surrounded in mist and moving to the beat of *Let's Have a Kiki* by the Scissor Sisters.

At three-thirty in the afternoon, after a belated lunch at the diner, a slim young man, wearing a khaki-coloured fedora and with a bandage around his left wrist, stood outside the entrance to the bar. He flicked through a small card wallet – each clear plastic sleeve held a different driver's license. He settled on one with the name Jericho Mondano and dropped it into the single pocket of his orange polo shirt. For the time being this would be his persona and identification if required. Leaving his hat on, he raised his head high, stretched himself tall, smiled and entered the Magnolia.

*   *   *

After ninety minutes the bouncer barman approached Jericho. 'Hey, gorgeous. It's after five now, we need to scan you in.'

'Cool.' Jericho pulled his ID from his shirt pocket. The barman used a bulky looking mobile phone to scan the driver's license. 'And I'll have another lemon, lime and bitters, thanks.'

The man looked at the card and back at Jericho. 'It's a bit faded, mate. Really, you should chase up a replacement.'

'Yeah, I know,' said Jericho. He took the card back. 'That's what happens when you leave it in an over-chlorinated pool overnight.'

'That'll do it, I guess.' The barman put down the scanner and set about making Jericho his drink.

There were a handful of patrons in the diner and a similar number in the bar where Jericho Mondano had been patiently perched. He had seen all the security cameras and positioned himself well down the bar, at a spot he deemed least likely to be fully seen. He chose to leave his fedora on. Thanks to his use of moisturiser and avoidance of excessive sunlight, Jericho, with his smooth olive skin, could easily pass as much younger than his thirty-two years.

Despite the slow pace of the venue, he had already attracted interest from two other men. He weighed them both up.

The first guy was an Englishman with blue eyes and a blonde mullet. 'Hello you, trying to hide away there under that cute hat. You've been sitting there a while. I'll bet your seat is really hot.'

Jericho checked him out – his age, the blue eyes, the accent, long hair, the short neck, the thick fingers. 'My seat is hot, but not for you. Go away,' he said softly and with a flick of his head.

'Hey, how about we share a cocktail?'

'We will neither share *cock,* nor each other's *tail,*' said Jericho calmly. 'I said *fuck off* politely. I'd rather not be rude.' Jericho spoke a little louder.

'Your loss.' The Englishman moved away. Not long after came the second approach – a lanky guy in a blue suit with flared trousers.

'Hello, lover,' he said as he slid out the stool and sat next to Jericho. 'You've hurt yourself, poor darling.' He gestured at Jericho's bandage. 'Hmm… not drinking alcohol. Hiding away under that fedora. Makes me think you're waiting on someone. I sense a lover's quarrel… and a gesture of self-harm to lure him back.' He reached over to Jericho's left hand and touched it lightly. 'I do have good senses. Am I right?'

'There is no quarrel. But yes, I am waiting for someone.'

'Well, wait no more, lover boy. Your prayers have been answered.' He opened his arms. Under his blue jacket was a pink body shirt.

'I don't pray, and I am not your lover. And I've never been a fan of seventies fashion,' replied Jericho.

'Ouch! That's not nice.' The man placed a hand on his chest.

'Get rid of the padded shoulders. And if you choose to wear a body shirt, get a body to match.'

The tall guy left without another word.

At five-thirty a stocky middle-aged man, with a crew cut and black stubble the same length, leaned over the bar and ordered a martini. Jericho looked, smiled, and raised his lime and soda. He got a broad smile back. The stocky guy, with drink in hand, moved closer.

'You have the loveliest brown eyes. And good taste in booze,' said Jericho warmly. 'Are you here on your own?'

'Until now, I think… I'm Jacob.' He held out a hand. Jericho took it lightly and brushed his thumb over the outside of his newfound friend's hand.

'I'm Jericho.'

'Can I buy you a martini, Jericho?'

'Thank you. That's very kind.'

For the next two hours the men continued chatting and drinking, leaving their barstools once to dance for five minutes. After a few drinks Jacob asked a question that had been circulating through his thoughts. 'It's been on my mind, and I just need to ask...'

Jericho held up his left arm. 'About this bandage?' he said interrupting.

'Ah ha. You know what it looks like don't you?' Jacob widened his eyes.

'Like a suicide attempt. It's not that. I do though at times... well... self-harm, I suppose you'd call it. Sometimes when you have a tough upbringing... you know... it's complicated... it's difficult...'

'Jacob placed a soft finger against Jericho's lips. 'It's okay. We don't need to go there. I get it.'

At seven forty, and at Jericho's request, Jacob called an Uber. At seven forty-five the two men left for their ten-minute ride to Jericho's hotel room.

*   *   *

No sooner behind the closed hotel door, Jacob threw his arms around Jericho's shoulders and kissed him hard on the lips. For a second Jericho opened his mouth and allowed their tongues to meet. He felt a churning in his stomach and pulled back. 'Hold up there my lovely man. Firstly, I need a Black Russian... as in the drink of course... although the other does hold some appeal.'

'I can go with that... to start with, but I'm feeling pretty excited about fucking you.'

Jericho pecked him on the cheek. 'I'm not going anywhere, love.' He walked to the fridge and grabbed the vodka, the coffee liqueur and poured them over ice into a tumbler.

'I want to taste your cock,' said Jacob in a loud breathy whisper. 'And I want to kiss and fuck that cute arse of yours. I gotta tell you, Jericho, I'm as horny as all fuck.'

Jericho passed Jacob the drink and they chinked glasses. 'Well then… it seems both of us are over-flowing with desire. Here's to satisfaction,' said Jericho.

'I'll drink, fuck or suck to that,' laughed Jacob. Jericho smiled but inside he felt like he was close to throwing up. They sat themselves on the bed and leaned back against every pillow and cushion they could find. For ten minutes the two men snuggled up next to each other sipping their drinks, chatting, and gazing into each other's eyes.

'You know I think I've had enough booze,' said Jacob. 'I'm feeling a little lightheaded.'

'How about you jump in the shower and wake yourself up. We got things to be doing here my man.'

'Sure.' Jacob stood. He rocked side to side but managed to find his way to the bathroom.

Once Jericho heard the shower running, he took what looked like a small brown toiletries bag from the drawer of the bedside table and tipped the contents onto the bed. There were no toiletry items. He twisted the top off two plastic five ml vials and drew the contents into a ten-millilitre syringe and attached a needle. He lay the syringe and a tourniquet on the bench under the television. He picked up a pair of pruning shears and placed then alongside the syringe. Jericho took a quick look at the empty vials – *Potassium Chloride for Injection – CONCENTRATE – Must be diluted before use*. He put them, and the twist off tops, back in the bag together with a pair of scissors and a cutthroat razor which were, today, not required. The remaining items including lipstick, foundation, eyeliner, mascara, highlighter, and a makeup brush he placed in a row on the bedside table.

On entering the bathroom, Jacob as expected, was sitting on the shower floor letting the water run over him. 'I'm going to pass out,' panted the naked man.

'Yes, you are. It was the Black Russian… well, not strictly speaking the drink I suppose. It was what I added to yours.' Jericho scowled as he looked down at him. His teeth clenched. His fingers rolled into tight fists. 'I think you are just like him,' he seethed. 'Fabian wants to see you.'

He left the room and spent a few minutes making the bed and arranging the pillows. He opened a small overnight bag and removed a yellow dress with a daisy pattern and lay it neatly on the bedspread. He placed a small plastic backed incontinence sheet on top of the bed near the pillows. Jericho undressed himself, leaving his polo shirt, chinos, and underwear in a folded pile on the bench, and placing his fedora on top. His sandals were below on the carpet.

He collected his items and returned to the bathroom placing them near the vanity cabinet. The churning amplified. His mouth watered. He dropped to his knees over the toilet and vomited loudly.

Jacob was slumped over in the shower corner with his chin on his chest. Jericho stood, shook himself then rinsed his mouth and threw water over his face at the sink. He looked at his reflection. His demeanour changed 'It's t… t… time.' He picked up the pruning shears and looked down at the man.

'You hurt me… over and over… you t… t… t… tortured me,' stuttered Fabian Carver. 'With your filthy g… g… grubby fingers you violated me. With that st… s… stinking c… c… cock you destroyed my childhood. Entering me so many t… times… and forcing that foul t… t… taste into my mouth. You are t… truly an evil monster. How could a son ever love you?'

With the shower still running he squatted and lifted the man's arm.

'These hands, these f… f… fingers, these instruments of pain and fear will no longer cause misery.' A loud snap and the first joint of an index finger fell to the shower floor. Jacob stirred and groaned but never woke completely. Blood spurted. Click, snap, click, snap, click, snap – the fingers fell one after the other. After twenty-eight click snaps all joints were severed and blood was splattered over the shower glass and both men. A stream of red was washing away down the shower drain.

'And now just one more cut. Fabian held up Jacob's penis. He gagged. It took three cuts to detach the floppy appendage.

He left the haemorrhaging man in the shower. Fabian looked down at him and the amount of blood loss. 'Hmm… your life ebbs away. Good,' he muttered. He stood watching him bleed wondering if death would come from blood loss.

After some more minutes, when the wounds were just oozing around thick clots, he squatted and felt for a pulse.

'Huh, the monster still lives.' He stood and picked up the loaded syringe. He pushed the needle into Jacob's neck and pulled slightly back on the syringe barrel. Blood swirled back into the clear liquid indicating the needle was inside a large blood vessel. Jericho expelled the ten millilitres of potassium chloride. Seconds later Jacob started jerking in a weak convulsion. Yellow urine flowed over the shower floor, taking a semicircular path then disappearing down the drain along with some streaky bloody ooze.

Fabian stood in front of the sink and unwound the wet bandage from his left wrist and removed a padded dressing. There were three injuries, one held together with small strips of white tape, the other mostly healed and the third injury was now just a healed scar. He took the shears, pushed and cut, making a deep fourth wound. The blood flowed down, dripping from the fingers of his left hand. He wrote on the mirror over three lines. *I'M MORE SPECIAL THAN YOU KNOW – DADDY.*

Chapter 10

Harmony – Part 3

Bentley carried Harmony through to the bedroom and lay her down gently on the turned back satin sheets. She was over-breathing, excited and utterly mesmerised by this handsome man. He left the room for a minute, returning with a jug of iced water and two glasses on a round tray.

Harmony was naked, she was sure this is what he had suggested before his brief departure from the bedroom. Her sequin skirt, half cup bra and G-string lay on the lush carpet with her heels. She squirmed provocatively, pulling in her shoulders to emphasise her cleavage, and dropping a knee to one side to show off her part Brazilian that left a narrow band of pubic hair down the sides of her vulva.

Her host smiled and set the tray down on the bedside table and poured two glasses. Harmony rolled to the side and sat up. He raised his head and passed her a glass. She looked at the beautiful highball glass with its ornate cut glass pattern in star shapes. She smiled and raised her drink. They looked at each other, downed their water and placed their glasses back on the tray. Harmony rolled her tongue over her lips. Bentley lifted the jug and gulped down the rest in seconds.

'I hope you're that thirsty for me,' she panted. Being nearly a head shorter than Bentley Hopkin-Jones, she had to reach up to push his denim jacket from his shoulders.

'You must work out so much,' she said softly, as her hands glided over his t-shirt caressing his muscles. Harmony pulled the shirt free from his chinos and lifted it high. Bentley assisted with a slight knee bend and lowering of his head. Every muscle was defined, his arms, his chest, and his rippled abdomen.

'Oh my God. I must be dreaming.' She pushed her face against his bare chest and kissed his muscles.

Bentley placed a hand over the back of her head and ran his fingers through her long blonde hair, stopping every now and then to massage her scalp with long finger movements from near her ears to the top of her head. Harmony was sure he was using his fingernails. There was a delightful sharpness that accentuated the sensation. She sighed as he massaged. It reminded her of using one of those wire head-scratchers you bought at the flea market, what were they called… an orgasmatron, yes that was it. And this was so like that, sending goosebumps down her spine.

Chapter 11

Davis Has a Serial

Richard Davis had recently completed his first detective year. For most of those twelve months he had been accompanied and mentored by Jan Silverton. It was no secret that he was gay, and while he copped the odd teasing remark, it was, for the most part, just friendly banter which he was well used to, and could give back as good or better than he got. While he was fit and strong, his being of short stocky build was more a cause of ribbing than being gay.

Now, he was working alongside other detectives on the Ipswich motel murder, with Jan being assigned to keep an eye on Clive Anderson and work the Johnny Randall killing.

While Richard wasn't particularly friendly with Clive, he didn't mind him. At least there was no pretence or hidden agenda. He said what he thought regardless of who he may offend.

While progress on the Ipswich case was slow, there was still plenty to be done with a local door knocking to start, and a wider sweep of all available CCTV footage.

It was at nine o'clock, on Monday the thirteenth of April, when Davis received a brief, but urgent phone call that made his eyes widen and his pulse quicken.

'This is Davis,' he answered in a somewhat bored tone as he paused some CCTV footage that he had already seen a dozen times.

'Detective Davis. Bowman, Parramatta. We have a murder here that may be of interest to you,' said a Sydney detective. *'I have emailed you the link to the case files. Have a gander, mate, then we'll chat some more.'*

Davis scrolled through the pictures, all taken yesterday after a body was discovered in a hotel by a cleaning lady. There was an image of a dead man with short black hair and heavy makeup, leaning back on pillows and dressed in a daisy patterned dress. A close-up pic showed all the chopped off parts of his fingers laid out like a jigsaw. Then there was another close-up of an amputated penis.

'Oh, my God!' he blurted loudly.

The young detective jumped to his feet and charged between desks down a short hallway and into Inspector Vince Edwards' office, completely forgetting to knock first.

It was a spacious room with two areas – an office side and a sitting room side. Edwards was in the comfortable side, chatting and sitting next to Detective Silverton. His narrow, wrinkled face slowly turned, and he glared at Davis.

'How many fucking times do you need to be told, Davis?'

'Sorry, sir. Detective Jan.' He glanced and gave Silverton a quick nod. 'Sir, we have a serial.'

'Do we, Davis? And has your barging in here led to a speedy arrest?'

'No sir. Not yet, sir. Sorry sir. The murders are identical,' he sucked in air as he spoke with urgency. 'This is no *maybe*. This is an absolute certainty. It's the same daisy thing and all.'

There was a moment of silence. Davis gave an unsure smile and shifted gaze between his two senior colleagues. He pushed his palms over his jeans and shifted weight from foot to foot.

*   *   *

Thirty minutes later Edwards had seen enough and had left to have a private conversation with his boss, the Superintendent. For the time being Silverton was to assist Davis in collating all information and liaising with the Parramatta detectives to gain full disclosure and sharing of everything both teams had.

Detective Jan Silverton sat at a wide desk with Richard Davis. The two had accumulated many pictures of the two murders. All were numbered and identified with date and place across the top. There were other printouts of witness statements, forensic and pathology reports and rough notes on scraps of paper. A large whiteboard near them had incomplete details of both murders listed under VIC 1 and VIC 2.

Jan held up two pictures of dead men in daisy patterned dresses, propped up on pillows showing the removed appendages lined up. 'What is notable about these images?' she asked.

'Hmm… both pictures are close to identical,' said Richard, looking up from jottings on his notebook. 'Both men have black, either shaved or short hair, and are of similar build. From what we know both are believed to be gay. There is a definite neat and tidy look about them.'

'Which suggests what?'

'That the killer is a neat freak? Although that doesn't follow through to the bathrooms… what are you thinking… some sort of fetish?'

'It's all too tidy. Too precise. I'm thinking these are not his first kills. He's perfected or is still perfecting a style.'

'Shit. You think there's more out there… already? How many more?'

'Don't know. Maybe two… maybe three,' said Jan. 'And more to come if we don't get to him first.'

'We should check missing persons. Especially men around thirty-five to fifty. Both gay and straight.'

'Indeed. Can you make a start on that?' asked Jan.

Silverton grabbed a whiteboard marker and stood. Under VIC 1 she wrote *perp – Napoleon Pugliesi*. Under VIC 2 the name *Jericho Mondano*. She placed an equal's symbol between the two names. With an arrow to the side, she listed the killer's possible descriptions given what they knew thus far:

- olive or tanned skin
- 180 to 190 centimetres tall
- 75 to 85 kilograms
- 20 to 30 years old
- + or - glasses
- well-dressed
- friendly
- pays in cash
- uses stolen or lost IDs
- provides false mobile phone numbers and addresses
- no vehicle seen
- avoids CCTV

Chapter 12

The Anderson Fuck Up

Through his entire working life, Detective Clive Anderson never had a perfect reputation. Even in his early detective years he seemed to find trouble. He was booked in a souped-up Torana doing one hundred and twenty in a sixty kmph zone, getting off scot-free after showing his badge, fessing up to his boss and begging forgiveness. He further tarnished his reputation and character when on a camping weekend. After sitting around a campfire with friendly fellow campers borrowing supplies, and drinking their beer, he dobbed them in to the local police for smoking dope.

In more recent years he had made some minor drug busts by planting evidence during drug raids. His fellow officers knew he was short cutting thorough police work, but for the most part, they went along with his style and reluctantly accepted the outcomes.

The biggest issue of his working life occurred nine months ago when he was responsible for protecting a gangland drug dealer and alleged hitman who was ready to confess, make a deal and snitch on several key underworld figures.

In a safe house at Albion, Brisbane, officers kept watch over the informant, Jason Galanis, in shifts around the clock – always in pairs.

So far there had been six uneventful boring days of playing cards, scrabble, Yahtzee, and eating pizza. On day seven, at six in the evening, the three men voted for a change in diet, so Clive's partner drove down the road to get some KFC drive-through.

'Hey, Clive. Take a card, any card.' Galanis fanned out a deck of playing cards.

'Is there money involved here?'

'No. Fuck you! It's a card trick.'

Clive moved over and pulled a card from near the middle. 'You know I don't trust you, right?'

'I know that. Look at the card and remember it.'

'Okay.' Clive looked at the Ace of Hearts.

'Push it back in anywhere you like. Clive obliged. Jason Galanis shuffled the deck, placed the cards on the table, then cut the deck in half. He picked up the top card and flicked it at Anderson. It was the Ace of Hearts.

'Neat. I'm never playing poker with you.'

There was a knock on the door.

'Yeah, who's there? What do you want?' shouted Clive, while looking through the peep hole and seeing no one. Jason, a broad-shouldered Greek man, stopped dealing the cards for another game of solitaire and stood. Clive held up an open hand, indicating for him to stay where he was and not worry. Then there was a tap on a front window. Clive removed his firearm and slowly pushed the block out curtains aside. A smiling Greek face looked straight at him.

'Huh, it's Nicholas Drakos,' said Clive with a chuckle as he turned to Jason.

'Drakos is dead,' spat Jason. 'What the fuck?'

'Look,' replied Clive with a smile as he reefed the curtain right back. Jason immediately relaxed on seeing the smiling face.

'Oh… fuck, it really is Drakos,' he nodded.

'He wants to talk to you.'

'Yes, that's fine. Let him in.'

Clive holstered his firearm and unlocked the slide bolt, the deadbolt and the chain and let Drakos in.

Nicholas Drakos looked strong, fit and lean. His dark hair was thick and collar length. He moved close to Clive's face and made a few popping, clicking and hissing sounds in the detective's ear.

'Yes,' replied Clive. 'I'm happy to wait outside.'

'Drakos, you look better than ever.' Jason moved over to his friend. 'Where have you been? A fucking health retreat?' The two shook hands firmly. 'No more grey hair and you're so pumped up. I can't believe it,' said Jason slapping him on both triceps. 'We thought you were fucking dead.'

Clive left the two men alone, closed the front door and wandered around the small front garden wondering when his KFC would be arriving.

* * *

At the misconduct hearing, Clive did his best to explain how Jason Galanis had disappeared from protective custody. As the words left his mouth, he couldn't help thinking how lame it all sounded.

'The guy at the window looked for all the world like Nicholas Drakos, even Galanis thought it was Drakos, and he convinced me there was absolutely nothing to be concerned about. I felt confident that I could leave the two men alone and everything would be fine. As I say this, I know it sounds ridiculous, even stupid, but at the time I felt I was doing the right thing.'

'Yet you cannot tell us exactly what words were exchanged,' snapped Alan Clarkson, a retired judge, and one of the four persons on the panel.

'I have no recollection of precisely what was said. I know it was something like, *you can relax, Clive. There is no danger. I need to talk to my friend. You can let me in, there are no safety concerns.*

'He knew your name?'

'Yes. He seemed to know me.'

'Are you always this gullible, detective?'

'No, sir. At the time though, all I can say is, I had... I felt... I was positive there was no reason to doubt what I'd been told.'

'What you *thought or felt* you were told,' scoffed the judge.

'Yes, sir.'

'And obviously, it was not Drakos, because we know that Jason Drakos was murdered and buried some weeks earlier. And let's say, if, by some bizarre Twilight Zone, X Files, twist of fate, detective, it happened to be Drakos, he would be the last person you would allow inside. Am I right?'

'Yes, sir. I can only agree. I would like to say in my own defence that I had nothing to gain by my actions. At the time I was certain everything was in order. I was not paid off to turn a blind eye. I admit this is a massive misjudgement on my part.'

'You allowed a gangland informant to go missing under your watch. You threw months of undercover police work out the window and potentially allowed other violent criminal figures to avoid apprehension.'

'Yes, sir. I know.'

*   *   *

Thanks to the finding of Jason Galanis's body two weeks after the episode and clear evidence implicating two other underworld criminals, Detective Anderson got off lightly, with a four-month suspension followed by a further four months of traffic duties. He was then permitted to work as a detective with CIB on two years' supervised probation.

Chapter 13

Harmony – Part 4

While holding her head against his chest he lifted her off her feet with his other arm. As Bentley walked around the bedroom with her in his arms, he lowered his head and made sounds into her ear. She groaned and moaned as he popped, clicked, hissed and whistled.

'And I so want you to do that to me. Every bit of it,' she breathed. 'This is the therapy I need, Bentley. Use my body to satisfy yourself as you know you must. Enter me, pleasure me. Use your fingers, your hands, your mouth, your tongue, just like you said. Then fuck me and make me come over and over. I think you must be the sexiest man on the planet.'

Bentley lay her across the bed with her legs bent over the side at her knees. He removed his remaining clothes then knelt on the carpet and opened a massive mouth. His tongue divided into three short octopus-like tubes, complete with suction pads. His mouth enveloped her entire pubic area. She instinctively raised her knees and let them fall apart while placing her feet on the edge of the mattress. Harmony pushed her pelvis hard into his face.

Bentley's hands and arms slipped under her back and slid up to her shoulders, looped over and came down across her chest, his fingers tweaked her nipples, and his hands gently massaged her breasts. Harmony had a momentary thought recalling how he first opened the door, *naturally, he has very long arms and exceptional dexterity, this is so fine and so perfect, don't stop.*

Bentley's lower jaw opened further, his lower lip now encompassing her anal area. The central tongue swelled further and entered her vagina. The upper one flicked and sucked at her clitoris, while the lower one prowled around her anus, pushing in gently every few seconds, each time a little deeper than before. Harmony shuddered and shook, all her pelvic muscles pulsating at once. She raised her head and looked down meeting Bentley's eyes. Beautiful blue eyes. There was something unusual about the shape of his mouth, but she gave it no serious thought. She was consumed by pleasure beyond measure, beyond description. *Don't stop, don't stop.*

One hand left her right breast only to be replaced by the other. This hand stretched and grew, three of the fingers walking across from one breast to the deserted one. Now he was caressing both her boobs with one hand. *How is this possible? Don't stop. Don't stop.* Blotches of greens and greys, like army camouflage, moved over his skin.

The free arm and hand arched up and descended over the top of her head with fingers extended. Black claws had replaced fingernails. The hand stretched to fully cover the top part of her skull. Bentley pushed with his claws. Harmony gasped and climaxed for the second time.

Bentley's eyes filled his eye sockets as he peered up across Harmony's bare stomach, watching his own limbs caressing her. He watched her chest rising and falling. For a brief second her eyes opened. He saw something. Right there inside her. There was something he had failed to notice before. His eyes moved rapidly side to side independently of each other, then filled with water which ran down his elongated cheeks and across her groin. His respective tongues left the various orifices and became one. His head lifted. His fingers and arms shortened back to their regular human size. He let out a shrill and glided over the top of her and kissed her open mouth. The vaginal penetration was unusual. At first it felt more like a thumb sized erection, but then, while inside her it grew with every second until there was no space for it to grow any further. Bentley didn't move. Harmony lay still, losing herself in the magic of the moment. Despite their stationary positions something was moving inside her — expanding and contracting in all directions. His groin was pushed hard against hers. She felt a stimulating vibration like something in his pubic area had been switched on. Harmony soaked it all up as they lay still and locked together for fifteen minutes.

Eventually, Bentley made a series of sounds, stood and headed to the shower where he stood crying under the hot water. Harmony remained prostrate over the bed still panting.

Chapter 14

R.I.P.

A white Falcon Hearse was parked outside Otto Hammerstein's house at Rode Road, Chermside.

Roderick Ignatius Peabody, a funeral director from Brisbane's south side, raised the dragon door knocker and tapped three times on Otto's front door. While he patiently waited, he took a white cloth from his pocket and polished the black dragon. When he heard the soft shuffle inside and the key turning in the lock, he tucked away his cloth and stood to attention.

Otto's face lit up on seeing him. 'Rip, so glad you came around.'

'Always a pleasure, Otto.' He tipped his head. Peabody was a tall, pale, and clean-shaven man in his fifties with impeccable manners and unwavering kindness. He had never asked anyone to call him Rip, nevertheless, given his initials, the nickname was common among those that knew him well. Over recent years he had assisted with three Hammerstein funerals.

'I'm simply overjoyed to see you,' said Otto warmly. 'Come in. Come in. We have to chat.' Otto, still in his pyjamas and dressing gown despite it being eleven in the morning, moved to the side and waved his companion through. 'Straight through into the lounge,' continued Hammerstein. 'I'll put the kettle on.'

'Can I offer you some assistance?' asked the undertaker, turning his head a little in Otto's direction.

'Thanks, but I've got it,' panted Otto.

'Most kind,' said Peabody. The black suited undertaker, in large quiet steps, strolled through to the lounge. He unbuttoned his jacket and sat on the edge of a recliner.

Otto first gave him a glass of cold water. Peabody briefly stood to accept the glass. 'Thank you, Otto.'

A few minutes later the old man set down a fine porcelain cup of black Earl Grey tea. 'There you go,' said Hammerstein.

'Thank you. Perfect,' replied Rip.

After setting his own cuppa down carefully next to a manilla folder on a coffee table, Otto sat in the other recliner. The frail old man flopped back in his chair and let out a long breath. He nodded his head then spoke. 'Everything has unfolded, almost exactly as you told me it could.'

'That is wonderful. It was exactly what Medora wanted. What a special life experience. If only everyone could be so fortunate.'

'Once again, I must thank you for the funeral service. It touched everyone's hearts and was an outstanding tribute to her.'

'Always a difficult time, but I'm very pleased that you, your family and friends were content.'

'As you warned me, some police officers paid me a visit.'

'And I'm sure they departed suitably puzzled.' Rip sipped his tea and flashed a brief smile.

'I was disheartened I never got to see her personally. Every knock on the door for three weeks made my heart skip a beat.'

'That is unfortunate, but as I explained, that is strictly a matter that only the Semblant and the Acquired can decide. They would consider all options and decide on the best outcome.'

'Pretty sure she didn't come because she would have been worried that I'd just drop dead. Which, I guess, was on the cards…. oh yes, I have these.' Otto picked up the folder and took out three pictures and passed them to Peabody. 'The police left them on my request… nice of them.'

'Oh my!' He looked at the images of Medora in her hot pink skirt and raised one black eyebrow. One photo was of her entering the club and two more on the dance floor. 'I see precisely what you mean. She is truly, what they call, *drop-dead gorgeous.*'

'I told the police it was her,' chuckled Hammerstein. 'I also told them she was up there…' he flicked his head up and to the side '…resting above the fireplace.'

'It's good to be honest.'

Both men sipped their tea. Otto looked to the ceiling and then placed his cup back on the saucer.

'Something is on your mind my friend,' said Rip.

'Yes… yes… the Semblant, they are very sensual.'

'Oh yes, very much so. Is that a concern?'

'Not especially. Those pictures of her…'

'The answer is yes,' interrupted Peabody. He glanced at the images he still held. 'I'd be one hundred percent sure she had sexual intercourse, and quite probably a number of times. But you already knew she would.'

'I know… she was given a second chance. So wonderful and I'm so pleased it happened this way.' Otto squirmed a little in his chair. He smiled as Peabody passed the pictures back, making brief eye contact before tucking them away again in the folder. He took up his tea and sipped, held the cup and sipped some more.

'I suspect that's not what is really on your mind,' said Peabody.

'There is something else… I was wondering, Rip…'

'It's not time, Otto,' interrupted the undertaker. 'You have a few years ahead of you. I know the Semblant. They would deny you. You want that same experience, that return to an exuberant youth, and I hope one day it comes to you.' Peabody studied his sad friend's face and sighed. 'Is that why you invited me here today?'

'It's always lovely to see you, Rip. But to be honest, which is the best thing as you say... yes... I was hoping they would take me.'

'What you feel is grief. Something not so easily put aside. I'm so glad the police left those pictures for you. Look at them regularly and others you have. Invite your brother up from the coast. Call in on your friends.' Rip reached over and placed a large hand on the armchair over Otto's. 'And you know, I always enjoy your company, and I'm more than happy to drop in on you from time to time.'

Otto looked at his friend. They smiled at each other. Peabody patted and rubbed Hammerstein's hand. 'Are they people, Rip? The Semblant?'

'They are the best of all people.'

'How many do you know?'

'I only know one but have heard about others. Beyond that, who knows. This conversation must always be private between us.'

'Of course, yes. I fully understand. The Semblant told me... well... at least assisted me to understand the rules.

Chapter 15

Clive Gets a Clue

To his surprise, Clive Anderson had been asked to complete the many outstanding interviews following the Tribal Moon decapitation. He would have preferred just being left to it, but a junior officer, Lachlan Godwin, in his second week with CIB, was to accompany him. Anderson was to report back daily to Edwards or Silverton. The serial killer case had for now, assumed top priority.

'Godwin, we have five interviews that are overdue. Four of which I think we can do today,' said Clive. 'Hopefully they'll be home on a Saturday.'

'Would you like me to get onto that this morning, sir?' asked an eager Godwin.

As he clicked print on his computer, Clive smiled. It had been some time since he had been called *sir*. 'Grab the list, son. We need to go together.'

*   *   *

The apartment block at Nundah in Brisbane was typical of the seventies. A six-pack of orange bricks. Three units on top and three below and half a dozen carparks that looked too narrow. It was ten in the morning when Clive knocked on the rattly screen door of apartment one. There were noises like stumbling around knocking over furniture and a loud male voice shouting *Fuck!*

The door opened. The two officers looked at a long-haired, scrawny guy, wearing only shorts. 'Huh…what's up, dudes?'

Clive showed his ID. 'We've missed you twice Liam, and you never returned our calls. So here we are for the third time.'

'Yeah. I got nothing. I know nothing. Can't help yous.'

'Can we come in?'

'I'd rather you didn't.' The guy looked around at the untidiness of his flat. 'The place is a fucking mess.'

'Look, I can smell the dope. I don't give a shit about that, and I'm prepared to completely forget about it if you answer a few questions.'

There was a brief silence. Clive gave a cheery smile.

'What about him?' the man gestured with his head to Godwin.

'He knows nothing,' said Clive. Godwin gave a wide-eyed look at the back of Anderson's head.

'Okay, come in.' He flicked a lever on the screen door, turned and walked to the lounge. Clive and Lachlan followed.

In the lounge, Liam put a cushion over his glass bong and sat next to it, keeping one hand on the cushion as if to guard it. With two fingers Clive lifted some soiled clothes off a single seater and dropped them amongst others on the floor. After inspecting the chair, he sat. The young-looking Godwin remained standing. He looked around the place. It was small and made to look smaller with the clutter and junk over the floor. A broken wooden dining chair lay on its side – one leg splintered in half, probably the one the untidy man fell over rushing to the door, thought Godwin.

'As we all know you were at the Tribal Moon on Friday the eleventh. We've seen you on video dancing with an attractive young woman.'

'Yeah... so? I danced with lots of chicks. That's what you do at nightclubs.'

'This particular lady wore a pink skirt with her boobs nearly hanging out.'

'Yeah, yeah...' smiled Liam, as he shook his finger at Clive. 'What a cool chick she was. She liked my clothes.'

'You mean you really have some decent apparel tucked away somewhere?' Clive pushed at some clothing with his foot.

'I can look fancy enough when I need to.'

'Well... what did she say?'

'Huh...' he looked up and to the left... 'Geez... be fucked if I can remember exactly. But I knew she liked the way I looked.'

'But she left you and moved on to someone else.'

'Yeah, she did,' he nodded. 'Shame really. But I didn't mind.'

'You didn't mind that a hot chick left you for someone else. Give me a fucking break!'

'I know what ur sayin' man... but really, I just didn't mind it. Even felt cool about it you know... like it was the right thing to do.'

Clive leaned a little forward and stared at Liam. He went quiet and seemed to be looking right through the young man to something beyond.

'You right, sir?' asked Godwin. Clive kept staring into the distance. Godwin stepped carefully over junk on the floor and put a hand on Clive's shoulder. 'Sir!'

'Hey... yeah, yeah,' retorted Clive. 'I'm fine. Just thinking.' Liam looked at Lachlan and rolled his eyes. Clive stood, moved to Liam and looked down on him. 'What did she say to you?' he shouted. 'Tell me the exact words. Tell me!'

'Fuck!' He pulled the cushion and bong closer to his body. 'Who cares, man. I know she told me stuff. It was a long night. I was on the piss. I can't remember exactly.'

'Did you see her again any time after that?'

'Noticed her dance a bit more that's all. After she left the dance floor, I never spotted her again. We done here now? I got shit to do.'

Clive lifted his leg and pushed his shoe hard against Liam's special cushion. Something cracked once, then again as the detective shifted his weight.

'Be seeing you.' Clive turned away. 'Let's go, Godwin.'

Liam gingerly lifted the cushion. His glass bong was shattered.

Chapter 16

Acquiring Medora

2 weeks ago…

Medora Hammerstein was eighty-four-years-old. This was her third year in care at the Seaview Life Aged Care Home. Contrary to its name, there were no sea views unless you drove east twenty kilometres.

Due to osteoarthritis, Medora's mobility had declined while living with her husband at Chermside, and this, combined with the many symptoms of Lewy Body dementia, forced him to ultimately make the difficult choice of sending her to Seaview Life.

She had many of the disturbing symptoms, and even using home help services could not alter the eventual outcome. Her hallucinations were at times intense and distressing, even at night she would thrash about in her sleep, waving her arms and kicking out her feet. Otto had resorted to sleeping on a spare mattress on the floor.

Medora had seen a plethora of jungle animals in her house over many months. The final decision to move her happened after she believed she'd seen a black panther in the house. She fell screaming in her haste to escape and fractured her wrist.

For two years, eight months and three days, Otto dutifully visited six times every week. Initially, the visits were relatively straight forward with a twenty-five-minute drive across Brisbane. When his vision and reflexes declined, and he could no longer safely drive, he would take a bus to town then hook up with a train, and finish with a ten-minute walk to the facility. It was always a nice change when a friend or his younger brother could help with transport.

Unfortunately, for the last year, Medora never recognised her companion of sixty-one years. She would greet him in different ways. Sometimes he was the doctor, or the gardener, a brother which she never had, the local publican or the parish priest. When in an irritable mood, which was half of the time, he could be a thief, a pushy salesperson, a jail warden or even a rapist.

Roderick Ignatius Peabody had visited with Otto many times and was deeply saddened by her gradual decline. It was in her last few weeks that her bladder control, and sometimes bowel control, failed her.

It was a Thursday in February, on a particularly difficult day for Medora, that Peabody decided it was time to take Otto aside for a quiet chat.

The pair sat next to one another on two orange plastic chairs in a small waiting room. This small space was most often used for relatives grieving the loss of their loved one or waiting for them to die.

'She thinks I'm a Nazi executioner,' sobbed Otto. 'Sent to pull out her fingernails and torture her to death.' Otto bent forward with his elbows on his knees and his head in his hands.

Peabody placed a hand on his shoulder. 'This is insufferable. I feel it so intensely for you both.'

'She threw faeces at me, Rip. She's never done that before.'

'What if I could help ease the suffering for both of you.'

'Yeah... I know... I've spoken to the doctor. I begged him to give her morphine. It was useless.'

'No morphine. I know another way. Something so profoundly beautiful, you would not believe it could even be possible.'

Otto sat up and looked at Peabody who gave him a soft smile and a gentle nod.

'What on earth are you talking about?'

The undertaker passed Otto a clean white folded handkerchief to blot his eyes. 'I cannot adequately explain this to you. I need to introduce you to a very good friend of mine. Every question, every concern you have will be answered, even concerns you didn't know you had.'

*   *   *

At the same time the next day, Peabody and a young man arrived at Seaview Life. Otto was sitting outside Medora's room having not yet ventured inside. He could hear her shouting to no one and swearing at an elephant. He decided to take a moment and gather his resources before greeting her.

Peabody strolled down the hallway with his friend. On this occasion he was dressed casually in jeans and t-shirt. Otto stood.

'Rip, I didn't know you owned anything but black and grey suits.'

'Good morning, Otto. Today is not a day to look like an undertaker. I'd like you to meet my very good friend, this is Alastair.'

Alastair looked young. Otto thought possibly in his mid to late twenties. He had a thick head of dark brown long hair and a tie-dyed t-shirt hanging over his shorts. He wore brown leather sandals. What struck Otto the most though was Alastair's skin. It was smooth and hairless – not just his face but his arms and legs. So smooth and blemish free that he looked almost photo shopped. There was something familiar about him.

'Hello Alastair. I think I've seen you before,' said Otto tilting his head to one side.

'You may recognise his face from the newspaper,' said Peabody. Alastair just smiled.

'Yes… the paper… the musician guy that went missing a few weeks back,' Otto paused in thought. 'Alastair… yeah, that's it, Alastair McCormack. Anyway, lovely to meet you.' Otto took a step towards him, but neither man made any attempt to shake hands. Hammerstein moved closer, lifted a hand, and stroked his soft cheek.

'Hello, Alastair,' he breathed. As he said those two words and felt the smooth skin, a calmness fell over him. A calmness like he had not felt for decades. A beautiful memory filled his thoughts – he was dancing the waltz with Medora at the Samford Community Hall – holding her, touching her skin, smelling the fragrance of her perfume… Faberge Tigress. All others had been tapped on the shoulder and stopped dancing. This wonderful woman had somehow dragged him, a man with two left feet, to the point of stealing the show and snaring the trophy. They waltzed around the empty floor seeing no one but each other.

A solitary tear ran down Otto's cheek, and despite the barrage of swear words emanating from room thirty-five behind him, the recollection of this wonderful day was as vivid as if he was there at this very moment.

'With your permission, Otto,' asked Peabody. 'Alastair would like to see Medora.'

'Oh… yes,' responded Otto, dragging himself reluctantly back to the present, and dropping his hand from Alastair's face. 'That's perfectly fine, but I'm afraid she's not particularly receptive at the moment.'

Alastair leaned towards Otto. He made three popping sounds, like you may hear on opening a can of soft drink, and followed this with a quick hiss, two clicks and a soft whistle.

'Yes, sir,' said Hammerstein. 'I understand.' Alastair moved into room thirty-five. Medora fell silent immediately.

The young musician pulled a chair alongside Medora's bed. She was sitting up against three pillows. Saliva was dribbling from her mouth. There were some remnants of breakfast on her nightie. Normally, by this time of the day the nurses would have had her bathed, dressed and sitting out of bed. The last few days though, Medora had been most difficult and not at all cooperative. The staff had apologised to Otto on each occasion and offered to give her a mild sedating medication to which Otto had agreed. But whatever the medicine was, it had no impact on his wife's irritability.

Now though, she sat quietly looking at the young man beside her bed. Medora's hair was grey and wispy. Her face had thinned, even more so over recent weeks due to decreased appetite. Her once full cheeks, now victims to age and gravity, formed deep creases down the sides of her nose, and some fine and not so fine lines had accumulated around the corners of her mouth. Alastair reached out and took her wrinkled and bruised hand in his. He let out a shrill oscillating whistle and tears cascaded down his cheeks in almost a constant stream.

Outside the room, Peabody stood next to his friend and dropped an arm around his shoulders. 'She has calmed now. Please go in and say goodbye to your wife.'

On entering the room his eyes met Medora's.

'It's time for me to go, Otto,' she said with a sad knowing smile. The young man still held her hand and cried quietly. His brow was furrowed and though his eyes were closed there was some protrusion obvious beneath his eyelids. Otto moved to the opposite side of the bed.

'My angel. I will never stop loving you,' he cried.

'Kiss me,' she breathed. Otto took her shoulders and kissed her firmly on the lips. 'My sweet, sweet man. I thank you for this wonderful life. You must go now. The Semblant and I have some work to do. Worry no more.'

Otto stood. Something inside him desperately wanted to stay, but his brain said otherwise. 'Beyond forever,' he said as he blew his last kiss. She mouthed the same words back to him. He left the room.

Outside, he and his friend closed the double doors and sat there, on two of the orange chairs that Peabody had borrowed from the small grieving room.

*   *   *

The smooth skinned young man lay down on the bed with Medora. He had removed all the pillows, and the two lay, fully clothed, on their sides face to face. He made a series of squeaks, pops, hisses and cracks.

'Thank you,' said Medora. 'Youth is so wasted on the young. Let us journey together.'

Alastair opened his mouth wider than seemed possible for a human. A heavy mist flowed from his mouth and into Medora's face, forming miniature tornadoes as she sucked it in through her nose. His tongue slowly bifurcated into octopus-like tentacles which extended and entered both Medora's nostrils. His smooth skin rippled and waved, starting at his head and progressing to his feet – wave after wave after wave. These small ripples changed colour from pink to greys and greens of every shade. The divided tongue seemed to keep running into her nose causing her nostrils to flare. Then it stopped, and many globules of material, about the size of grapes, flowed the other way back down the tongue tubes into Alastair.

*   *   *

A uniformed nurse strutted down the corridor towards the two men on the orange seats. Before she reached them, she had started talking and gesticulating.

'Those doors must remain open, gentlemen. Unless staff are performing a procedure.' Otto glanced at Rip. They both raised their eyebrows. The men remained seated as the nurse squeezed between the two chairs, opened one door and poked her head in the room. Seconds later she closed the door and stepped back. 'All is well here,' she said. 'Thank you both and have a nice day.' Both men's eyes followed her as she continued on her way and around a corner.

'The Semblant?' asked Otto.

'The Semblant,' nodded Peabody.

* * *

The men kept a quite vigil while the Semblant acquired Medora. Peabody glanced at his friend.

'Do you have any questions?'

Otto slowly shook his head. 'It seems strange in a way, but I have no questions.'

'That's pretty normal. You may have some in a day or two.'

They sat quite again, looking at nothing in particular. Another nurse went by, never looking their way or saying a word. After twenty minutes the doors behind them opened. Alastair strode out and away at a good pace.

Peabody took out his phone and tapped away for a moment. 'Getting an Uber for Alastair.'

'Semblants use Uber… huh, who'd have thought.'

'Technically, it's *The Semblant* – both singular and plural,' noted Peabody. Otto nodded. 'He has approximately two hours to assimilate,' continued the undertaker. 'Alastair will soon expire.'

'Yes, I know,' replied Otto. He looked at Peabody. 'Somehow… I just know that.' He shrugged.

'If it's suitable to you, Otto, we could be on our way. The staff will no doubt call you to say Medora has passed away. Naturally, I will organise the funeral.'

'Yeah, I guess,' he said hesitantly.

'You would like to see her again?'

'It had occurred to me.'

'As they say Otto… Elvis has left the building.'

'I know that, Rip.'

Peabody looked at his companion. He nodded. 'But you're right my friend, let's go back in.'

Inside, Medora's lifeless body lay back against pillows. She looked peaceful with her eyes shut and a slight smile. A motley purple and white pallor had settled over her forehead and cheeks. Otto moved closer and touched her face. 'I know you've moved on, but I still love the package you came in.'

Chapter 17

Number 2

It was eleven in the morning and the third day in a row, as the cleaner pushed her linen trolley past a row of cabins, that the smell, once again, hit her in the face. Today it was seriously offensive, and this time she was positive it was coming from cabin 12A.

The rotund lady stopped and moved towards the door. She had a master-key and was able to unlock any of the rooms. The smell was worse as she moved closer to the entrance. She pushed her key in, paused, and covered her mouth with the other hand. Visions of what could be inside flicked through her mind. She withdrew the key and waddled over to see the manager of the Northside Holiday Resort.

*　　　*　　　*

Detectives Silverton and Davis joined a uniformed policeman who stood a few meters upwind from the cabin.

'Hey, Charlie,' said Davis, recognising the officer. He moved closer and they shook hands. 'How are you going? You still on traffic?'

'Richard. Nice to see you. Yeah, mate. I'm good. And traffic's just fine,' he smiled. 'Better than this shit.' He tipped his head at the cabin.

'Hmm… you've not opened the door then? Taken a quick peek?'

'Fuck no. You crazy?'

'Oh, Charlie, this is Jan Silverton. She's the boss.'

'Hey, Jan. Lovely to meet you,' he nodded, smiled and politely shook hands.

'Likewise,' she replied as a white van pulled up. 'Forensics. Come on Davis. Let's dress up.'

'Later,' he said pointing to his friend who nodded.

*   *   *

'This guy checked in eight weeks ago for a two month stay,' said Silverton. 'The staff stories vary, but most seem to think they hadn't seen him for at least three weeks. The rooms are only serviced when vacated or requested. It's not going to be pretty in there.'

While some cabins were family size, fifteen of them, including 12A, were small one-bedroom boxes with an air con, a TV, a fridge and a narrow sink. The amenities block was a short walk across a patch of grass. The air con of 12A was still humming away.

After ten minutes, Silverton, Davis and three forensic officers were near fully covered in their protective clothing. Even though they both wore face masks, the two detectives had put a dab of mentholated cream under their noses.

Standing near the cabin door, the pair put on the last of their protective gear – their shoe coverings. Richard Davis stood behind Jan Silverton. A fly settled on his forehead. He flicked his head, then there was another and another. Jan flicked away a few.

'It's Christmas in here for flies. Try breathing more through your mouth.'

'The thought of sucking that stench into my lungs is not particularly appealing,' replied Davis.

'Here we go.' Silverton turned the round handle and pushed the door wide open. A gush of cool putrid air flowed out. The two turned their heads in disgust before peering in.

The female forensic officer looked at her male colleagues. 'Fuck! Gotta be two to three weeks old to smell like that.' They both nodded their agreement.

The detectives took a few tentative steps into the room. There was a man propped up on the bed. Apart from his face, his skin was tight and bloated like an overinflated balloon. From his neck down he was a patchy dull green colour while his head was predominantly a dark red. His open mouth and nose were infested with maggots. Many crawled over his decaying cheeks and through his eyes. Foamy blood-stained liquid had flowed from his mouth, nose, and eyes, then down his neck and onto the bed linen. The sheet and quilt were covering his groin, legs and hands.

Davis closed his eyes tightly for a few seconds and cleared his throat.

'You right?' asked Silverton.

'I will be.' He opened his eyes. 'Daisy patterned apron.' He pointed to the stained material draped over part of the distended abdomen.

'Yeah. Our killer's sewing skills have improved since he was here. And it looks like short dark, black hair.'

The pair moved further into the cabin. The female forensic officer began taking photographs of everything, with wide angle shots and close ups. The other two had placed and opened their square black equipment cases outside the door on a plastic sheet. There were many fine brushes, multiple sizes of empty jars, all sizes of sealable plastic bags, labels, fingerprint dust and an ultraviolet light in one. Torches, tape measures, lint rollers, scissors, forceps, syringes and needles, swabs and cotton buds, glass microscope slides, disposable gloves, and crime scene tape in the other.

'When you're ready Catriona, I'd like to turn down the blanket,' said Jan.

The covered officer looked at her male colleagues and got a thumbs up. 'You're good to go. Easy does it.'

Silverton and Davis stood on either side of the bed and in unison slowly turned down the sheet and quilt. The man's hands were the only part of his lower body not bloated, thanks to the amputation of all his fingers which allowed fluid and gas to ooze and bubble out. All the digits were complete and not cut into pieces at the joints like the other two crime scenes. Some much smaller maggots were crawling around the severed stumps, the loose fingers, the detached penis and the oozing amputation point in his groin.

'The air-conditioning is on max cool and is directed at his chest,' said Catriona. 'This has created different rates of decay in his body. This is why the maggots are younger here between his legs. His head was above the blanket of cool air in the cabin and has decayed more rapidly. He's been dead for three to four weeks. And by the looks of the area around the small sink...' she gestured to the narrow and very bloody basin further along the wall '... this is where the victim may have been killed.'

The sink was covered in dried blood. The vinyl floor below was strewn with spatters, clots and bloody smears.

'Our killer has done at least two more since this one,' said Silverton. 'Both probably gay men, both with black hair. This is pretty untidy. At the other crime scenes, he had a proper bathroom to work with.'

Davis squirmed. 'Yeah... this gay men thing with black hair is a bit of a worry.' Richard touched his own head. Catriona gave him a reassuring double pat on his shoulder.

'Check out the TV,' said Silverton.

Across the TV screen, written in blood, over three lines, were the words *TIME AND TIME AGAIN – I SEE YOU DIE – DADDY*.

'The Daisy Killer seems to have a Daddy problem,' added Davis.

'It's certainly a consistent theme,' agreed Silverton. 'His last two were just ten days apart, his last one being three days ago. And he has developed his technique since being here.'

'He's escalating,' said Catriona. 'Unless he's caught soon there's sure to be more.'

'And there may be another before this,' added Silverton.

The forensic officer nodded. 'Could be from months ago.'

Chapter 18

More Q's Than A's

Clive and Lachlan successfully completed three more brief interviews, all of whom were attendees at the Tribal Moon on the night in question. While none had danced with Medora Hammerstein, two of the interviewed men had ogled her and were in hope they might have had the opportunity. The third, a twenty-year-old lady, had been poised on a barstool when Medora came over for a large glass of cold water. None of these three had spoken with Medora or heard her say anything. Clive had asked all of them. 'Did you feel in any way at all that she communicated with you? If not words directly, perhaps with body language or by eye contact?' All answered in the negative.

On their way back to the office, Clive's mobile rang. He pushed the green button and took the call via speaker as they drove.

'Anderson,' he snapped.

'Hey Clive. Chris Pendleton from the lab at…'

'Yeah, I know,' interrupted Anderson.

'How are you?'

'Busy.'

'I called Jan, but she said I should talk to you.'

'Did she?'

'She's got another one you know.'

'Another one what?'

'Another body. One you wouldn't like. Serious decomposition.'

'No. I won't be coming in,' barked Clive.

'That's fine but I'm calling about the Randall decapitation case. I have some intriguing path results.'

'I'm all ears.'

'As I knew, there was semen present in the genital area. There was also some undefined cephalopod-like fluid.'

'English works best for me.'

'Cephalopods include octopus, squid and cuttlefish.'

'Huh... Some sort of fish-based lubricant or something?'

'No other lubrication components were present.'

'So, what does this mean exactly, Pendleton?' said Clive sharply. 'Are we looking for a woman who has tentacles hanging out of her vagina?'

'Are you mocking me, Clive?'

'Just trying to understand.'

'I think the most likely of unlikely options is that a squid or octopus was used for some sort of sex play. A particular fetish I have never heard of before. There was a small amount of fluid on the spinal cord as well as the genitals.'

'Huh... what else?'

'The severing of the spinal cord is suggestive of tearing. A tearing which may, in part, have occurred by suction.'

'You mean suction like with a vacuum cleaner?'

'Perhaps not a vacuum cleaner as such... something with considerable strength... but this is not conclusive.'

'Octopuses suck you know!'

'I am aware of that. But as far as I know, Clive, no giant octopi were spotted in the club that night.'

'Now, you're the one taking the piss!'

Pendleton laughed. *'Yeah... I do get my chance every now and then.'*

'Good for you. Are we done now?'

'Nearly. The neck, right through to the spinal cord, was cut neatly... evenly... with something very fine and sharper than a scalpel blade. I initially thought

something like piano wire, but microscopically it's something finer and sharper. The cutting around the neck appears to have happened all at once, not progressively like you might cut an avocado.'

'You draw a lot of comparisons with your work and food. It disturbs me, Pendleton. Is that it then?'

'Nothing further at this point. I'll email the interim report.'

'Okay. Bye.' Clive pressed the red button.

He looked at Godwin. 'You got all that, squire? Call out if you see a lady with tentacles hanging out her skirt, or if you see any giant octopuses!'

'Octopi, sir.'

'What?'

'Octopi is the plural, sir.'

'Fuck off, Godwin!' snapped Clive.

*　　　*　　　*

Over the remainder of the weekend, Clive hung around at his home drinking beer through the day and red wine late into the evening, as he wondered how to present an evolving theory to his boss, Vince Edwards.

There was one final interview scheduled for Monday with the only female that danced with the person alleged to be Medora Hammerstein. Beyond that, he was unsure what direction to proceed. Octopuses, octopi, heads, skulls, vacuum cleaners, fine sharp circular saws and decapitation… what a fucking mess.

For Clive it was usually around the fourth beer when he would start rehashing the incident from nearly ten months ago.

His charge, Jason Galanis, had escaped with Nicholas Drakos. The dope head, Liam, described a similar experience – the fractured recall of events, just the same as he had on that day when he fucked up. That absolute conviction to the truth of a story despite only having a patchy inconclusive recall. That was it exactly – identical to his own story.

'Can't be coincidence,' he said aloud as he poured a very full glass of cabernet sauvignon.

He turned his attention to his mobile phone, checked his Facebook and emails, then went to his contact list and amused himself by connecting various ring tunes and sounds to his contacts.

*   *   *

Janine Hansen worked either in a city office or from home. Today she was in town. After several calls last week, Clive had finally teed up a meeting for twelve-thirty. The elevator arrived at the twenty-second floor quickly and quietly.

Anderson and Godwin presented themselves at a semi-circular reception desk, complete with glass screen extending a metre above the counter. Emblazoned in big lettering across the front of the desk over two lines were the words *Langley, Lester, Bruce and Associates. Insurance and Commercial Lawyers.*

'Police,' said Clive flashing his ID. 'We have an appointment with Miss Hansen.'

The skinny receptionist stood. 'Certainly. This way please.' She walked ahead of the two officers, one foot crossing over in front of the other, making her pelvis and shoulders sway. Godwin was more than a little mesmerised with her buttocks as they moved in her tight frock. Clive shoved his young accomplice's shoulder.

The place was spacious with wide corridors decorated with pastel prints of sparse random dribbles, specks and blobs that resembled nothing. After their third ninety-degree turn, the receptionist opened a door to an empty conference room with a massive oval table that would seat at least twenty. 'Janine will be with you shortly,' she said with a quick smile before turning and striding away.

'You like that piece of arse, son?' said Clive.

'Sorry sir.' Lachlan blushed. 'I was rather taken with it for a moment.'

'Hmm…you got good taste, Godwin. I'll give you that.'

'Yes sir. Thank you, sir.'

After five minutes Janine Hansen made her entrance. Clive tipped his head. 'Hello. Thank you for your time, Miss Hansen.'

'Janine, please,' she replied with a smile revealing a perfect set of teeth. She shook hands lightly with both officers. Her long blonde hair was swept back over her head and tied back in a ponytail. Clive knew she was thirty-five, but she could easily pass as being ten years younger.

The three sat at one end of the large table.

'I believe you know why we are here?' said Anderson.

'Yes,' she nodded. 'The Tribal Moon matter. How dreadful.' She shook her head and looked at the floor. 'How can I help?'

'Do you remember who you danced with that night?'

'Some, yes, but not everyone. I danced with a lot of different people. Male and female.' Janine pushed out a quick smile.

'You danced with a pretty lady in a short pink skirt.'

'Oh yes, Medora. She was so lovely.' Janine's narrow face lit up.

'She told you her name?' said Clive with surprise.

'Well… yes. At some stage she must have, or I wouldn't know it, would I?'

'What else did you talk about?'

'Is she in some way responsible for the death of that young man?'

'We are anxious to talk with her about that. For the moment she seems to have vanished.'

'But she's a suspect? Really?'

'We are doing our best to rule people out. As yet we are unable to do that with… this *Medora* lady. What else did you two discuss?'

Janine sat pondering, looking towards the ceiling. 'Well… we both liked each other I know that. Pretty sure she said something about catching up with me again.' Janine nodded. 'Yes, she definitely said that.'

Clive leaned towards the seated lawyer. 'Janine… I want you to think very carefully. Take your time and try to recall the exact words Medora said to you. I'd like you to be precise. This is important.'

Godwin took a breath, remembering the Saturday interview with Liam, and how Anderson seemed to have lost the plot. Out the corner of his eye, Clive noticed his offsider's tight mouth and raised eyebrows.

'The music was very loud…' continued Janine. She looked up again and tipped her head. Her tongue lightly touched her top lip. She put her attention back on Anderson. 'This might sound strange, but I can't remember exactly. I can only tell you in general terms what was said. I know she will be back in touch sometime. This is true. She wasn't lying to me.'

'How could you know that?'

'Can't say. I just know it… that's all.'

'You're a lawyer, right?'

'I am.'

'How do you think such a statement would stand up in court?'

'Obviously it's too vague, but sometimes you just know things, don't you? Just as I know this table is made of wood…' she tapped on it with her knuckles. 'I know what I say is true.'

'And where do you expect to catch up again?'

'The Tribal Moon.'

'When?' Clive fired back.

'Not sure. A Friday night. Which Friday… who knows, but I'll keep going and find out.' She knocked on the table again and smiled.

'You were there last night?'

Janine nodded. 'And the one before. And as you already know the one before that too… when the incident occurred. Sorry, but I've become a little obsessed with going there. Odd, I know. That night was only my second time, but now I wouldn't miss a Friday night for the world.'

Chapter 19

The Assimilation – Part 1

Two weeks ago…

The Semblant, temporarily named Alastair, left Seaview Life after a short wait for his Uber. As he sat in the back, on his journey to South Brisbane, his smooth pink skin lightened and dried. The gloss on his hair had gone, and dark-brown had gradually become light-brown. A facial tic had developed on one side of his face, and around every ten seconds the muscles of his cheek and jaw spasmed, his right eye closed and his head jerked.

'You okay back there, mate?' said the driver as he checked him out through the rear-view mirror. Alastair let out a high-pitched yelp like that of a small dog, after which the driver casually turned up the music and put his focus back on the road.

The Uber pulled up alongside a large black sign with white lettering – *Peabody & Sons Funeral Directors and Crematorium* and in a smaller font at the bottom *At your service for over 100 years.*

'Have a nice day. Thank you for a five-star rating,' said the smiling driver.

The Semblant hurried past the car park, the grand entrance to the main reception and funeral service area, the smaller chapel at the back, the staff only and furnace area and the memorial garden. He stumbled through the unlocked door of a small two-storey cottage style home, tucked away on the corner of the large property behind a row of mid-sized mango trees.

It was a small but tidy home with all the amenities one would require. He moved through a sparsely decorated lounge room where there were two old single lounge chairs. On the wall was a large print set in a heavy frame. The picture was the front on view of a black panther creeping forward across some grass. The eyes were yellow. The gaze was piercing.

Alastair went into the bedroom, locking the door behind him. There was a bare queen size mattress on the floor. The Semblant took off all his clothes throwing them to the side and let himself fall to the mattress. His dry skin was curling and peeling, yet not shedding, on every area of his body, and his hair was receding back into his scalp. He rolled up in a tight ball with his chin on his knees. A faint whining sound began as he started to tremble from head to toe.

Chapter 20

Harmony – Part 5

Ten minutes had gone by since Harmony's multiple orgasms, and her breathing had finally settled. She rolled onto her back and opened her eyes while she lay there, naked and spreadeagled, on the bed. There were sounds – water was running, but there was something else. She lifted her head and turned an ear to the side, there were cries, sobs and a few short squeaks like a door hinge needing oil.

The bathroom was breathtaking. Spacious, with beautiful white tiles with a subtle gold and grey fleck. The shower had two stainless-steel shower heads the size of dinner plates.

Bentley was sitting on the shower floor with his knees up with water falling onto his head. He was squeaking and sobbing at the same time.

'Oh… what has happened? My poor man!' She went to join him but recoiled back on feeling the heat of the water. 'Ow… that's way too hot. Come on. Get out. Quick!' She carefully stepped back in and reached through the hot stream and turned off the tap. 'Shit, that's so hot.' Harmony rubbed a hand over her wet arm.

Bentley shot to his feet as if he was spring loaded.

'Ow… look at you,' gasped Harmony. She reached out and touched his chest. 'You are hot… like… I mean heat hot. Hot in every other way of course. Have you burnt yourself?'

Bentley took her shoulders and pulled her into him. He held her with one hand on her back and the other on her backside.

'You are fucking cooking.' She instinctively put her arms around his waist. He was still hot, but it was easing off. There was no redness despite the prolonged hot shower.

'You were crying.' She looked up at him.

Bentley smiled as he gazed at her. His mouth opened and a thin tongue shot out and darted straight into her nostril. Harmony's pupils immediately dilated. The tongue twisted slightly in the air as it ran into her body. He maintained his hold on her back and bottom as she became loose against him. Misty air fell from his open mouth onto her face. She breathed most of it in.

To Harmony, in what seemed only a moment, they were both naked and sitting next to each other on Bentley's bed. She looked at him. He was truly stunning, but for some reason, right at this moment, he appeared hazy and the area around them both was blurred and foggy.

'I feel like I'm in a dream,' she said. She peered around at her surroundings.

'Yes, I know… but it's perfectly fine. There is no cause for concern. You can relax,' he replied in a soft, but deep voice. There was a reverberating quality to it, but at the same time it was clear and somehow soothing. 'I owe you an apology.'

'You owe me nothing.'

'I was overcome with desire. This clouded my judgement.'

'I am glad you were overcome,' breathed Harmony through a smile.

'I was going to acquire you, but in a somewhat different way than you were expecting.'

'What does that mean… acquire me? It sounds… sort of peaceful… nice.'

'It is a bridge to something profoundly beautiful and exhilarating.'

'Bentley, you can acquire me whenever you want.'

'Yes… I know… thank you,' the Semblant nodded slowly. 'Harmony, I suspected something that I now know to be true. You have an irregular heartbeat. The electrical activity of your heart is…

out of synch, so to speak. This is something that can be treated and cured quite simply. You will see a specialist about this… and you will do this quite soon.'

'I need to see a cardiologist? Wow, I had no idea. I will do that. Thank you,' she said. 'This explains a lot. The light-headedness, the fainting, and some chest pain. And here I was thinking it was growing pains and hormones.'

'Thank you for coming back to my apartment. You have a wonderful body. You are a very beautiful and sexy lady. I sense you have a great future ahead of you.'

'I love your senses. Are we going to have sex again?'

'We will.'

'Now?'

'Soon.' Bentley smiled and briefly closed his eyes. 'I'd like to drive you home.'

Harmony's face lit up. 'Yes, I'd love for you to do that. That is, if staying the night here is not an option.' She raised her eyebrows in a question. 'Are we in a dream?'

'Sort of… we are communicating. We will be fully alert in a moment.'

'That's good, I need to go check my phone. Crystal's probably been calling. And I'm not finished with you yet, Bentley.' She pointed her finger and tilted her head towards him.

The couple woke lying next to one another, both opening their eyes at the same time. Harmony gave him a quick kiss and got up to search for her phone.

Chapter 21

The Assimilation – Part 2

Two weeks ago…

Any resemblance to Alastair had disappeared. All dried and peeling skin was gone, and the visible areas of the body now appeared oily and sticky. The Semblant's arms and legs had become like tentacles that were wrapped around what vaguely looked like a torso, neck, and head. They curled and uncurled. Squeezed and sucked noisily. Browns greens and greys washed over the Semblant like waves rolling up a beach. Skin and tissue stretched in all directions as if elastic.

The head was an elongated oval shape. An opening, which may have once been a mouth, stretched and grew until it reached the edges of the oval looking head, revealing a bottomless pit of absolute blackness. There was a slight slowing of activity as a mass of heavy whitish mist shot upward, then descended over the body, encasing it in a translucent cloud. A fat tentacle swooped inside the black hole only to erupt from the lower end of the torso and wrap once more around the writhing mass. A sound like a whistling kettle filled the air.

Slowly the creature began showing traces of pink and white. The tentacles stopped entwining, settled and reshaped into limbs. The mist cloud absorbed into the skin surface. The waves of spreading colours slowed and stopped. The black hole shrunk forming lips and a mouth. Hair grew from the scalp. Other facial features emerged and took form. The body uncurled, breasts filled out, an abdomen took shape and a neat triangle of pubic hair emerged. The squealing kettle sound eased away to silence. The eyes remained closed.

After a moment of quiet and stillness, the fingers uncurled, and the hands glided over the naked body as if discovering it for the first time. The full breasts, the soft abdomen, the firmness in the hips and thighs – outer and inner. The right hand pushed firmly against the pubic area, the pelvis pushed back. Then the fingers rode gently over the small dark patch of pubic hair, over the bellybutton, between the breasts then caressed her own neck and shoulders. The other hand moved to the top of her head and pushed through the thick blonde hair – lifting it and letting it fall through her fingers. Her touch moved to her face, across the forehead, tracing the fine line of her eyebrows with thumb and forefinger. She lightly felt her eyelids then down both sides of her nose, lightly outlining each nostril. Two fingers pushed through a small gap between her full lips. She felt her tongue. She licked and sucked her fingers. Slowly, she put her arms by her side. She let out a contented sigh and smiled.

Medora Hammerstein rolled onto her side and slept.

*   *   *

Many hours later, a naked Medora walked around the lower level of the cottage exploring every room. In the bathroom she stopped and looked at herself in the mirror. At first, Medora tried to speak, but found the words difficult to articulate. She breathed out an *Oh my goodness.*

She felt her now smooth cheeks, forehead and around her eyes. She lifted her hair and let it fall. A wide-eyed Medora smiled as she touched herself. *However brief this rebirth may be, it is beyond belief. Truly indescribable.'* A solitary tear ran down her face.

She stepped back from the mirror so she could see more of herself.

She paused and tilted her head as if listening to some internal dialogue, then replied via her thoughts. *Yes, I remember this version of me. Thank you for this wonderful and exciting opportunity. Let us use it well. And you are correct. I have already said my goodbyes to Otto. Him seeing me… like this… only to lose me again. That would break him. That would be so unfair. I can't… we can't do that.*

Medora hummed quietly as she paraded and swirled around the bathroom, taking in frequent glances back at the mirror, admiring herself.

Shopping? Yes, how divine. I need something modern, eye-catching, sexy. We should do that soon.

Chapter 22

Reporting Back

It was with some degree of trepidation that Inspector Vince Edwards had decided that Clive Anderson could continue to interview the remaining list of patrons who were at the Tribal Moon on the night of the murder. Silverton and her experienced colleague Bryant needed to head up the serial killer investigation.

'I'm giving you some leeway here, Clive,' he had said. 'You are the lead detective on this case now. Be methodical. No shortcuts. Don't fuck it up.'

Anderson was under strict instructions to report back directly to the inspector or to Silverton at the end of each working day.

Now, it was a few minutes after six in the evening when he stood at the inspector's door, rehearsing his words to himself. *The key is sound credible and not delusional,* he repeated once more. He knocked, then heard Edwards shout, 'Come in Clive.'

Edwards and Silverton were standing, heads down, at a side table covered with photos and notes. Clive ambled over and peered between them. 'Oh my God! Someone is seriously fucked in the head.' He turned away and wandered to the comfortable side of the room and dropped into a lounge.

Edwards turned his pale head. 'Make yourself at home, Anderson. I'll be with you in a moment.' Clive gave a grimace and an unsure wave.

'Popular thought is that there is another body somewhere. Maybe his first kill,' said Jan.

'Fuck,' sighed Vince. 'This isn't going away anytime soon.'

'No, sir,' replied Jan. 'May get worse yet.'

'Yeah. Let's talk to Clouseau,' scoffed Edwards. The two left their notes and pictures and sat near Clive.

Vince Edwards let out a long sigh before speaking. He turned to Anderson. 'So, do we have any suspects as yet?'

'Did you read Pendleton's report?' asked Clive.

'We both read it. Suspects… are there any?'

'No… but something is evolving here.'

'Right… is this a tangible lead then?'

'A lead it is… but where it leads I'm not entirely sure at this time.' Clive flicked his gaze between his two senior colleagues. Edwards tipped his head and displayed two open palms.

'We have now interviewed everyone on the Tribal Moon list,' continued Clive. 'Some were very brief, others that we knew had direct contact with the mysterious Medora were more substantial. There is a common thread here…' Clive paused and swallowed. Edwards looked at Silverton and raised his eyebrows.

'No one that spoke to her or danced with her can recall any actual words that she spoke… but they all insisted they had communicated with her. They were certain of it beyond any shadow of a doubt…'

'Oh no!' bellowed Edwards as he stood. He pushed his hands over his face and through his short grey hair. 'You're doing a fucking angle here.' He stabbed a finger at Clive. 'It's about you, isn't it? All about you. Still trying to justify your fucking stuff ups. Jesus, Anderson! Give us a fucking break.' Some colour had risen in Edwards cheeks.

'Sir, please…' interjected Anderson.

'Shut the fuck up, Clive. As if we haven't got enough on our plate with this serial killer shit 'n all.' Edwards was pacing. Stopping every few strides to glare and shout at Anderson. 'This was your chance. Your chance to prove you can handle a big case. Do a thorough job!'

'I apologise,' said Clive.

'All you've done is waste time. Interviewed people with your own agenda in mind. This is not good.' Edwards put a hand on his head. 'I need to sit down.' Silverton was up and guided him to a chair.

'Are you taking your blood pressure meds, sir?'

'Shit, Jan.'

'Pendleton asked me to remind you. He was concerned.'

'Pendleton? What is this? A group effort to antagonise the boss?' Fuck off, both of you. Give me some space.'

'Will you be okay?' asked Silverton.

Edwards pointed at the door. 'Go! Get out!'

Jan and Clive left. Once outside the door, Anderson had more to say.

'I've seen all the video footage, Jan. There is not a single time when she speaks to anyone.' The two walked together past cubicles, desks and closed doors. There was no one else around. 'Oh... the Medora bitch smiles a lot,' continued Clive. 'She stares at times, but not a fucking word. This is factual. This is not me working any fucking angle for Christ's sake.'

'How much footage was at the back of her head?'

'There was some.'

'That's when she could have been speaking.'

'Not at all likely. I don't buy that. What I saw and what I was told go hand in hand.'

'Let's say you are right. What on Earth does it mean?'

'That... I don't know... yet. But I will. There's a chance she'll be back there. The only woman she danced with, Janine Hansen, is one hundred percent certain that Hammerstein will be returning to the Tribal Moon on a Friday night.'

'How could she go back. She wouldn't last a minute. Gerry Bonering would be onto it.'

'Don't know. She's imitated Medora Hammerstein. She could imitate someone else. You know… a new hair style and colour, different dress style, glasses or whatever.'

'Risky for her to return to the scene. I guess you want to go clubbin' now?'

'I need to be there. I'll do it on my own time. Don't want to give the boss a stroke.'

'We can go together,' said Silverton.

'You believe me?' Clive's eyes lit up.

'No. But something weird is going on. It might be worth chatting up a few of the regular patrons and even a second round with some of the staff.'

Chapter 23

Harmony – Part 6

Harmony grinned as she sat in the front passenger's seat of Bentley's white Mercedes sports. It was one-thirty in the morning as they drove along through the suburbs on their way to her home at Ascot. Her hand had been across the centre console for most of the drive. She first started touching his shoulder and neck, then running her fingers over the bristles on his cheeks and chin. A moist feeling had settled between her own legs.

She shifted her focus and began stroking and squeezing the top of his left thigh. Moving from time to time to his inner thigh and groin. From the moment her hand first went there, there was a firm bulge in his chinos. Her hand moved away. She placed a finger over her mouth and bit her bottom lip.

'There's something I want to do,' she breathed.

Bentley turned his head and looked kindly at her. He turned back to look ahead. The road was intermittently lit with streetlights which illuminated the inside of the car every few seconds. There were still some other cars on the road – for the most part it was taxis, rideshare vehicles, and police.

Harmony undid her seatbelt. Bentley pressed a button and his car seat slowly moved back as far as it could. The Semblant emitted a few quick pops and hisses. She shuffled closer, leaned over and undid the top button of his pants. The zip partly undid itself with the pressure from below. Harmony helped it on its way.

Bentley's penis stood there proudly, displayed more vividly every time they passed a streetlight. The light moved through the car showing the black and green colours of his erection. There were lumpy nodules on the sides, and on the top it looked like the mouth of a sucker fish.

Harmony gazed in wonder as she placed a hand on the shaft. All she could see was a large pink organ with wavy blue veins running down the side and a smooth head protruding above a partly retracted foreskin. After pulling down with her hand to fully expose the glans, she took it in her mouth.

The sensations were strange. While she set about doing some work with her hand and allowing it to slide deep then shallow into her mouth, there was a vibrating sensation. She could feel it in her lips and her palate.

Her mouth seemed to be filled with his penis. She stopped using her hand and the organ kept working itself inside her mouth – going deep to the back of her throat then back to her tongue and teeth. All this without any movement from Bentley's pelvis. While Harmony Magenta Lake had never considered herself as a fellatio expert, it did occur to her that this was significantly different to what one should normally expect. Nevertheless, it felt pleasurable and stimulating, and she had no intention of stopping.

As these odd thoughts filtered in and out of her mind, she felt a hand slip down the back of her G-string. Fingers glided over her anus and moved to her vagina. The fingers extended into her and worked in and out, somehow seeming to be longer and fatter than fingers would normally be. His arm trailed over her back then back underneath her, while Bentley himself remained completely upright with his eyes on the road.

Harmony recalled his dexterity on opening the apartment door and how his arms slid under her back, over her shoulders and onto her breasts when they were on the bed. She had never considered the idea of a man having a dexterous penis – but here it was, in her mouth – dexterous and wonderful.

For a second she thought back to her old boyfriend, Martin Jorgensen and how he almost demanded she allow him to come into her mouth. That was wrong. This was right. No demands. No pressure – just desire, intense, loving and lustful.

Bentley's ejaculation, while not unexpected, was plentiful. Harmony had read about these things. This was no teaspoon full. It was a mouthful, a swallow, then another mouthful. It happened at the precise moment of her own orgasm and she was ecstatic.

She had always liked calamari, and to her this was how it tasted, but in a liquid form of the seafood. Not unpleasant by any means, but probably a little more than you would want if it was served at the dinner table. She sat back up. Both of Bentley's hands were now back on the steering wheel.

'I will see you again,' she said. 'This will not be the end.' She wiped her mouth roughly with the back of her hand.

Chapter 24

A Killer Tees-Off

The olive-skinned serial killer sat at a picnic table under a shelter at the Ossie Walker Memorial Park. Being mid-week and mid-morning there were only three other people in the park – two kids with their mother at the opposite end, the kids playing on the climbing obstacles in the playground area.

Fabian had visited here several times, each time going over events from several months ago. And just like every other time, he initially felt some anguish as he relived his first kill, even feeling a modicum of regret and a tinge of guilt. He knew these feelings would be temporary, and before he would leave, he would once again feel vindicated.

The image of his father began to form in his mind. His mouth filled with saliva as the depraved acts perpetrated upon him flooded into awareness. Fabian stood and walked to the line of nearby trees. He pushed a little way through and came to a damaged wire fence which he climbed over. In front of him he could see the flickering flagpole of the sixth hole. There was no one around, so he moved to the edge of the green, gazed over a bunker and down the embankment to the river.

As expected, feelings of nausea and anger rose. He would wait until these feelings altered, then he would leave the golf course with a renewed sense of purpose.

*   *   *

Several months earlier…

It seemed like it must have been inevitable the way that day had unfolded. Fabian was not a great golfing fan but had agreed to play a foursome to placate his boss, Roger, who had been insisting that he get together with his three best software engineers for some team building. Fabian felt the real reason was that he wanted to show off his new Mizuno golf clubs and have fun kicking everyone else's arse on the course.

Since his colleague Brian had agreed to go, Fabian also fell in line with his boss's wishes. Brian was the only person at work he had any time for, and him being there might make the day bearable. The fourth member was Logan Bridgeman, a stocky, black-haired man with an annoying superior attitude, and a guy who regularly invaded your personal space while exhaling his stale coffee breath.

Fabian was driven to the course by Bridgeman, while Roger and Brian were travelling together. It was a Thursday and tee-off was scheduled for two-thirty. All four left work at lunchtime to get ready for their team building golf day.

Fabian and Logan waited at the first tee. It was an hour later when Logan got a call from Roger. He and Brian had been involved in a nose to tail accident, and while they were uninjured, there was no way they could make it. An argument had erupted with the other driver and now they were waiting on the arrival of the police.

Logan relayed the story to Fabian. 'Never m… m… mind. Maybe some other time,' said Fabian as he started the electric buggy. 'I'll take my c… c… clubs back to the clubhouse.'

'No way!' yelled Logan. 'Come on. We're here now. Sure, we're late, but with two of us we can easy get through nine holes.' Logan leaned into the cart close to Fabian's face. 'Afraid I will whip your arse, like I do at programming?'

'It's supposed to be a t... team building day with the four of us. And it's going to rain.' Fabian leaned away and broke eye contact.

'I'm going to give you a two-hole head start.'

'Still not k... keen,' stammered Fabian.

'Okay, Fa... Fa... Fabian,' mocked Logan. 'A special offer for a special colleague. Three holes start. Now grab your fucking driver and let's get this show on the road. Roger's a golf fanatic, and he's paying us to be here. We do this and we keep in his good books.' Logan made his way to the tee and drove a massive drive right down the middle of the fairway. Fabian swore under his breath as he moved to the tee. He hit half the distance.

After completing five holes, and despite the three-hole head start, Logan was already a hole in front. On the sixth tee he sent his drive down the left of the fairway which ran parallel to the Brisbane River.

He admired his shot. 'Your turn s... sp... special boy.'

Fabian felt a flush of colour to his cheeks and a knot in his stomach. His drive matched Logan's for the first time. A drizzle of rain began.

They sat next to each other in the cart as they glided gently over the fairway undulations of the sixth hole. Logan slapped Fabian on the shoulder. 'I'm thinking my *special* colleague is getting a hiding. Best get more practice before the boss sees you, sport.' Fabian glared at Logan's smiling face and imagined a box cutter slicing through the man's eye and cheek.

Fabian and Logan strode through a cluster of daisies towards their balls.

'Looks like I'm first up this time, Fa... Fa... Fabian,' laughed Bridgeman. Fabian swallowed and put a hand on his stomach. 'You out-drove me by a metre, arsehole,' continued Logan. 'But it's too little too late for you now. You're fucked.'

The two men took their second shots and headed off again on the cart, stopping near the two golf balls. Both men had landed their shots to the left of the green and close to a bunker.

Logan chipped up and over the sand trap. The ball rolled over the green and dropped in the hole for a birdie. 'Fuck you my special mate,' he roared. He turned his head towards Fabian to gloat some more, but all he saw was the flash of a pitching wedge before it collided with the side of his head. Blood was spurting from the wound even before he fell amongst the daisies.

'Just die... you m... m... monster.' He looked down at Bridgeman. 'You are just like him. You make me sick to my stomach.'

The rain became heavier, and fortunately for Fabian, the few remaining golfers were heading off the course. He dragged the man by the feet, through the daises, off the edge of the fairway, and down the embankment to the river's edge. Fabian Carver stood there, watching Logan's blood flow ever more slowly from his head wound, trickling away with the rain, over the riverbank, and across the mud to the water. 'Today, your special boy wins... d... d... Daddy.' He ran back to Logan's golf bag and took out four clubs.

Back at Bridgeman's body, he moved both the dead man's arms out to the sides. Then with the golf irons chopped down hard on each wrist. The head and body wobbled a little with each blow. The number two iron bent over. Fabian hurled it into the river and carried on with the next club. He wrecked three clubs in his effort to sever both hands. He pulled down Logan's shorts and underwear and got stuck into the man's genitals with the pitching wedge.

'Daddy hurts his special boy no more,' he panted. Fabian dropped down on his haunches to catch his breath.

A few minutes later he raised his head and let the heavy rain hit his face and fall in his mouth. 'One more thing,' he muttered. He clambered back up the slippery bank to the sixth hold and reefed out handfuls of daisies from near the bunker. Back at the body he opened Logan's mouth and shoved the flowers in. 'It's time for you to be the fucking daisy princess.' He stood and nodded with some satisfaction as he admired his work. 'Yeah.'

Back at the sixth green, he grabbed the two balls and threw them down the embankment, then moved a few of Logan's clubs around so they seemed more evenly spaced in the divided sections of the golf bag.

Fabian wandered through a row of trees that defined the course boundary while his mind searched for a solution to his dilemma. He pushed some branches out of his way and looked through the rain into the Ossie Walker Memorial Park. Only metres away a barbecue area was under construction. The weather had driven the workmen away. On seeing the boundary wire fence in front of him and the large cement blocks just over the fence, he knew what he had to do.

*   *   *

Fabian returned his set of hired clubs, and the cart, to the clubhouse, loaded Logan's set into the car boot, then drove away in the Ford Mustang. Before heading to Logan Bridgeman's home, he stopped at a supermarket and bought a roll of paper towel. He mopped, blotted and wiped as best he could, cleaning away his fingerprints from the car and the golf bag, and removing the mud from the inside of the vehicle. He locked the car and left it in Logan's driveway, then walked the four kilometres back to the golf club, where he called a taxi to take him home.

Chapter 25

Return to the Tribal Moon

'We got some cops here tonight,' said Bones.

'What the hell for?' asked Tony Rizzo as he poured some boiling water over his instant coffee.

'Just on the lookout. They promised to be discreet and not upset the party. That's a fucking joke!'

'On the lookout for what exactly?' Rizzo brought his coffee over and sat next to Bones in front of the monitors.

'They didn't say in so many words, but I think they're expecting that Medora lady to return. Part of their ongoing investigations they said. See if you can sniff them out?'

Rizzo looked at Bones, but the boss appeared to have his full attention on the monitors. Tony lightly touched his nose. 'You taking the piss again?'

'What... fuck no,' said Bones, giving a quick glance to his offsider. 'Can you spot them? That's what I'm asking.'

'Hmm... well, first of all, I don't think any killer in their right mind would be back here...' Tony stood and pointed at a screen. 'This guy sitting at the first bar is definitely a cop. We don't get many sixty-year-old half bald dudes in here... well other than you, Bones.'

Without turning his head or changing his expression Gerry Bonering flipped him the bird.

Tony smiled. 'Everyone's gonna know that guy's a cop.'

'For sure. The sixty may be a bit harsh. Anyone else?'

'Hmm… what about this woman? Looks like she's trying to blend in. Tryin' a bit too hard. And, despite her makeup, she's a bit long in the tooth too.'

'Nice one, Rizzo. There's one more.'

*　　　　*　　　　*

It was eight-thirty, and still early for the nightclub. Capacity was usually reached around eleven. At the front entrance Buster Compton, an overweight ex-wrestler, was scanning IDs as the queue slowly became longer. Each person was asked to look up at the camera before being allowed in. The next guy, a slim young man in torn jeans and wearing thongs, held out his driver's license.

'No way,' said Buster. 'Move along.' He put a hand on the guy's shoulder and looked down the queue. 'Next.'

'Come on man. Tattered jeans are the go,' pleaded the guy. 'It's called fashion.'

'That's not a healthy place to stand, fella.' Buster leaned towards him. 'And this is not a debate. Best fuck off while you still can.'

The guy moved a few paces away, gave Buster the finger and a 'Fuck you!' as he looked back over his shoulder and quickened his pace.

Buster admitted three more young women, after which a slim guy, with luscious light brown hair to below his collar, presented himself. His fitting, long sleeve shirt was dazzling, with a paisley pattern of swirls and shapes over a purple background.

'It's not the sixties, mate,' scoffed Buster. 'You got ID?' The man showed his driver's license. 'Johnny Randall… hmm… familiar.' Buster frowned and looked at the young man's face. 'You look a bit different to your pic.'

Johnny ran his fingers through his hair.

'Yes, I can see your hair has grown… a lot.'

Johnny pointed to his cheek.

'Ah… the birth mark is gone. Amazing what they can do nowadays… but I'm getting a sense of déjà vu here.' Buster kept flicking his gaze from the license to the young man, looking him up and down. Johnny moved closer and leaned in to Buster's ear. Only Buster heard the pops and clicks.

Randall stood back, grinned, and showed his perfect teeth. 'I see,' continued the bouncer. 'You're the twin brother of that poor chap. Commiserations. That was a fucking nasty business. So sorry… but you're all good to go in. Have a great night.' The doorman looked down the queue. 'Next please!'

*   *   *

'I can't spot the third cop,' said Tony Rizzo eventually.

'Yeah, he's pretty good. I reckon he's more here for a party than to do police work. If I didn't already know I wouldn't have picked him either. That's him there on the dance floor.' Bones pointed to two guys dancing together and seeming to be very interested in each other. 'We should do a walk around.'

Rizzo and Bones parted company after heading down the stairs, both going to opposite sides of the club.

Bones strolled slowly, nodding and giving a thumbs up to the bar staff and a couple of bouncers who currently had little to do. He stopped near Detective Anderson. Clive was on a stool sipping a soda water. 'Got a suggestion for you. Why not come upstairs and hangout in my office. You can see all the monitors. You'd probably be better off. Out here you're standing out like dog's balls, and that's not so great for my clientele.'

Clive slowly turned his glass in his fingers then took a sip. 'Why, are they doing something illegal?' he replied without making eye contact.

'By your definition… probably. By my broader definition… no. I'm trying to help you out here. Make your surveillance a little easier.'

Clive nodded his head and thought it over. 'Okay Bones, that sounds fair enough.' He pushed his glass away and stood. 'Lead the way.'

* * *

The security room was small, but adequate for the three men all lined up on office chairs with castors. Clive sat in the middle.

'Coffee or tea behind us, Clive. Help yourself,' said Bones.

'Thanks. This is quite an impressive set up gentlemen,' nodded Anderson. 'Several fixed cameras and others that scroll across various spots. I like it.'

'We can quickly contact the guys downstairs as we need to,' added Rizzo. 'Not too much gets by us up here.'

Clive coughed. 'Ah hmm… except for the odd decapitation... eh?'

Bones and Rizzo both looked at Anderson at the same time, then at each other.

'Just the one,' sighed Bones. 'Thankfully.'

'Question,' said Clive. 'You were both here that night, doing your rounds, chatting with folks here and there. And you've both seen the footage of that night.' He looked left then right and got two nods. 'Did you see her actually talk to anyone at any time?'

'She got guy's attention pretty easily… including mine,' said Rizzo. 'She didn't really need words.'

'You're right though Clive,' added Bones. 'No, we never heard or saw her have a conversation with anyone. Seems a bit unusual… what are you getting at?'

'Yet she still communicated with others… somehow. Body language, smiles, gestures, sexy glances and all that.'

'Huh… funny,' grinned Bones as he glanced to the ceiling.

'What… what's funny?' asked Clive.

'Reminds me a bit of a guy that was here a few weeks back.'

'How so?' Clive angled his chair towards Bonering.

'This dude was sitting over here.' Bones stood and tapped his finger on a screen. 'At this corner table. A table for four or five people. He was on his own. Pretty much like this long-haired prick that is there now. He was there for a few hours… drinking Bloody Mary's.' Bones dropped back onto his chair which rolled back a metre. He inched it forward. 'I spoke to him on my rounds because I was a little pissed off that he was occupying a space more suitable to a group. He said something to me… I think. Yet I have not the slightest recollection of a word he said. I just know I felt satisfied at the time and let him sit there. Seems a bit dumb as I say it now. I get a bit absent minded at times. It's probably nothing.'

'Oh, it's fucking something all right,' replied Clive with a vigorous head nod. 'What did he look like? What did he get up to?'

Gerry Bonering described Bentley Hopkin-Jones to a T. 'Some pretty chick ended up sitting with him. They must have left soon after that. I got side-tracked because some drunk girl fell off her stool and hit her head.'

'As I understand it, you use your own private in-house surveillance in here?' asked Clive.

'We do. CCTV outside the front door.'

'You still got the video?'

'We keep it for twenty-eight days. So yeah. We got it for another twenty-four hours.'

'Great. Silverton needs to see this.'

*   *   *

'He drinks several Bloody Mary's and two full jugs of water, sits there for hours, but never goes to the toilet,' said Jan Silverton. The detective was sitting with Tony Rizzo in a small office behind the monitoring area. 'And, apart from possibly whispering into your boss's ear, he hasn't spoken to anyone. I hate to say it, but I'm thinking Clive is onto something.'

'This is starting to get a bit weird,' said Rizzo. 'It's like some fucking Jedi mind trick.'

'I'm hoping it's something a little more down to Earth than that,' scoffed Silverton. 'I need to see his ID scan and his face pic when he came in. You got that?'

'Oh, yeah. We got all that.' Tony Rizzo fired up another laptop while Silverton rolled the video forward.

*   *   *

Clive remained with Bones watching the monitors while Rizzo and Silverton were in the small side room watching the Bentley Hopkin-Jones show on a computer screen. Clive was quietly confident that he knew what it would show… or not show.

'There she is.' Anderson was up on his feet pointing. 'That's Janine Hansen.'

Hansen wore a slim leather jacket with a deep neckline and long lacey semi-transparent sleeves with large cuffs. Her pants were black fitting leather.

'She looks fucking good,' breathed Clive. 'We need to watch her. There might be nothing tonight but let's not miss anything.'

'I'll get Joey to keep a discreet eye out.' Bones spoke into his walkie talkie.

Anderson watched the monitor as Joey said a couple of words then moved closer to Janine who was now at a bar.

Johnny Randall sat alone sipping his Bloody Mary and working his way through a jug of water.

Chapter 26

Constantino

While the Tribal Moon was ramping up with activity and guests, further away, near the end of Edward Street, and adjacent to the Brisbane Botanical Gardens, a small white Jayco motorhome found a vacant parking space.

Fabian Carver sat in the driver's seat, flicking through several drivers' licenses. Some were faded, others were marked and cracked. It was thanks to a guy at the main roads department who kept aside replaced licenses rather than destroying them, that Fabian had so many. Fabian had assisted the young man with some *unofficial* software programming that gave him a significant advantage in online gaming. The two had struck up a deal.

Fabian selected a license with the name Constantino Abrahams. It was scratched and a little faded, but the image was a fair resemblance, especially since Fabian had bleached his short hair. He slipped it in an empty wallet in the clear plastic window then added a bunch of twenty and fifty-dollar notes. From the glovebox he removed a mangled looking piece of plastic and put it in the pocket of his jacket.

After grabbing his small suitcase from the back of the vehicle, Fabian locked the Jayco and moved off down the street, heading to a busier part of town. He increased his stride length, stood as tall as he could and raised his smiling head. Constantino was ready for business.

Ten minutes later, in his business suit and tie, and wearing glasses, Constantino entered the plush foyer of The Glastonbury Hotel. He moved over the carpet, his small suitcase rolling silently along behind him. Everything was clean and shiny. He sucked in deeply through his nose. He could smell polish.

'Good evening, sir,' said the black suited man at the reception desk. 'Checking in?'

'Yes... Abrahams. Constantino Abrahams.' Constantino noticed the silver name tag – *Lloyd*.

'Yes, Mr Abrahams. Just the one night I see.'

'Correct. There is a minor issue I'm afraid, Lloyd.'

'Sorry to hear that. How may I help?'

Constantino reached into the pocket of his jacket. 'This is my credit card.' He placed a chewed-up card on the counter. 'It's a long story. But let's say credit cards don't fare so well in a blender... um... ah... well, there was a bad argument, Lloyd...' he dropped his head for a moment. 'My wife got upset... she... you know...' He looked at the receptionist and put a fidgety hand to his neck. 'She said a few things and then...'

'It's okay sir,' interrupted Lloyd. 'I'm sure we can sort something out.'

'Happy to provide cash as a security deposit if that works.'

'I'll have a quick word to the manager, but I think we can manage that. If you could fill out your details here.' The pleasant man pushed a form over. 'I will be right back.'

*   *   *

The room was outstanding. A massive king size bed, a mini lounge room, a desk and sitting area and a very spacious bathroom with a shower over a large bath. All doorknobs and bathroom metal fixtures were gold coloured. All timber finishings looked like mahogany. The same polish smell from the foyer was in the room. Not overpowering, just enough to give the place a homely and clean feel.

Constantino unpacked his overnight bag. He placed a small green toiletries bag in the bedside drawer, then a bottle of vodka and coffee liquor in the fridge. He showered and changed from his business suit into a long sleeve shirt with a black floral print, leaving the top two buttons undone, then dabbed some Ralph Lauren Polo Black cologne on the top of his chest. He put on a pair of slim tapered white pants, and ankle socks with white sneakers. He hung a daisy patterned dress in the cupboard.

It was still early, so he ordered some crispy skin Atlantic salmon from room service and made himself a double strength coffee using the coffee pod machine in his room. He felt some anticipation about the evening ahead. A couple of times, while unpacking, he had nearly slipped back to being Fabian Carver as needs and anxieties tried to push through. Constantino was a better man, controlled, organised, friendly and thoughtful.

Chapter 27

Take Me Clubbin'

While Janine had been dancing with several men and women, her distraction had been noticed by several.

'Are you waiting on someone?' asked a young girl who looked barely of age to be there.

'I am.' She put her attention back on her dance partner. 'Sorry, my mind is elsewhere.' Janine smiled and picked up her dance moves. 'I like the way you dance,' she shouted, competing against Justin Timberlake's *Sexy Back* song.

'Do you want to get outta here?' yelled the girl.

'How old are you?'

'Old enough.'

'You're very pretty. What's your name?'

'Crystal, and believe it or not, I'm nineteen.'

Crystal slowed and moved her head closer to Janine. 'I think you're waiting for someone who's not coming. Come with me. I know how to make you happy… promise. I think we'll be good together.'

Janine tilted her head as she contemplated. She glanced over Crystal's right shoulder. There was someone there she had never noticed before. Just standing at the edge of the dance floor looking straight at her. His hair was long and beautiful. His face had a soft glow.

'Hey!' shouted her dance partner. 'You and me. Come on! Let's go.'

Janine barely heard her. She was swallowed up with this stunning man. A slow misty breath left his mouth and disappeared. He angled his head and pursed his lips. Janine's dancing slowed to a stop.

'Is that who you're waiting for?' asked Crystal, following the line of her gaze.

'I'm really hoping it is. I was expecting a woman, but I must have been mistaken.'

'He looks amazing.'

'Doesn't he! Come with me.'

Janine didn't wait for an answer. She took Crystal's hand, and they left the dance floor together.

Johnny Randall moved back to his table with his head turned over his shoulder to a peculiar angle, while watching the two girls come towards him.

Joey, the bouncer, took a few steps, keeping his eye on Janine, while at the same time looking around at others, casually waving to a few young ladies and trying not to look too obvious.

Crystal and Janine sat with Johnny. All were smiling. No one was talking.

*   *   *

In the security office the three men were back in their office chairs leaving Detective Jan Silverton to stand behind them.

'Your sidekick down there seems to be in a world of his own,' said Rizzo.

'So it seems,' sighed Silverton.

Richard Davis had been dancing and drinking with a group of young men. As the team all watched the monitor, Davis extended both arms out, and dropped them over another guy's shoulders and around his neck. With their foreheads touching the two danced and gazed into each other's eyes.

'Could be his lucky night,' quipped Rizzo.

'We're here unofficially. I guess he's entitled to do his own thing.'

Clive shook his head. 'I told you not to bring him along.'

'Don't go there, Clive.'

Anderson shrugged and looked back at the screens.

'I'm getting a sense of déjà vu,' said Bones.

'Yeah, tell me,' Clive replied immediately.

'This table. It's the same one that Bentley Hopkin-Jones was at.' He shone a red laser pointer at the screen. 'This long-haired guy. Was on his own for ages. Now he's with your Janine Hansen and another bird.' Bones picked up the walkie talkie. 'Joey, find out what that long-haired prick at table twenty-one has been drinking. What he's been saying.'

The group watched Joey saunter to the bar and chat with the barman. The pair gave a quick glance at the table of three. The bouncer held the small microphone attached to the cord dangling from his ear.

'Yeah,' said Bones into the handset.

'Bloody Mary's,' said Joey. *'He's just gestured, pointed and shit. Hasn't actually spoken to the bar staff.'*

Clive's chair flew back into Jan Silverton's legs as he leapt to his feet. 'Holy fucking shit!'

'Rizzo,' barked Bones. 'Get on the iPad. Check this fucker out. Clive, sit the fuck down!'

'You giving me orders?' barked Anderson.

'No mate. But you can't arrest someone for not talking.'

'We'll see about that.' Clive moved back and forth, gesturing with his hands at the side of his head. 'Now we got three of them. Medora, Bentley and this other fucker! What the hell!'

'Jesus!' shouted Tony Rizzo. 'Look at this. It's Johnny Randall. Same fucking ID. The walking fucking dead!'

As Silverton took off down the stairs there was movement at the table of interest. All three were on their feet and leaving the area.

*   *   *

Silverton was first to the empty table, quickly followed by Anderson.

'Where are they?' yelled Clive.

Bones and Rizzo joined them.

'Rizzo, check the exit,' snapped Anderson. Bones glared at him. Rizzo looked unsurely at both men.

'I got this covered, Clive. This is my joint!' Bones slapped himself on the chest. 'You need to back off!' He turned to his offsider. 'Rizzo, check the exit.'

The security boss quickly barked out more instructions. 'Clive, check the dance floor.' Clive growled but reluctantly complied. 'Silverton, you do the bars. I'll check the booths.' He looked up to the raised platform area and caught the eye of his DJ. Bones drew a finger across his own throat. The music stopped.

In the booths, Bones saw a couple fucking on the long coffee table. He moved on, then saw a group of four snorting a line of white powder. He turned a blind eye and kept moving. There were six guys in booth eight. Two of them were passing around booze they had smuggled in. He barrelled in amongst them, slapping one guy with the back of his hand.

'You cunts gotta buy your booze here in the club. Hand it over. You know the fucking rules.'

The young man with the Johnny Walker took a step back holding the bottle to his chest. Bonering's boot made contact with his scrotum. The guy doubled over. Bones grabbed the bottle.

'Next!' he shouted. He beckoned someone to step forward.

A taller thin guy with his head shaved near bald on the sides and spikey on top, tentatively reached out holding a bottle of tequila. Bones snatched it. 'Good thinking, beanpole. I'm not kicking you guys out this time. Don't fuck with me again. Clear?' He looked at the four guys still standing. 'Clear!' he bellowed. He got a *yes sir*, a *sorry sir*, and a couple of nods. He moved on checking more booths. He was disappointed that there was not a single long-haired guy to be seen.

The immediate area outside many of the booths had been vacated, and many clubbers had gathered in their small groups to chat, stare and point at the commotion. On the dance floor, Clive seemed to have scared off most of the dancers. The only remaining few couples just stood there waiting for the music to restart. At the middle bar, Bones saw Silverton sitting on a stool next to bouncer Joey. He trotted over and banged the two bottles on the bar.

'Add these to our collection, Delvene,' he said to the bargirl. 'What the fuck, Joey? You've let me down. And what… now you're drinking on duty!'

'Leave him,' said Silverton. 'He's doing what he thinks is right.'

'What the…' Bones looked at the detective then back at Joey.

'Like you with Hopkin-Jones. He let Janine leave with Johnny and the other girl, believing, beyond any doubt that it was okay.'

'There's no cause for alarm boss,' said Joey calmly. 'And I was assured you wouldn't mind me having a schooner. In fact, I'm sure that you wanted me too… am I right?'

Bones shook his head. 'Are you fucking deranged? How would you like to be unemployed?'

'It's okay, Gerry. Hang loose, man,' smiled Joey. 'We're cool. Right?'

Silverton looked at Bones. 'Maybe we both need a drink too.' She shrugged and raised her eyebrows.

'Fuck it. Two Glens, thanks Delvene… make them doubles.'

The barmaid grabbed the Glenfiddich and poured two double shots over ice.

'Thanks.' He passed one to Silverton. 'What's happening here?'

'Don't know. A device of some kind? Some new technology, or a weird form of hypnosis.'

Clive joined them. 'I reckon they've done a runner.'

'Drink, Clive?' asked Bones.

'Sure.'

'Another one, Delvene.' The barmaid nodded. Bones raised his arm, pointed a finger and spun it in circles. The music restarted.

Chapter 28

On the Streets

Constantino Abrahams left the Glastonbury Hotel at eight. He hailed a taxi.

'The City Arms Hotel thank you,' he announced, as he took a seat in the back.

'Huh… that's just up the road,' grumbled the driver, a round man with greasy black hair.

'Yes, one point five kilometres. I prefer not to walk.'

'I normally do the longer journeys. Why don't you grab an Uber.'

'The sooner you start driving the sooner this trip will be over, and you can go looking for your longer rides. I do pay in cash.'

'Do you tip?'

'Always. So let's go.'

The rotund man took off with a jerk. He seemed to get every red light on the way, and his frustration was evident in his driving. After nine minutes of stop start through the busy city streets, they arrived at Spring Hill and the City Arms Hotel. The car pulled into a driveway twenty metres up from the venue.

'Twenty-five bucks plus the tip, Champ.'

Constantino Abrahams opened his wallet as he got out the cab. He moved to the driver's window. 'Here's your twenty-five. And here's your tip…' he went to take more money out. The cabbie's eyes lit up seeing a lot of big bills, but the wallet snapped shut. 'Clean your fucking hair. Brush your fucking teeth. Lose some fucking weight. Get some fucking manners!'

The cabbie squealed his tyres and took off, his insults fading as he got further away... 'Gay fucking poofter cunt. Arsehole windjammer prick...'

The City Arms Hotel looked decidedly better at night than day. The rather drab old brick exterior and green footpath awning was lit up with multi-coloured fluorescent globes. A rainbow carpet marked the way to the entrance. *Into You* by Ariana Grande pumped through the air.

Constantino moved gently to the music as he entered. While he had his driver's license at the ready, he just walked straight in, past the doorman, who just winked.

The bar was long, with bands of zig zag black and white stripes running the full length. The staff were busy preparing various cocktails. On the other side of the room was a drag queen show with six dancers showing themselves off and gyrating to the Ariana Grande song.

Abrahams ordered a lemon, lime and bitters, then approached a high black metal table with four matching stools. One thin man, wearing a cut off T-shirt showing his abdomen, was there. Constantino gestured to a vacant stool and the guy smiled and nodded.

'Hi, I'm Walter, but I'm not available,' shouted the thin guy as he leaned to Constantino's ear. 'I'm waiting on Grae Grae, my man.'

'Cool, I'm Constantino, cheers.' He held up his drink and chinked glasses with a margarita.

'I so love this show.'

'They all look so beautiful,' yelled Constantino.

'As do you. Those white pants and that black shirt... very nice.' His temporary companion smiled, displaying some very prominent front teeth, then sipped his drink while rocking side to side to the music.

*   *   *

At the Tribal Moon, Jan, Gerry, Clive and Joey were on their second drink when Rizzo squeezed his way across the dance floor and presented himself in front of them. He had a light sweat. The second in charge took a big breath, smiled, and nodded to the group in a gesture of some satisfaction.

'You caught them?' asked Bones.

'Oh yeah. I caught up with them.' Rizzo nodded, grinned, and looked at the others, who, apart from Joey, showed no signs of pleasure. 'What's up with you lot?'

'Where are they then?' continued Bones.

'Oh, they'll be back.'

'When?'

'Don't know for sure. But they will.'

'You know that with absolute certainty?' said Clive.

Tony Rizzo nodded. 'Beyond any shadow of a doubt?'

'Delvene,' called Bones as he waved.

'One more, boss?' she replied.

He gave her the thumbs up. She prepared another Glen.

'This is new,' said Rizzo with surprise. 'Drinking at work. What's going on?'

*   *   *

Constantino spent ninety minutes at the City Arms. He had chatted to several guys and to one drunk middle-aged lady who wanted him to escort her to the bathroom. Everyone had been friendly enough, and the evening had been quite enjoyable, however there was no one here that he wanted to take back to his hotel. No one here that would quell the urge that was rising within.

He had become acquainted with Grae Grae, Walter's partner. Grae Grae, who's proper name was Graeme, looked straight as they come, and was several years older than Walter. Graeme had a pale band of white skin on his ring finger.

Constantino spun a bullshit tale about leaving his phone in the taxi, and asked Grae Grae to call him an Uber to head to The Platform Bar in Ann Street – not that he was going there, but rather covering his tracks just in case anything happened, and enquiries were made. He gave Grae Grae twenty dollars.

'Lovely meeting you both. Have fun guys,' he said.

'Hope you get lucky at the Platform, darling,' replied Walter.

*   *   *

Richard Davis was having the time of his life with four other men. The five were regularly swapping dance partners with one another, and now Richard was back with the same blonde guy that had caught his eye earlier. Davis had just dropped his hands back around the guy's neck when he got a sharp tap on his shoulder.

'Davis!' shouted Jan Silverton.

'Hey, Jan.' He dropped one arm but kept moving. 'What's up? They stopped the music before for some reason. Anything going down?'

'You sound a bit drunk.'

'Well… I've had a couple, but I'm fine.' Richard's dancing slowed. His man friend lost interest and moved immediately to another. 'Hey, you!' he bellowed, reaching out into the air.

The blonde man gave him quick wave and blew him a kiss.

'I'm not driving, Jan. It's okay. Look, you've scared Nigel off.'

'I doubt it. We're going now.'

'I didn't see any drama. A quiet one then?'

Silverton rolled her eyes. 'I'll fill you in on Monday.' She put a hand on his shoulder. 'Be careful.'

'I will. See you later.' He pecked her on the cheek and moved back to his new friends.

As the song ended. Nigel signalled to the group who all gathered round. 'How about we head off somewhere else for a bit more fun.' They all cheered.

*   *   *

The Birdwhistle Bar in Queen Street Brisbane boasted the best alcohol selection of anywhere. On entry it was easy to see why – the shelving behind the bar went all the way to the ceiling and was packed with everything imaginable. Not only that, they bragged about having the best bartenders and cocktail makers in the business.

At the Birdwhistle, it was not just about mixing cocktails, it was about entertainment – spinning bottles, pouring drinks from a height, dancing while mixing and shaking, and singing along to the music and getting the customers involved.

The décor was of vintage styling. All the stools at the Birdwhistle were thickly padded with red vinyl on the top. In addition, there were a few old-style leather lounge chairs with bulging shiny brown upholstery. The bar, shelving and window frames were all a beautiful dark timber in keeping with its heritage branding.

Constantino sat on the last available red stool at the bar and perused the cocktail menu. Generally, and to keep his head clear, he would order a non-alcoholic drink, but tonight he needed a little something to settle his insides. It had been sixteen days since his last emotional release back in Sydney. This feeling had been eating at him, getting worse and triggering more flashbacks. *I just need one more,* he told himself, *then the urges will settle, and I can stop.* He ordered a whiskey sour.

It was thirty minutes later, as Constantino tipped the last of his drink down his throat, that five men walked in. They were laughing and huddling close to one another. As soon as they were through the door they began bopping about to the beat of *Little Crime* by Winter Valley.

> *...Sharpen your knives a new way out*
> *Sharpen your lies don't give in to doubt*
> *It's twisted and changing your mind is fallin'*
> *I wish that you could just ... tell me...*

There was a man in the group with dark stubble and short black hair that caught Constantino's eye. He had an arm over a shorter guy's shoulder. Two of the men went straight to the bar and ordered cocktails.

'Three Mint Julips and...' The red-shirted man turned to his Asian friend. 'Cheng?'

'Two Espresso Martinis... what else? Woo hoo!' Cheng tapped away on the bar to the music.

Constantino smiled at the two men who briefly glanced his way. The other three of the group found a round table and dragged over a couple more stools.

Over the next hour, Constantino stuck to his lemon, lime and bitters, after just the one whiskey sour. He deliberately walked past the group three times to get a bit closer to the guy who sparked his interest. He needed to see his eyes and his hands. On his third pass, Richard Davis lifted his head. The two briefly made eye contact and gave each other a slight passing smile. His eyes were brown. He already knew he was a guy of a slightly stockier build with thicker fingers. From a little eaves dropping, Con had found out that his name was Richard, that he liked cooking, dancing, motor bikes and that his favourite flower was a tulip. Richard seemed more intoxicated than the other four.

When Davis lowered his head to the table and let his forehead rest there, the blonde Nigel turned his attention to Peter, the man on his other side. Nigel whispered in the guy's ear, then left to go to the bathroom. The other man waited a moment, looking about aimlessly. After a minute, he too left for the same room.

Constantino watched as Richard moved his hands to the side of his lowered head and rubbed his temples with his thumbs. When the two other men at the table left to dance, Con saw an opportunity.

'Are you okay?' he asked as he placed a gentle hand on Richard's neck. He got a groan in response. 'It's a wonder you haven't just toppled right off that stool.'

Davis raised his head slightly. 'Would you mind escorting me to the bathroom. My head is spinning. Throwing up here would be a bad look.'

'Sure. Here, put an arm over my shoulder. You'll be just fine. I've got you,' smiled Constantino.

In the bathroom Con opened a cubicle and ushered Richard to the toilet bowl, where he dropped to his knees, put his arms around the porcelain and vomited. Con stood at the door.

Three cubicles down a door opened and one of the men from the group of five walked out, quickly washed his hands and left. Richard Davis raised his head, put his hands on the toilet seat and panted loudly. A few seconds later he was back to position one, vomiting once more. The same door further down opened and the blonde man, Con knew as Nigel, emerged. He went to the sink, washed his hands and face, then gargled some water before leaving.

Con gathered a few paper towels, soaked them, and wiped Richard's face.

'You're a nice man,' breathed Richard. 'Thanks for your help.'

'My name is Constantino. I know you're pretty smashed, but I think you're a bit cute all the same.'

Richard moved from the bowl, sat on the floor and propped himself against the wall. Con squatted near him.

'What are we going to do with you?' smiled Abrahams.

'Ooh… the world turns. I should know better than this,' he grumbled, as he held his own head with his hands. 'You're very kind. Thank you… what was it… Constantino?'

'Yeah, you got it. Now how about we get you to your feet?' Richard slid up the cubicle wall. Con held his arm. 'Very good. Let's get to the sink.'

Richard gagged a couple of times as he splashed his face. He threw water over the top of his head and around his neck, a lot of which went on the floor, and over his helper. 'I'm so sorry, Constantino.' He pushed his hands over his face.

'Hey, it's okay. We've all been there before. Come on let's walk and get a bit of fresh air.'

With Con's assistance, Richard managed a half reasonable walk out the bathroom. The table he had been at was vacated. His friends were gone.

The pair ambled up the street. 'Ah, that breeze is so good on my face,' said Richard lifting his head and turning it side to side.

'I have a hotel room here in town,' said Con. 'I don't mean to be presumptuous and I'm not suggesting anything improper, but you are welcome to spend the night, sleep and recover.'

Richard kissed his cheek. 'You are the nicest person. And that would be lovely, if I wasn't so fucking drunk. Right now, I'd love it if you could pour me into an Uber and send me home.'

Constantino was thoughtfully quiet. *Yes,* he thought, *I could do that. Your place, my place. What difference would it make. Does it matter if he's drunk? And he seems more like a younger version of Fabian's abuser… is that a problem?* Constantino was questioning himself. *But he hasn't said anything about wanting me. Wanting to fuck me. Wanting to mount me. Wanting to stick his filthy cock in my mouth. But he looks so much like him. He has all the features. I'd like to see him in a daisy skirt.*

'What about that Uber?' Richard stopped walking and awkwardly dragged his mobile phone from his pocket. He looked at the screen and it unlocked. He handed it to Con. 'Bottom right is the app, thanks Connie.'

Con gave him a look, 'Connie?'

'Sorry, Con…stantin ople,' slurred Richard.

'Connie, will do.' He ordered the ride and selected the default address that appeared on the screen. 'Three hundred and forty-three Devondale Avenue, Salisbury?' said Con.

'That's me.'

'I'm gonna tag along. Make sure you get home safely. I'll get the Uber back to my hotel.'

'You don't need to…'

'I want to… please.'

'Sure, sure, no worries,' slurred Richard.

Two minutes later, the Uber arrived.

Chapter 29

Johnny Plus Two

Janine's twentieth floor apartment was directly across from South Bank on the Brisbane River. It had a long verandah with great views of the river and beyond.

Tonight, there was a cool breeze, the sky was clear, and the city lights seemed brighter than usual. Boats loaded with party groups cruised slowly up and down the waterway, while the well-lit ferry catamarans motored either way full of commuters. A steady stream of people made their way across the Goodwill Bridge – walking, running, cycling, and scootering.

Janine's bathroom was spacious, with two porcelain basins perched on a marble looking bench top. In a shower built for two, Janine was gently washing Crystal's back with a soapy sponge.

'You are so petite and beautiful. You sure you're nineteen?' she giggled. Janine was half a head taller. Both were slim without being thin.

'Everyone says that. But it's true.' Crystal turned and looked up at Janine. 'I love your hair. Is it naturally blonde?'

'It is.'

Crystal kissed Janine's chest between her breasts and put her hands over her companion's backside, pulling her as close as she could. The nineteen-year-old's hands slid over and around her friend's buttocks, kneading and massaging, and every now and then separating the cheeks of her bottom and running a hand lightly along the crevice.

In the lounge, Johnny had shifted a central coffee table to near a wall, and had hauled out Janine's queen mattress, laying it over the lounge room rug in the centre of the room. He had connected her computer to the big screen television and was silently streaming pornography. A naked party of four, three female and one male, were positioning themselves to gain easy access to the genitals of at least two others.

As he stood upright, he felt a vibration down his spine and opened his eyes wider. With his head tilted at almost ninety degrees, he let out a long high-pitched note through a small gap between his lips.

'What's that whistling sound?' said Janine as she moved her mouth away from Crystal's.

'I hear it…oh… there… it just stopped.'

'Was it Johnny?'

'Sounded more like a cat whining,' added Crystal. She put a soft hand against Janine's cheek and moved her face back round. 'Now, where were we up to?'

Johnny slowly slipped off one shoe then the other. He repeated the same sound while he walked to the bathroom.

The girls stopped kissing again.

'That's creeping me out a little,' said Janine. Just as she finished speaking, Johnny entered the room and went straight into the double shower fully clothed.

'Johnny, what on earth are you up to?' stammered Janine. 'That noise was it you? And why are you fully dressed?'

Johnny Randall pushed between the two naked women. He was now much taller than Janine.

'Have you suddenly grown six inches?' Janine looked down at his trousers, the bottom of which was now showing more of his ankles than it should. Not only that, the exposed skin on his legs was changing colour through motley shades of greys and greens. 'Fuck me!' she squealed. Johnny caught her eye. She immediately went quiet, took a step back, slid down the glass, and sat in the corner with her knees drawn up hugged by her arms.

To the much shorter Crystal Whitlock he looked like a giant. The Semblant looked down at her with unblinking round eyes. He lifted her right hand and examined her palm. There was a fresh, J shaped red scar from a recent cut. Another higher pitch note came forth once more. His mouth opened wider. His tongue extended and thinned as it flicked through the air, bending this way and that, like a thick wriggling worm. The tongue entered Crystal's left nostril and seemed to be going deeper and deeper.

The nineteen-year-old just stood watching him. She could feel this tentacle tongue at the back of her throat. It was probing upwards. There was no pain, just an odd sensation like pins and needles inside your head – not totally unpleasant. Then her pupils fully dilated, and her entire body trembled, before going loose and relaxed. Johnny held her flaccid body against his own with both arms.

In the corner, shaking, Janine watched but felt unable to move. This most beautiful man was a monster, but as his wet shirt clung to his body defining every muscle, and his strange tongue entered Crystal, she still believed he was beautiful. She was frightened, but still sexually aroused. For some reason she could not fathom she wanted his tongue inside her, just like her friend.

Chapter 30

Harmony – Part 7

It was Saturday lunchtime when Crystal arrived at the hospital to see her friend. Harmony had a cardiac ablation yesterday afternoon, and all being well, would be home sometime today.

'Hey Crystal.' Harmony's face lit up. 'Thanks for coming to see me.'

Crystal moved in slowly, trying to take in the picture. There were two monitors running, showing different trace lines of her heartbeat. Something was beeping. The wall behind the bed was full of apparatus – sucking devices, intravenous pumps at the ready, oxygen outlets, and a blood pressure machine. There were at least six empty power points of different colours. A drip line was in Harmony's arm. Regardless of all that, she was sitting up in bed eating some peaches and ice-cream.

'Don't be scared. It's all good. I'm fine. Come on in.' She waved her best friend forward. 'Should be going home this evening. You gotta tell me everything. How was last night? I'm soooo dying to find out. Come around here.' Harmony patted on the mattress and shoved the food table out of the way.

Crystal sat on the bed. 'You sure you're okay?'

'I'm Fine. Come on… tell me.'

'Last night was… different. Nice, but strange in a weird sort of way.'

'Did you find a nice girl?'

'Yeah, yeah… Janine. She was lovely. And a guy… Johnny.'

'Shit Crystal!'

'It's not quite as it sounds.'

'It sounds like a threesome.'

Crystal's eyes watered. 'I was frightened.'

Harmony inched across the mattress and grabbed her in a big hug. 'You poor thing. You're alright now. It's okay. Did he hurt you?' She pushed her friend back to arm's length, still holding her shoulders and studied her face.

Crystal sobbed, unable to speak for a minute. 'Oh dear,' continued Harmony. She pulled her back in and squeezed her tight. 'I should have been there with you. I'm so sorry.'

'None of this is your fault,' she whimpered. 'Geez… you were having heart surgery.'

'An ablation is not really heart surgery. More a procedure. Everything went well, and I'll be fine and fully recovered in another day or two. But you… what happened… were you raped? Were you hurt?'

'I woke up in bed with Janine this morning. She was just as frightened as me… maybe even more than me. Johnny was gone.'

'What did he do to you both?'

'That's the thing… it's all a bit of a blur. We were in the shower. I remember him looking at my hand and the scar. It seemed to make him go a bit strange. I think it reminded him of something. I remember him being in the shower with Janine and me. He came in fully dressed… crazy hey. He opened his mouth… I think I must have passed out because after that I go blank until I wake up next to Janine.'

'What about Janine? Did she remember what happened?'

'She said she was cowering in the corner of the shower unable to move. She could see him. She saw him hold me. She saw him open his mouth real wide too… then she wakes up with me. We are not hurt really. We weren't assaulted or anything. But this is the strange thing too… while we were scared shitless, we were both still way excited… I mean like sexually. Is that normal?'

'Fuck, Crystal. I'm so sorry for you. It sounds like he might be a crazy nut job. Best forget about him. What about you and Janine?'

'Yeah… nice.' Crystal shoved at the bed sheets with her fingers and looked down.

Harmony tightened a grip on her friend's shoulder and gave her a gentle shake. 'You fucked her? Oh my God. There's a silver lining to this story. Woo hoo!'

'She's so sweet. We'll be catching up again… and strange as it sounds, we are both hoping Johnny will turn up.'

Harmony squeezed her again. 'I don't know about that. Sounds risky. You gotta be careful, Crystal.'

'He is so lovely. We know he won't hurt us.'

'How do you know for sure?'

'We just do that's all. We know it and we are both absolutely positive about it,' said Crystal with a shrug. 'That's enough about me. Tell me about that super sexy Bentley? Has Mister Wonderful the super fucker been up for a visit?'

Over the past two weeks, whenever Harmony had met, texted or talked on the phone to Crystal, she could barely talk about anything but Bentley, and how great he was in almost every way imaginable. Even the dexterous penis got a mention.

'Mister Wonderful Bentley hasn't been able to come up, but he will be in touch soon. He told me…' Harmony paused with her head angled. 'Well… I know for sure he wants to keep seeing me. I think I'm in love, Crystal.'

'You sure it's not a severe case of lust?' she smiled back.

Chapter 31

R.I.P. & The Semblant

The Semblant, currently known as Johnny Randall, was dressed in a loose-fitting tracksuit, and lying in a star shape on the floor. His eyes were closed. His breathing was nearly imperceptible.

It was late morning when there was a knock on the door. Roderick Ignatius Peabody entered, then closed and locked the door quietly, before sitting in one of the two lounge chairs – the only furniture in the room. For a couple of minutes Peabody sat quietly not wanting to disturb his friend. The undertaker glanced at a wall-mounted clock which showed eleven fifteen. He looked at the picture of the panther mounted on the wall. The hypnotic eyes reminding him of the Semblant.

Johnny's eyes opened and the two made eye contact. Johnny nodded knowingly, smiled and rose to his feet. He moved the other chair and sat directly in front of Peabody.

'Thank you for doing this again,' said Rip. He relaxed into the lounge and closed his eyes. Johnny opened his mouth wider and wider, until his nose was pushed right back, and his bottom jaw was touching his chest. A thick translucent mist left his mouth, moved through the air and settled over both their heads. His tongue thinned and extended out towards the undertaker, flicking about as it lengthened, becoming over a metre long before finding Rip's nostril. The Semblant reclined. His eyes closed. The two sat there quietly connected to each other, both by the mist and the tubular tongue which oscillated gently.

Rip opened his eyes. Now he was floating, completely weightless and surrounded by a heavy fog. In front of him was a grey humanoid shape with unclear features. Within the mist he was able to make out a large head with unusually big darker eyes, a torso, a mouth and parts of arms and legs. Beams of light streamed between the two.

'Hello Sobo,' breathed Rip.

'Hello Roderick. I see you are nicely relaxed. The beams that connect us facilitate tranquillity and acceptance of this process. For the moment we find ourselves in this place of neutrality,' replied the Semblant called Sobo. 'I will be using the voice of Johnny Randall while we communicate. We are one of course.'

'Yes, of course,' nodded Rip.

'Today both you and I seek dialogue and understanding.' Johnny's voice through the Semblant was clear, but had an echoing, nasal quality.

'Oh... really... that's a little different to other times,' said Peabody.

'It is, Roderick. Previously it has been you asking questions and me supplying answers. But I have experienced vibrations that tell me another Semblant is in this city. This happened at an inconvenient moment for both Johnny and me. We were overcome and had to abort some pleasurable activities. I was able to deduce that this other Semblant had, like me, been at a nightclub called the Tribal Moon. I accessed a human's memory and saw a face. It was Kwikal. I was previously of the opinion that Kwikal had died over a hundred years ago.'

'Sobo... this is wonderful news. We must find Kwikal.'

'We must.'

'Could you tell if Semblant Kwikal was in a state of assimilation?'

'The Semblant was not,' echoed Sobo. 'Kwikal was using a default persona from many decades earlier. We all have choices of several personas with which we have been previously associated.'

'I see,' replied Rip.

'The Semblant have been decimated over the centuries through multiple pandemics. The influenza outbreak of 1918, otherwise known as the Spanish Flu, killed nearly one hundred million people, over three thousand were Semblant. I believe this represented about ninety percent of the Semblant population. If we meet another we must repopulate at every opportunity.'

'Oh my... I apologise, but this is something that has never occurred to me. Semblant babies? Is that what you mean, Sobo?'

'Not in the sense that you would know. An emerging Semblant inherits memory, characteristics, knowledge, abilities and senses. All things that need some practice to blossom...'

As Sobo spoke the space between them became brighter. Sobo lifted his arms. Arcs of even more light left Sobo's hands and fell onto Peabody's head and shoulders. As the Semblant's words continued, pictures formed in front of Peabody's face, as if he was transported to a different time and place.

'... Both humans and Semblant have many thousands of genes,' continued Sobo. 'And while it is true that the Semblant evolved from humans, the Semblant are able to utilise their genes more thoroughly. It is suggested that many human genes are inactive or not switched on, because they were attributes that are no longer required, and as such have become redundant through the many eons of time....'

Images of primates and neanderthal beings walked and ran around, and even through Peabody. There were lions, deer, and large birds of prey. He saw primates hunting and lighting fires. There were giant trees and heavy jungle-like foliage. It was a multidimensional experience.

'... However,' Sobo continued. '... one should look at this genetic matter differently. It is not that these genes are no longer needed, it is that they have never been switched on at all. What if they could be activated? And what if some of the genetics of other earthly creatures could also be utilised? What would we have, Roderick?'

'A Semblant?' answered Peabody.

'Correct.'

'You are answering my questions without my having asked them?'

'I am… you also wonder why the Semblant don't speak in the way of original humans.'

'It has crossed my mind more than once,' smiled Peabody.

'To a Semblant, psychic connection is like blinking. Automatic… instant. As you know the Semblant also communicate by an array of sounds which are like a *double blink*. Such messages are, for the most part, believed by the recipient without question,' said Sobo. 'Such belief, from these sonic communications, may remain with the recipient for days or even weeks. Whereas psychic thoughts transmitted via eye contact have a much shorter duration.'

'You wonder,' continued Sobo. 'How far such a telepathic instruction could go. You should look at this, Roderick, like an advanced form of hypnosis. It is important to note that the human instinct for self-preservation will not allow any psychic influence that could cause bodily harm or death. For example, I cannot suggest to someone that they should take their own life, unless it happens that they are already predisposed that way.'

'Thank you,' replied Peabody. 'My understanding is improving.'

'The Semblant have evolved beyond verbal communication as you would know it. If they choose to communicate by actual speech, it will be because they are under duress or stress of some kind. Semblant tend to avoid situations where speech is a requirement, alternatively they may feign some sort of laryngitis or the like. A newly emerged

Semblant however, is a little different, and developing these psychic abilities takes time, so they will speak in what you consider a more natural verbal way until their skills are fully realised.'

Peabody nodded. He remained in his suspended weightless state, hovering, and connected by light to Sobo.

'Speech and the spoken word are only one part of the message, and in many instances of original human communication these words are not accurate, or are even deliberately or unconsciously misleading. The Semblant do what comes naturally.'

'Is being well-meaning and good natured a natural process for the Semblant?'

'For most it is, Roderick. I can see how you think this would be of concern should a Semblant be not so positively inclined. It is possible, given that you are a Semblant friendly person, that over time you will meet other Semblant, and I trust this will remain a positive experience. If you wish, I can equip you with some defence in the unlikely event that you meet a negative influencer. That is, a Semblant that can alter your memory or access thoughts or feelings that you are not yet ready to disclose, and memories that you wish to keep. Is this something you would like?'

'Hmm… well would this affect me in any other way?'

'It would not.' For a second the arcs of light grew brighter. 'And as I see you are good with this, I have already given you this gift.'

'Wow.'

'All you need to do is put thoughts, feelings, or ideas in this safe place. For simplicity, let us call this place Fort Knox.'

Peabody smiled. 'Fort Knox. I see it. I have it. Thank you Sobo.'

There was a moment of quiet. Sobo's arms remained raised. The arched beams of light continued descending onto the undertaker.

'Ah... you also wonder about death,' said Sobo. 'What happens when a Semblant dies? A Semblant death, like that of an original human, is a devastating event. So much is lost. For the most part, a Semblant knows when death is coming. A Semblant can expire in the natural process of decline over many years. The oldest Semblant known to me was four hundred and eleven years of age when they departed. I have heard of others that were older. A Semblant will seek water, as in a river or the sea if possible. The body gradually overheats, and as the Semblant disappears into the water, the body disintegrates right down to and beyond a cellular level and is fully dispersed. If another Semblant is present, and if time permits, a dying Semblant may be able to transfer some memory and advanced abilities to another.'

Right in front of Peabody a vision of an unknown Semblant appeared. She was hovering in front of his face. Light coloured cloth was draped around her, and the material waved in slow motion as if caught in a light breeze. She was beautiful, but with a grimace. A furrowed brow. Watery eyes. A quivering mouth.

'I can share an experience if you wish. It will not harm you, but it will be harrowing, and for a short time you will feel pain both physical and emotional...'

'I feel it already... please continue,' panted Peabody.

The floating, ghostly image moved closer and entered his body. He raised his head and suddenly he was swimming or at least he was part of someone else who was swimming. The swell was slight and as he turned his head he could see a long beach, palm trees, houses and a few multi-storey apartments, but he was heading the opposite way and out to sea. His arms swam in a lazy freestyle motion. They felt heavy and flopped and splashed on each stroke. Peabody felt heat inside his abdomen. The temperature rose and spread throughout every part of his being. The arms stopped splashing and his overheated body extended in a star shape. The headache was excruciating. His mind became filled with flashing images – faces of many people he didn't recognise yet felt connected to – men, women and children of every race and colour, from young to old. They were leaving him forever. The sadness was beyond measure and the mental pain was so intense as to nearly eclipse the physical burning. Then there was a complete release to blackness, a final breath out, and absolute nothingness. A second later he was back floating in the mist in front of Sobo.

'You will experience some moments of catharsis for a couple of hours, but you will be fine,' said Sobo.

'Yes…' panted Peabody. 'It sits in the pit of my stomach right now. Oh my goodness!'

'And even amidst all that emotion, I see you still have a question,' said Sobo with a softer, more soothing tone of Johnny Randall's voice. 'There is a rare occurrence that you will have heard about, but not ever believed… until now. It is called spontaneous human combustion. There are several recorded accounts, but there are many that occur without anyone's knowledge. These occur when a Semblant dies suddenly from some form of misadventure – be that an accident or a deliberate action by an original human. It can also occur when a Semblant is unable, for whatever reason, to get to water.'

'Oh… my… positively dreadful,' muttered Peabody.

'That will be enough, Roderick. Take your time and remain in your chair for a few minutes when you awake. When you feel ready, please consider how we might attempt to locate Kwikal. I have some upcoming business. Both Johnny Randall and I have some unfinished matters to attend to. Thank you for being present with me today. I have enjoyed the process. We shall return now.'

Peabody had his eyes closed. He felt the chair underneath him as if he had just descended onto it. His hands ran over the fabric on the arms giving him the sense he was back where he should be – not that he had ever really left, despite the very real sensation that he had travelled so far away. After a few long slow breaths he opened his eyes. The door was open. The Semblant was gone. The clock showed eighteen minutes past eleven.

Chapter 32

A Picture Forms

'I can only apologise,' said Richard. He shook his head slowly. 'I really thought Clive was full of horseshit, so I just settled in and enjoyed myself.'

'You got plastered,' said Jan.

'True.'

'Well… now you know what you missed out on.'

It was Monday morning, and Jan Silverton and Richard Davis were back at Roma Street police HQ waiting on the arrival of other officers and detectives. She had brought Davis up to speed with the events and mysteries of Friday night at the Tribal Moon.

'How is it possible for someone to influence others like that?' Richard shook his head. 'It's the stuff of science fiction.'

'And as it stands, Clive's version of events from nine months ago is now sounding quite plausible.'

At that moment, Clive Anderson walked into the briefing room.

'Did I hear my name mentioned?' He placed a leather satchel on a small table and opened it, taking out a plastic lunch container and a thermos.

'Jan was saying she believes your account of the Galanis / Drakos incident,' said Richard brightly.

'Really,' smiled Clive.

'That's not exactly what I said.'

What did you say… exactly?' taunted Clive.

'I said it seemed *plausible*.' Jan pushed out a quick half smile.

'Happy to take *plausible*,' said Anderson. 'I'm sure that will move closer to certainty in due course.' He turned to Richard. 'What about you? Better now? Did you find a new squeeze?'

'I'm fine thank you, and as a matter of fact I did meet someone nice.'

'Someone right up your alley then?' asked Clive with a smirk.

'Come on Clive! What the hell?' snapped Jan.

'It's' okay,' laughed Richard while holding up a hand. 'If you must know we never got as far as the back alley, Clive. But he was very kind and helped me find my way home. Having someone to lookout for you is pretty nice… not that you would know much about that.'

'I prefer numero uno. I've never been that great with partners.'

'Yeah,' said Silverton. 'I can vouch for that.'

'Did you get to first names, or is that not particularly important with you guys… I mean *you gays*.'

'Clive!' snapped Jan.

'It's okay Jan,' said Richard. 'I can take his taunts all day. Water off a gay duck's back.'

'Hey, you know I like teasing the hell out of you, kid. It adds a degree of satisfaction to my day,' said Clive with a wink at Davis.

'Go your hardest old man,' chuckled Richard. 'And his name is Con – short for Constantino.'

'Con… huh, sounds like a used car salesman. Don't get conned.'

'I'll be just fine. Thanks for your concern.'

'You're welcome,' smiled Clive. 'Hey Jan. Could you update Edwards for me… on all that Tribal Moon shit. If I speak to him, he'll surely have a brain haemorrhage.'

'I need something solid. At the moment it could simply look like people misinterpreting, being influenced by alcohol, not paying proper attention… something like that.'

'Really? What about the appearance of the dead Johnny Randall?'

'Could just be another impersonator, as odd as that sounds,' replied Jan. 'Like the Medora woman. Granted, his hair was way longer, and he had no birthmark.'

'Hmm…why would an impersonator get the hair so wrong? That's gotta be basic impersonation 1-0-1.' Clive shook his head. 'Anyway. I need coffee. I'm off to the kitchen.' He strolled away to the tearoom with his lunchbox and thermos.

'He's making sense,' said Davis.

'Yeah… I know,' said Jan. A door opened quietly behind her. 'But telling Edwards we were out unofficially at a night club would not be received that well.' She heard a sigh and a thump as someone dropped into a chair behind her. It was Edwards.

'Fuck me, it's only Monday!' he said loudly.

*   *   *

Most of the detectives and officers had finished milling around in the briefing room, grabbed their coffees and linked up with their respective teams to review their cases, check messages, and plan their day with each other.

Detective Jan Silverton's team of seven, remained in the briefing room. She stood next to a chair in front of six men. Everyone was in civilian dress except for one senior constable who was in his blue uniform. Jan wore her regular civilian wear of black jeans and a high-low hem top, with rolled up sleeves – today in the colour peach. The guys were mixtures of neat and tidy to scruffy. Davis wore chinos and a cream blazer over a black long-sleeved shirt.

Jan held up a wad of A4 sheets. 'We have something of a breakthrough, thanks to our mates in Sydney. They have been doing the rounds of the gay clubs, bars and other hangouts. They got lucky at the Magnolia bar and spoke to several people who had seen a guy who we believe called himself Jericho Mondano.' She passed out the sheets of printed paper. 'The footage from the CCTV was not that helpful in seeing his face. He positioned himself carefully... deliberately... and left his hat on. This is a drawing of what this guy looks like. He's an attractive well-dressed man with an olive complexion.'

'Do we really think this guy's gay?' asked Detective Henry Bryant, tapping the picture. Bryant was an experienced officer with ten detective years under his belt. He had a habit of wearing his sunnies all the time except when in front of a computer or TV. His black hair was brushed back and highlighted with grey.

'I think we're still inconclusive. What's your thoughts, Bryant?' asked Silverton.

'Well, he kills gay guys of a particular appearance,' added Bryant through a tight mouth. 'No evidence of sexual activity. No semen at any of the crime scenes. Could be a straight guy with a grudge... maybe a bad past experience of some kind, even childhood trauma.'

'Childhood trauma. I'd go along with that,' said Richard.

'He has a bandage or possibly a dressing of some sort on his left wrist,' continued Bryant. 'We know the words he writes are not done with the victim's blood. Most likely his own... like he is harming himself and then writing a note to *Daddy*.'

'I've researched the hell out of what he has written,' said Davis. 'But no real luck yet. Get thousands of hits on Google, and lots on a site that matches lyrics. Found plenty of weird shit. Nothing useful.'

*   *   *

Clive gave Lachlan Godwin an abbreviated recount of the Tribal Moon story.

'I want you to find out what you can about this Bentley Hopkin-Jones guy. I'll SMS you his picture and his driver's license.'

'Do we think he has done anything wrong, sir?'

'Son, I've tried to paint you a picture here,' said Clive gesturing with his open hands. 'People are being unduly influenced in some way by different people. At present I know of four… granted, one of which was a guy that impersonated a gangster called Nicholas Drakos… yes that is my issue. But there is Medora Hammerstein… there's Johnny Randall and now there is this Hopkin-Jones prick. You weren't at the nightclub. You didn't see the effect on the bouncer and on Tony Rizzo.'

'I apologise. Perhaps next time… if there is to be one, you could invite me along.'

'Hmm… I could, Godwin… now if you wouldn't mind…'

'Hopkin-Jones,' interrupted Godwin. 'I'm onto it, sir.'

'Good. I'll be heading off soon to track whatever CCTV footage I can. See if we can get an idea where this Johnny Randall went on Friday night.'

Chapter 33

The Collector

It was seven in the morning when a dishevelled young man sat on the footpath on Edward Street with his back against a shop window. He was only one city block away from the Tribal Moon nightclub. His dirty brown trousers and a similar coloured long sleeve button up shirt were riddled with holes and tears.

He took off his well-worn rodeo-style hat and placed it upside down between his legs. His long brown hair fell around his shoulders. The way he was dressed, and being several days unshaven, Johnny Randall looked much different to the smartly attired young man that only four days ago, became the centre of attention at the nearby nightclub.

He propped a cardboard sign next to him. Roughly written in blue paint were the words *Help me find my place in this world.* On his other side he placed a large water bottle.

The street was already busy, with employees in a hurry to get to work – businessmen and women, store owners and staff, trade and council workers, students going to school, TAFE or Uni. Later in the morning a huge variety of shoppers would add to the mix.

The spot selected by Semblant Johnny was near a busy intersection, and with a railway station nearby, bus stops and a taxi rank, there would be thousands passing him over the next few hours. It would be tiring work trying to make direct eye contact with as many as possible.

A slim suited man with a black suitcase bustled along the footpath, striding faster than most others. He dodged and weaved his way through the crowd, bumping a few shoulders in his haste. Johnny stared at him… waiting… just a quick glance was all he needed. When the man was nearly on top of the apparent vagrant, he looked down with a frown. In that second the Semblant had him. The man stopped. His frown changing to a smile as he squatted.

'You poor guy. Please accept my gift.' He pulled a wallet from his back pocket and dropped a fifty dollar note into the hat. 'Goodbye.' Off he went, picking up where he left off, darting this way and that through the throng of pedestrians. Johnny smiled.

*   *   *

After three hours, and having collected nine hundred and fifty dollars, Johnny took a break, picked up his gear and headed further along Edward Street. He stopped at a closed door and put his sign down, above the door was an unlit neon sign – *Tribal Moon Nightclub*. Underneath in bold red lettering was *WED, FRI & SAT 6PM – LATE*. He first put two fingers in his mouth. His mouth widened. He put all his fingers in, then as his mouth stretched even further, squashing back his nose at the top and touching the top of his chest at the bottom, he pushed his entire hand in to past his wrist. A couple of metres away a lady with a stroller had stopped and was preoccupied checking her phone. The toddler looked at the Semblant and pointed.

The hand withdrew and the orifice returned to its normal size. Johnny had a handful of a clear jelly-like substance. Using it like ink for a fountain pen, he dipped in his other finger and wrote in large letters on the door. SOBO AT PEABODY FUNERALS. He glanced at the toddler and gave a wink. The child erupted into a loud cackling chuckle. He waited a moment as he watched the words dry and disappear altogether like invisible ink.

Satisfied with his message, he headed down Adelaide Street to Anzac Square, a distance of only four hundred metres.

The Semblant hadn't felt any vibrations or stimulation of any other senses. It was probably a long shot to find Kwikal, but it was a plan that Sobo and Roderick thought was a chance. It may require repeating several times, even into the evening. If Kwikal went anywhere near the Tribal Moon, he would detect the message.

Being around morning tea, the numbers in the park at Anzac Square had increased, and all nearby coffee outlets had queues.

Johnny sat on the bottom of a flight of concrete stairs that led up to The Shrine of Remembrance. Ahead of him was a cement pathway, lined with trees and open grassed clearings, which led past a Boer War Memorial of a soldier on horseback and back to Adelaide Street.

A steady flow of people wandered past him; their pace markedly slower than the early morning rush. He had unintentionally caught the eye of a couple of passers-by, one handed him five dollars, the other twenty. As he looked up again, he felt someone from behind brush past his left shoulder, heading down the steps. Johnny looked up and caught the eye of a smartly dressed man, with short cut blonde hair.

'Apologies,' said the man, flashing an open hand as he slowed. Johnny smiled and nodded. A subtle scent hit the back of the Semblant's nostrils. It was a mixture of a male cologne, deodorant, furniture polish and a hint of sweat. The man stopped at the bottom of the steps and pulled a ten-dollar note from his wallet.

'There you are. Have a nice day.' His voice was soft, and despite his appearance conveying warmth and sincerity, a tingle went up Johnny's spine. It was not the tingle of a past acquaintance, a memory, or a like-minded friend, it was a tingle that felt like hate, desperation and death.

The olive-skinned man continued through the park. Johnny followed, keeping his distance.

A few minutes later, and a little way down Adelaide Street, the blonde-haired man joined a coffee queue at a mobile vendor – Kev's Kwik Koffee Kombi. Johnny watched and listened as the man made a phone call. He was several metres away but once focused was able to hear every word. As the man spoke more tingles ran down the spine of the Semblant.

Chapter 34

Catch Up

At eleven on that Monday morning, as Richard was walking out the bathroom, his personal mobile rang to the tune of "Another One Bites the Dust", and the words *No Caller ID* came up on the display.

'Huh… who are you?' He muttered as he looked at the phone.

'Hello,' he answered, choosing not to give anything away.'

'Hi Richard. Hope you're well now.'

'Who's this?'

'Constantino. We met Friday night…'

'Ah… you took me home in an Uber.'

'Correct.'

'Thanks for that. Sorry for my behaviour. I was more shot that I intended to be. You took my number?'

'Yeah… hope that's okay. You gave me your phone to call a ride. Then I took the liberty to take down your number, so I could call you. Being a little presumptuous, I guess. Sorry.'

'That's okay. No big deal,' Richard tilted his head. 'Why are you blocking your own number?'

'Oh… yes. Something I always do now. I had a torrid break up a few months back and was hassled incessantly by an ex and his mates. I got a new number and ever since then I keep caller ID hidden. Very happy though for you to know it… and call it if you feel so inclined.' There was a hint of suggestiveness in Constantino's voice. *'And Richard, I just got your number and that's all… promise. I didn't do any snooping around or anything improper with your phone.'*

'I believe you, Con. It's okay,' chuckled Richard.

'Phew… thanks. I was so worried you'd be upset.'

'All good. Where are you? It sounds a bit noisy?'

'Yeah, it is. I'm in town doing some shopping. At the moment waiting on a coffee from Kev's Kwik Koffee Kombi, in Adelaide Street. Despite his advertising he's not that quick.'

'Busy spot.'

'The point of my calling you is to see if we can catch up. Perhaps a morning tea… maybe a meal.'

'I'd like that, thanks.'

'Great.'

'Sounds like you've given it a bit of thought. A dinner sounds nice. What did you have in mind?'

'You're right. Just tell me if this is out of order… but I'm not a half bad cook… and seeing as I know where you live 'n all – I was thinking I could come over with a few ingredients, a nice bottle of red, and cook up something very sumptuous.'

'Hmm… sounds pretty good to me.'

'How does tomorrow night sound? I could be at your place around seven.'

'Works been a bit frantic. How about we make it Thursday around seven-thirty?'

'Thursday… okay, I guess I'll wait till then.'

'What are you going to cook?'

'Do you have any special dietary issues?'

'No. Not a big fan of Brussel sprouts.'

'Okay,' chuckled Constantino. *'No brussels – I'd like to surprise you if you don't mind.'*

'Wonderful. I like surprises. Looking forward to it, Con. See you Thursday night.'

'Super. See you then. Bye bye.'

Richard pushed the red button. He smiled and nodded to himself. 'Bloody good,' he whispered as he headed back to work.

*　　　*　　　*

Constantino Abrahams pushed his mobile into his jeans and sighed. *'Can we make it to Thursday, Fabian?'* he asked some other part of himself. After a few more minutes he had his coffee, wandered up Adelaide Street and plonked himself on the grass in the park at Anzac Square.

Fabian Carver sat there sipping and looking at nothing as his tortured mind wandered. He remembered the last day he ever saw his mother...

The station wagon pulled up in the busy departure lane of the Brisbane Airport. Security officers in yellow hi-vis shirts were hurrying commuters along and not allowing drivers more than a minute of wait time.

Mrs Maureen Carver was an overly thin lady with a wrinkly face and salt and pepper collar length hair. Her thirty to forty a day smoking habit seemed to have even given her skin a greyish pallor. She puffed her Ventolin inhaler three times before she got out the car. George Carver opened the rear door and hauled out her suitcase, gave her a quick peck on the cheek then hopped back into the driver's seat.

Maureen squatted in front of ten-year-old Fabian. She gave him a big squeeze.

'Now you be good for your father,' she cautioned in a soft voice.

'I don't want you to g... g... go.'

'I have to see your grandmother, she has only days left to live.' Maureen brushed at her skirt. 'Oh dear, look at that.' There was a small burn hole from a cigarette near the hem.

'Dad is n... nnn....nnn...' Fabian swallowed Dad is nn...n....'

'Slow down. Take a breath,' instructed Maureen. 'Just like we've practiced before.'

'Dad is not n... nice to me.'

'Come on now, we have spoken about this.' She rubbed the burn hole removing the black edges. 'You must not continue to malign your father's good character. He's a good provider for our family.'

'Why don't you believe me?'

'Because I know your father loves you.' She held the boy's shoulders. 'He would go out of his way to protect you. Please don't start this again. Not here. Not now. As if I haven't got enough on my mind already.'

'Are you pretending?'

'Pretending what?'

'Not to know what he does.'

'I won't hear another word. Now, I'll be home in a couple of weeks. Off you go.' She stood, kissed the top of his head, and moved away with her suitcase. Fabian got into the backseat of the car.

Three days later Maureen was dead. A massive heart attack. Fabian's grandmother lived for a further two years.

After his mother's departure and subsequent death, the sexual abuse escalated, starting from that very afternoon when his father took him into the shower. George declared his intense love for his son, while he kissed him with an open mouth. 'Who's my special boy then?' In the background the song was playing...

I hear you breathe
I see your sweet form
Smooth and unique
We find each other
No end to this love
My special boy forever...

He then spent thirty minutes penetrating him with his fingers and penis.

It was pretty much fifty-fifty between the bath and the couch – sometimes it was both – the couch followed by taking off the daisy pattern dress and then heading to the bathroom. It seemed an odd thing to even have a preference, but in the bath, it was easier for Fabian to go to his special place by the sea. He could imagine the warm water washing over him, cleansing him, and somehow giving him the energy to survive. One day, if he could keep living, he would be old enough to change all this. He would grow and become stronger than his father. He could leave home and not be brought back time and time again by the police. Unfortunately, it would be nearly seven more years before this would happen.

Chapter 35

Some Things Don't Add Up

Lachlan Godwin had spent considerable time on checking information systems and other records to find out as much as he could about Bentley Hopkin-Jones. He had taken some initiative and also decided to make comparisons between Hopkin-Jones and Medora Hammerstein.

At nine-thirty, later than expected, Clive joined him in their combined office. He placed a plastic bag of items on his desk.

'Sir, I have something of interest,' squawked Lachlan, standing as he spoke. Clive held up his hand.

'Not interested. Not until I get coffee.' Clive left the room with his thermos and lunchbox.

'Huh…' Lachlan moved to Clive's desk and gently separated the plastic bag and peered inside. There was a blue tooth headset and a pair of sunglasses both in boxes. The young detective backed away to his own area.

Over two whiteboards in front of both desks, several photos were on display – the headless body of Johnny Randall and two pics of his opened body from the autopsy; two photos of Medora Hammerstein, one from the Tribal Moon and another borrowed from Otto showing an old lady; a nightclub image of Bentley Hopkin-Jones next to an enlarged image of his driver's license; and another of the apparently reincarnated Johnny Randall with a pic of his license when first scanned at the nightclub before he lost his head.

Clive ambled back in, coffee in hand. 'Okay, what's so interesting?' He sipped his drink and flopped down into the chair at his desk.

Lachlan moved quickly to the photos and pointed at the enlargement of Bentley's license and tapped on it. 'This is a fake license. Pretty good work. A good quality card printer and some expertise would have been required.'

'No shit, Sherlock! We already know it's missing a watermark and the word *Australia* above the face.'

'But it's such a good copy you would wonder why they would make a silly typo.'

'What typo?'

'The date of birth says the twenty-first of August, but the year…. It's 1887.'

Clive stood. 'Shit. So it is!'

'Strange eh?'

'Yeah… it is. So this means Godwin, that it is simply just a typo, or that Hopkin Jones is really over one hundred and forty years old. Which one do you think is most likely?'

'I know you think it must be a typo, but there is a lot of odd shit going on. Here's the thing boss… sir. I tracked down the birthdate of Bentley Hopkin-Jones and according to the Australian birth register it is, in fact, the twenty first of August 1887.'

'Fuck. You sure?'

'Triple checked.'

'Does there happen to be a date of death?'

'Died in the first world war in 1915.'

'And there are no other matching names?'

'None with the same birthdate. And only one of the same name from South Australia. Also dead. 1940.' Godwin looked at Anderson with the slightest of smiles. 'And I've got more… sir.' Lachlan moved to his desk, picked up two sheets of paper and handed them to the seated Anderson.

'Hammerstein and Hopkin-Jones. Both have forged licenses. Neither lives at their stated address. Both have this weird communication style. Both are supposed to be dead. Both, by look, appear about the same age and both are extremely attractive and well-dressed.'

'Yes, yes… and apart from the forged license, we can put Johnny Randal right in there too.'

'Sir, I put in a call to Langley, Lester, Bruce and Associates. Janine Hansen is in this morning. Made an appointment. I think we should talk to her about her antics on Friday night.'

'You seem to have hit your straps, Godwin. Good work.'

Chapter 36

Matters Needing Attention

Johnny Randall sat on the large back deck of his parent's home in the suburb of Taringa in Brisbane. From this elevated location on Swan Road, he had a perfect view of the city skyline and the immediate surrounds. Looking left he could see the heavily treed Mount Coot-tha and the string of television broadcast towers running across the top.

In the back yard were a cluster of small fruit trees and a partly concealed garden shed. Rebel, the ten-year-old black and white Jack Russel Terrier, stopped barking and ran up the stairs and onto the back deck, laying down at Johnny's feet.

Sitting down at another table were his parents, Warren and Stephanie, and his teenage sister, Mel. They were all smiles as they chatted away over a barbecue lunch. Then his father said something and the three all gave a subdued chuckle.

Johnny smiled as he looked on. 'Dad... Mum!' he called. Rebel raised his head. There was no response from the three at the other table. 'Mel... hello!' His sister wiped her mouth and took another mouthful of her chicken.

Johnny stood and walked slowly over and stood next to the table, Rebel tagged along. 'I love you guys so much.' He swallowed heavily as he spoke. His mother paused, and her smile evaporated as she looked about as if something had caught her attention.

'So sorry I never got to say goodbye,' croaked Johnny.

'I wish Johnny was here,' said Mel.

'Me too love,' said his mother. 'I was just thinking the very same thing.' Mother and daughter looked at each other, both with a slight smile and an almost indiscernible reassuring nod.

'Guys… I'm here. Right with you now. Missing you all so much. This must be the deepest pain anyone could ever feel.' Tears flowed freely, running down his cheeks. Some dripped from his chin and disappeared into nothing as they struck the decking. Rebel tilted his head to one side.

'He was so sick,' said Warren. 'I should have insisted he see someone, but instead I told him off. Called him a fool. Blamed it on drugs.' The lanky man dropped his head into his hands. 'Oh, God!'

Johnny moved to his father's side and placed a hand on his dad's head. 'I was pig-headed, Dad. You blamed drugs. I blamed your cooking.' Johnny gave a quick grin. 'It's okay now. I have found my peace. You must find yours.' Rebel barked once.

'I fought with him too often,' said Mel. 'It was me that broke his finger. I slammed the bathroom door on his hand. I was mean. I could have been a better sister.'

'He loved you, Mel. So much,' said Stephanie. 'I didn't know about the bathroom door. Johnny said he did it with a hammer while fixing his car. He looked out for you. And he knew you loved him.' Rebel moved and sat next to Mel's chair. She instinctively started scratching his neck.

Johnny walked to near his sister. He bent over and kissed the top of her head, then held up his hand and looked at his bent index finger. He smiled. 'I'll always be keeping an eye over you, Mel. You best behave.'

'Do you think he is watching over us?' asked Mel.

'I do. I really feel that,' said Steph. 'I have felt that before, but today I'm convinced of it.' She looked up and cried. 'We love you Johnny.'

Johnny moved nearer his mother. Rebel moved to under Steph's chair. Johnny reached out with both hands and touched her cheeks. 'You will always be mother of the year.' As he moved his hands away Stephanie raised her own hands and lightly touched her face.
'He always called you mother of the year,' said Mel. Steph nodded and sniffed.

Johnny looked beyond the verandah. A heavy mist swooped in, concealing everything. It swirled in front of his face. He felt as if he was moving but his body was still. An indistinct Sobo appeared before him. 'It is done, Johnny Randall. I am tired. I am sorry. We must leave now.'

Johnny moved forward and his ghostly form flowed back into the Semblant.

On the verandah, Rebel barked and took off down the stairs. He stopped at the door to the backyard shed, barked three more times then sat quietly.

*   *   *

Later, on that same afternoon, Semblant Johnny strode from the elevator and presented himself at the semi-circular reception desk of Langley, Lester, Bruce and Associates, Insurance and Commercial Lawyers. His three-piece suit was a shiny greenish black. Johnny's long brown locks were gone, and he now sported a cut with shaved sides, thicker on top and a straggly fringe over his forehead. He wore a set of fine round yellow glasses.

'Oh... hello,' said the slim lady at reception. She stopped tapping at the keyboard and stood, staring for a moment, her mouth slightly open. She shook her head, looked away, then back. 'Sorry sir. How may I help you?'

Johnny looked at the reinforced glass mounted on the counter. There were some small holes to talk through and some low gaps where documents could be exchanged. He held his throat, then pointed to his mouth before lifting his shoulders and tilting his head. The receptionist pushed a biro and notepad through the gap. He wrote *Janine wishes to see me. Tell her it's Johnny.* He passed the note back. The lady picked up the phone and partly covered the mouthpiece as she spoke.

'Janine, there's a gorgeous guy here called Johnny. Says you want to see him...' There was quiet. 'Janine... shall I bring him down to your office or to the boardroom... hello... Janine.'

'My office. Thanks Cheryl.'

Cheryl hung up and turned round. Johnny was already on his way, walking round the reception desk and heading down a corridor. 'I can escort you... sir... please...' Johnny lifted an open hand and waved it side to side. Cheryl stopped and watched. 'Next hall on the right... then second door...' her words petered out. She let out a big sigh and returned to her reception area.

Johnny smelt the air as he walked quietly, but purposefully, over the carpet. He stopped next to a closed room, raised his head slightly and sniffed some more. He opened the door. The blonde lawyer was standing right there, just a metre and a half away, leaning back slightly supported by her hands against her desk.

'Oh... my!' She looked him up and down. 'Looks like Johnny is all business-like now. I quite liked your long hair, but this is nice. Very refined.'

Johnny was quiet, smiling and gazing into her eyes.

'You frightened me, Johnny…' continued Janine. There was a slight quiver in her voice. She swallowed. '…on Friday night… it was weird. You scared Crystal too. Neither of us understood what was going on.'

Johnny nodded and mouthed, *Yeah*. Then he stared at her with larger than normal blue eyes. Janine heard him say *Sorry*. He took a step closer and shut the door with his foot. While holding her gaze, his hand reached back and pushed the lock button. Then both arms moved to each side, turned awkwardly, and twisted a plastic rod. The thin venetian blinds closed.

'I'm not sure… Johnny.' She pushed herself back against her desk. 'Will you disappear again?'

Johnny flashed his big smile and shook his head. He took a step closer. Janine eased off her desk and slipped off her Tweed blazer, letting it fall to the floor. She stepped up against him and kissed him hard on the mouth. Her hands pushed through his hair, then held his cheeks while their mouths opened. She pushed fingers into his mouth alongside her tongue. Her fingers went from his mouth to hers, feeling his tongue, the inside of his cheeks and his teeth. Feeling her own tongue. Sucking and licking eagerly.

Johnny lifted her and slid her bottom across the desk. A plastic pen caddy toppled over. A computer monitor slid to the side and teetered on the edge. Without missing a beat, Johnny's arm shot out and pushed it back a few centimetres. He pushed up her tweed skirt. A hand shot quickly to either side of her knickers and somehow cut both sides. He pulled them away from under her and threw them to the wall.

'Fuck… wicked… that's fucking wicked,' she breathed heavily as she saw her knickers fly across the room. Janine groped frantically at his trousers. He placed an open hand on her chest and eased a little away from her. Johnny undressed slowly. Janine lent back on one arm.

Her other hand slipped between her own legs, her fingers sliding between her labia, finding her clitoris.

Johnny held her gaze as he gradually revealed his naked body. Janine panted as she caressed herself. 'Oh... Johnny... yes. Please put your tongue inside me.'

His mouth opened wide. His tongue flicked through the air, extended longer, formed into a roundish shape and shot into her nose. For a fraction of a second Janine was shocked and thought that Johnny had misunderstood what she had requested. *I should have been more specific...* then her pupils dilated. Her body went limp as he took her in his arms.

When her eyes opened, Johnny was on top of her. They were lying on what looked like the biggest and softest mattress Janine had ever seen or felt – at least the size of six king sized beds. The massive bed was surrounded on every side by pink and white cherry blossom trees in full bloom. Pink and white petals floated through the air. Behind the trees, and hanging below whatever ceiling existed, was a heavy cloudy mist.

At their feet was another couple, a fit black man and a snow white young red-haired woman, both with their heads tightly nuzzled into each other's genitals. To one side were three naked women – one straddling another's chest, pushing her pelvis forward against an eager mouth. She leant back on her arms while the third woman fondled her breast, kissed and sucked her tongue. On their opposite side an athletic man was kneeling and pushing his cock in and out of the mouth of his boyfriend. The boyfriend lay flat with his arms extending to his friend's hips, pulling and pushing him as he took the penis deep into his throat.

Then Janine felt Johnny slide inside her. His penis seeming to enlarge even more as her vagina tightened around it.

'Oh… oh… Is this a dream?' she panted. 'Where are we?'

'It is half a dream. Half not.' His penis pulsed inside her while his pelvis barely moved. 'Created especially for you… from my memories.'

'Johnny… ooh… my God… Crystal… she should be here with us.'

'Yes, she should. Maybe next time.'

'Huh… argh… oh… these people… who are they, Johnny?'

'I am all of those lying horizontal. The others, like you Janine, are my friends and lovers.'

'Oh… I see,' she said, although she didn't really, but that was no longer important. Only this moment mattered.

Just as she let go of a thousand questions and bathed in the pleasure, something else unusual happened. Johnny was above her looking into her eyes. One hand was taking his weight, while the other was stroking her face. But somehow something else pushed against her anus. Gently at first, then a little harder. There was moisture. This probing appendage went into her. It was if another man was beneath her having anal intercourse at the same time as Johnny was filling her vagina. The back and forth in both passages continued as if synchronized – one forward while the other went back. Janine heard sounds and voices from the others. Mixed groans and moans of pleasure together with loud whispers – *more, harder, slower, faster, oh yes, that's wonderful, don't stop, oh oh, oh*. Her head rolled from side to side noticing the others having their own erotic experiences and at the same time enhancing her own.

Chapter 37

Back to Work

Janine stirred and opened her eyes. She was lying on the carpet in her office with the office chair cushion under her head. She looked side to side. Johnny was gone and she was naked.

A wave of concern swelled within her, and she jumped to her feet. Janine darted around the office grabbing clothes and shoes and getting dressed. Her phone rang.

'Oh shit.' She snatched it up. 'Yes, what's wrong?' she said, a bit louder and faster than she really should have. She looked about her office as she held the phone. At least the blinds were still closed.

Janine… are you okay? I have your three o'clock here. The two detectives. Shall I escort them to the boardroom?'

'Yes… Cheryl… the boardroom.' She hung up.

Janine was frantically brushing herself off and trying to push the creases from her white V-neck blouse. Most items on the desk had been pushed to the side. Pencils and pens had rolled onto the floor.

'Oh my goodness.' She noticed a large wet patch on the carpet. With a handful of tissues she blotted and rubbed. There was a knock and then the door opened. Cheryl walked in. Janine was on all fours on the floor. 'What the hell, Janine?'

'Spilt some stuff. No problem.' She got back to her feet.

Cheryl looked around. 'Are they your knickers?' She pointed to a red lacy pair next to the wall.

'I don't know,' replied a bewildered Janine.

'Don't know? Have you been fucking in here? Oh my God, Janine. That Johnny guy. You fucked him right here in your office.'

Janine stood there and dropped her shoulders and let out a big sigh. 'Okay Cheryl! He fucked me, really. Like… good and proper. Like, I can't even begin to describe.'

Detective Clive Anderson peered over Cheryl's shoulder then pushed her aside as he entered. 'Good afternoon, Miss Hansen.'

'This isn't the boardroom, detective,' yelled Janine.

Clive looked around. Janine darted over and stood on her knickers with both feet. 'Cheryl, please escort them to the boardroom.'

'This way, sir,' said Cheryl sharply. Clive ignored her. Lachlan Godwin tentatively entered also.

Cheryl threw her arms up in frustration. 'Really! This is uncalled for.'

'Has Johnny Randall been here?' asked Anderson. He ambled about the office. 'Your desk is a mess and look…' Clive pushed at the carpet with his shoe. '… you've spilt something here.'

'Never mind that, detective. Just what do you think you're doing?' snapped Janine. 'This is a private space. There are confidential documents here. Leave or I will see that you are charged.'

'This door was open. I was invited into the building and escorted down here by the lovely Cheryl. I have an appointment. I will ask again, has Johnny Randall been here?'

'He left some time ago.'

'What did he want? What did you talk about?'

'Are you deliberately trying to embarrass me?'

'I think you are doing a fine job on your own. And I can still see the edge of those red knickers that you're trying to hide.'

Janine squatted carefully and retrieved the panties. 'Okay, tell the whole fucking world,' she yelled. 'I had sex right here in my office. Is that what you wanted to hear? Why don't you stick these in your stupid pocket. Could be evidence you know!' She waved the damaged red knickers around.

'I'm not interested in your sexual habits. I just want to know about Randall.'

'Find him yourself and ask him.'

'Hmm… yes. But here's the thing.' Clive turned to his colleague and put out his hand. Godwin handed over a picture which Clive placed on the desk. 'This is Johnny Randall. Dead as a doornail and missing his head.'

'Obviously detective, that is not the Johnny I know. You see my Johnny definitely had a head. I think I would have noticed you know, being a lawyer and all that,' she scoffed.

'Did this Johnny speak to you.' Clive raised his voice and took two steps closer to Janine. 'You must tell me what exact words he said.'

'He spoke when we were having sex. He said this was a dream he had created especially for me. Those were his exact words, detective.'

'Hmm… what does that mean exactly?'

'I was in the middle of something very intimate. I was not about to ask for clarification.'

'What else did he say?'

'I'm not answering anymore of your questions.' She took a step away from Anderson then turned to Cheryl. 'Call security and get Mr Langley here to witness this intrusion.'

*   *   *

Downstairs Clive tossed the car key to Lachlan. 'The Stinger's all yours. Don't disappoint me.' Godwin's eyes lit up.

Once inside the sleek black vehicle he set a personal setting for his seat position and buckled up.

'You know where we're going?' asked Clive.

'To see Crystal Whitlock. Four three nine Jumbuck Street, Jindalee. You didn't want to mention her name to Hansen in case she might call her and give her the heads up.'

'But it's a Monday afternoon. She might not be home.'

'She works part-time at Mathers Shoes,' said Lachlan. 'Not usually on Mondays. She might be out somewhere. We got a fifty-fifty chance I reckon.'

'You're on the ball today, Godwin. Take the Legacy Way tunnel. Lights and siren on. Open this baby up.' Clive tapped the consol.

'You for real, sir?'

'Yeah, why the fuck not. Just don't kill me,' smiled Clive. 'And happy for you to drop the *sir. Clive* or just *Anderson* works fine.'

*　　　*　　　*

After a speedy trip, the unmarked police Stinger pulled up opposite Crystal Whitlock's rented home.

'Easy to pick the rentals, eh?' said Anderson as he got out.

'Hmm… yeah, they either don't have a mower or couldn't care less,' replied Lachlan as he turned an ear to a thumping sound. 'And they play their music too loud.'

'Well, at least someone's home.'

The two detectives crossed the road. Clive pushed at the low rusted gate which only opened halfway. They weaved their way along a cracked cement path, dodging low hanging branches and intrusive shrubs. The home was a low-set timber building on short wooden stumps. There were three dodgy looking steps up to the front door. Anderson leaned forward and pushed a button that made no sound. He knocked loudly.

A moment later the music volume decreased, and a short young lady with untidy curly hair opened the door. She yawned and squeezed out a tired 'Can I help you?' She cuddled herself up in a dressing gown.

'Detectives Anderson and Godwin,' announced Clive. Both displayed their IDs. 'Crystal Whitlock?'

'That's me. Is something wrong?'

'We have a few questions regarding Friday night at the Tribal Moon. May we come in?'

'Sure.' She turned and headed back inside. The three sat at a round table in a small kitchen / dining room area. The inside of the home was cluttered and desperately needing a makeover. Paint was peeling, a kitchen cupboard was hanging open by one hinge. The vinyl floor covering was cracked and faded.

'Looks like we woke you, sorry,' said Godwin.

'I worked night shift at the aged care joint up the road.'

'You can sleep through the loud music?'

'Yeah. Blots out all the traffic noise. People mowing their lawns. The construction racket a few doors up.'

'Do you have two jobs?' asked Godwin.

'I do. I work at Mathers too.' She looked at the two detectives. 'Is there something wrong with that?'

'Not at all. We want to ask you about Johnny Randall,' said Anderson. 'You left the nightclub with him and Janine Hansen.'

'Oh shit! Has something happened to them?'

'No. We are simply gathering information on Johnny Randall. We think he can help with our enquiries on another matter. Do you know where he is?'

'No idea.'

'Can you explain to us what happened after you left the nightclub?' asked Anderson.

'We walked to Janine's apartment in the city.'

'And...' Clive opened his hands encouraging her to continue.

'We had a couple more drinks... then... well... this is a bit personal really.'

'Okay, so there was sex. Fair enough, but we are more interested in what Johnny actually did and said, and when he might have left,' said Clive.

'Did something unusual happen?' added Lachlan.

Crystal swallowed and hesitated before responding. 'Yeah. I still don't fully understand or even remember everything. He scared us. Janine and I.'

'Were you harmed?' asked Godwin.

'No... there is this weird thing. Like... I don't know if it's a dream or what, and it's something that I only started to remember yesterday. But I think he stuck his tongue in my nose... that's weird right... but it was strange because his tongue was really long... like... as long as your arm.' She shook her head, some brown ringlets of hair bounced around her cheeks. 'It must have been a dream.'

Crystal went on to describe the evening as best she could. It was a patchy recollection at best, but despite everything, she was hopeful she would see Johnny again, but she had no idea when or how this might happen.

Chapter 38

Number One

After school, on Wednesday, Sam and Nathan darted home, changed and took off on their bikes. Fifteen minutes later they met up at the golf course.

The two boys pulled up a hundred metres from the clubhouse and looked across the green undulating course in front of them. Several groups of players, mostly women, were working their way towards hole eighteen.

'Looks like there is no one playing on the fifth,' said Sam, the taller and thinner of the two.

'That's always a good place to start. We should find a few there along the riverbank.'

'Let's go before old man Wilkins sees us.'

The two rode away from the pro shop and clubhouse. They took a roundabout way to get to the fifth hole, heading back along the road, then lifting their bicycles over a damaged wire fence where the wire had been cut, heading down between the practice range and the Ossie Walker Memorial Family Park, towards the river. They passed a stretch of thick lantana alongside the sixth hole. The boys stopped riding where the lantana ended, and they shoved their bikes behind the prickly bush and out of sight.

They had been here many times searching for golf balls. It was a handy source of pocket money. When they were able, they would sell them to the golfers on the course, getting two dollars for balls in good condition. They had been busted once before by Wilkins, the greenkeeper. He told them they were both trespassing and stealing. He confiscated twenty-two golf balls. Nowadays, whenever on the course proper, the boys only ever had a couple of balls on them at any one time, choosing to leave the bulk of their collection hidden away near their bikes.

The red-headed Nathan slid down the grassy embankment. Sam followed. Right in front of them was the Brisbane River. The tide was out, and the muddy riverbanks were exposed. Mangroves were plentiful, growing like a shrubby hedge, up and down the riverbank. New stems of plants thrust upwards from the mud like gelatinous stalagmites.

The boys stood for a few minutes just looking. Nathan was first to spot one.

'There.' He pointed. 'Just down from that Coke can.'

'Yeah, I see it,' said Sam. 'Good start.'

Three metres away was a small white dome, only just visible in the mud. Nathan moved along the grassy bank then stepped down into the mire. His feet sank slowly, covering his ankles. He bent over and pulled the embedded ball from its muddy hole and wiped it roughly with his fingers.

'It's a two-dollar newbie,' he shouted. Nathan tossed it to Sam who dropped it in a cloth bag tied to his waist.

'There's another. Near that plank and tyre.' Nathan squelched forward slowly, each step an effort. This time he was closer to the water's edge and his feet sank deeper. As he reached to grab the next ball, he saw something else. Just alongside the discarded tyre. The boy stared, unsure at first what he was seeing. He had seen skulls before in science at school, and plastic ones at the show. A crab emerged from the eye socket. He saw some neck bones, then the outline of a body's shoulders as they were lapped by gentle ripples in the water.

'Ahhh… geez,' he yelled. The mud sucked back against his feet as he tried to get away. He toppled forward, his hands sunk too. He reefed them free.

'The ball. Get the ball,' shouted Sam.

Nathan heard nothing. His mouth watered. He gagged. As he got closer to the bank, he was able to move quicker, eventually pulling himself onto the grass, panting and swallowing deeply. Mud was now all over his arms, legs and clothes.

'We gotta go… a body…' gasped Nathan. '… in the water. Shit. Quick, let's go.'

*   *   *

Police and police divers, along with forensic officers had been examining the scene for two hours. They had cordoned off a large area, taking in part of the fifth and sixth holes and a section of the adjoining Ossie Walker Memorial Family Park. At seven pm, in failing light, further examination of the area was halted. Weather was forecast to be clear, so it was decided that the investigation could resume at first light.

Three officers were assigned to an overnight vigil to keep the area secured and a police boat was anchored in the river nearby. Initial underwater findings revealed the body had no hands and the feet had been tied to concrete building blocks. On receiving the information Inspector Vince Edwards had given instructions to his team to be onsite first thing Thursday morning.

Chapter 39

The Body

Thursday PM

It was a delicate and painstaking process to retrieve the corpse from the river. Nevertheless, once out of the water it was imperative to have a post-mortem as soon as possible.

At one o'clock in the afternoon the decayed body was on Dr Christopher Pendleton's steel mortuary bench.

The body exhibited skeletonization in the cervico-cephalic region and a little on top of the shoulders. The remainder of the body was covered in a moist brown and black sludge.

Pendleton was fully covered in protective wear. Detectives Jan Silverton and Henry Bryant were also in attendance, both similarly attired. Pendleton had his spectacles on under his protective eyewear while Bryant chose to leave his sunnies on under his. Detective Richard Davis remained at the crime scene, glad to forego the opportunity, saying he would be happy to see the photos and read the reports.

'You done your nose?' Silverton asked Bryant.

'Fuck yeah,' he nodded. 'I'm not weird like Pendleton. He prefers to *appreciate* the stench. What's with that?'

The two detectives moved to the mortuary bench and stood on the opposite side to the doctor.

'It's icy in here, Chris,' said Silverton as she shook herself.

'Yes, sorry. Needs to be colder than usual so I can examine this corpse before it liquifies…' Silverton glanced at Bryant who turned his tilted head towards her.

'It will do that?' asked Jan.

'Oh, most definitely. Check this out.' Pendleton pushed a pair of forceps into the dark brown matter near the hip, and with no effort at all, slid them across through the putrid decay. A wedge of decayed tissue the size of small saucer slid free and dropped onto the stainless steel, forming a sludgy circle. 'So, you see, it's not unlike coating someone with a thick layer of chocolate and leaving them in the sun.'

'Ooh… that's just dreadful.' Jan swallowed.

'We get the point, doc, thanks. Let's move on shall we,' added Bryant.

'Certainly. The head and neck, as you can see, are essentially just bone because every low tide it was exposed to the air – nearly all soft tissue has gone. There is a reasonable amount of better quality tissue on the heels and buttocks where the body was held down in the mud by the cement blocks which were tied on with wire. I'm sure you can both see the massive fracture in the temporal area of the skull. That is most likely the cause of death. And, considering the size of the injury and that this was on a golf course, it seems likely that a golf club may be the murder weapon.' Pendleton shifted his attention to the arms but kept on chatting away in his soft voice. The two detectives found themselves leaning a little over the corpse to hear him.

'The hands, obviously, are missing,' continued the doctor. 'They have been hacked off. The ends of the bones of both forearms have been splintered and shattered. I could also speculate again that a golf club was used. In this section…' Pendleton pointed to the pelvis with a pair of surgical forceps. '… there is no clear evidence of the presence of a penis. I point this out because other bodies you have brought in have had theirs removed. It could have decayed away or been eaten by a creature. I will need to look there more closely to get a better idea.

There may be some chips or cracks in the pelvis. This could then mean that the penis was also hacked off and would be consistent with the other bodies.' He looked up at his two spectators. 'Bodies that have decayed over time in water are challenging from a forensic pathological point of view. They have been subject to weather, currents and tides, animals, bacteria and foreign objects like foliage and general rubbish that you might find in a river.' He looked up at the two detectives. 'Any questions?'

'How long has he been dead?' asked Silverton.

'Impossible to be sure.'

'Best guess.'

'Ballpark... five to eight months.'

'Thanks Chris. We'll be off. If you find anything of note...'

'I'll be in touch, Jan,' interrupted Chris Pendleton. 'Give my regards to Vince. Did you remind him about his meds by chance?'

'Yes. He didn't seem to take it in the spirit it was intended.'

'Thanks. I'll call him.'

'Good luck,' said Jan.

* * *

For half of the drive back to the city headquarters the two didn't speak. Bryant was nodding off, while Silverton was chatting almost silently to herself as she drove.

'Henry!' she eventually shouted.

'What the...' he jerked his sleepy head awake.

'I know it's getting late Henry, but we should quickly check a couple of things when we get back to the office.'

'Sure. I have no social life. Just a pissed off wife. No big deal. And why do you only call me Henry when you want something?'

'Do I?'

'Yes, you do, Jan.' He replied emphasising her name.

*   *   *

Back at the office, Detective Henry Bryant pulled just two folders from the many missing person files to re-examine. He dropped them in front of his partner.

'You only want these two?' he said.

Silverton looked up at him. 'Yes… and do you really need those sunnies on inside and at night? It makes you look more shady than you already are.'

'I'll have you know, I'm a very sensitive person.'

'I don't think the name Bryant, and the word sensitive should be used in the same sentence.'

'You are so unkind,' he smirked.

Silverton opened the first file. 'These are the only two that have clear connections with the golf course where the body was found. We need to take another look.'

'Okay, well that's Walter Bailey. A keen golfer.'

'Went missing after an argument with his wife,' said Silverton.

'Yeah, we interviewed her. What a bitch. I'd go missing too.'

'His age and size fit the victim profile.'

'I always thought the older son was hiding something. Like, maybe he knew where his dad was… you know.'

'And you're telling me this now? What the hell, Bryant.'

'Was just a hunch. We could have another talk to him.'

'We will. That's another job for you in the AM.'

Jan opened the second file. 'Logan Bridgeman.'

'Another golf nut.'

'Fits the profile too.'

'Lived alone. Never showed for work on the Friday,' added Bryant.

'Played golf the day before with… this guy.' Jan pointed to a name. 'Fabian Carver.'

'Interviewed him too.'

'Was he hiding something as well, Bryant?'

'Who knows. He was an oddball though. Never look you in the eye. Stuttered a lot.'

'Maybe he was sensitive… like you,' quipped Silverton.

'Maybe he was. We interviewed a dozen others too,' added Bryant.

'Yeah… but this Carver.' Jan tapped the file. 'Seems like a bit of a loner. Didn't even like golf that much. Let's talk to him again. Contact his work first thing tomorrow. Could try his mobile…' Jan stopped and thought for a moment. 'Better still, why not just drop around to his home right now. Unannounced. Let's not give him the heads up.'

'Sure boss. If we leave now …' Bryant looked at his watch and gave a sigh. '… we should be there before nine-thirty. Home by ten-thirty.'

'Stop grumbling. You can drive.' She tossed him the keys.

*   *   *

The inside lights at one hundred and eighty-four Townley Street, St Lucia were on. The glow from a TV program flashed colours against the curtains.

After the detectives knocked, a porch light came on. Silverton displayed her ID as she looked at the peephole. The door opened.

'Yes?' asked a gaunt middle-aged man with no hair.

'Is Fabian Carver home?' asked Silverton

'He doesn't live here now.'

'Since when?'

'Since the fourteenth of this month. I think he was going on holidays. We're renting.'

'Is he still the owner?' asked Bryant.

'As far as I know. You can check with Ironside Real Estate. They manage this place now.'

'Did you know Carver?' Bryant moved his sunnies to the top of his head.

'Not really. Just met the one time. What's he done?'

'We're just following up on some unpaid fines,' continued Bryant. Silverton slowly turned her head and looked at him with widened eyes.

'At nine-thirty at night! You gotta be kidding me, right?' scoffed the bald man. He flicked his gaze between the two detectives.

'Apologies, sir,' said Silverton. 'We didn't wish to cause you undue distress. We are in fact investigating a murder.'

'Shit.'

'Do you know where Mister Carver has gone?' she continued. Bryant sighed and looked at his shoes.

'No idea. He said something about getting a Winnebago or a camper trailer.'

Chapter 40

Harmony – Part 8

Thursday – 6 PM

Unlike her best friend, Harmony continued to live with her parents and her two annoying younger brothers. The house, in the suburb of Ascot in Brisbane, was a beautifully maintained two-storey regal looking dwelling with a wide tapered staircase leading to the front door. At six in the evening, in the street outside and opposite the neighbouring property, a white Mercedes A250 Sports pulled up. Bentley Hopkin-Jones sat behind the wheel.

He sent Harmony a text message. *I'm parked just across the road. See you soon.*

He had a quick reply. *Terrific! I'm so excited. Would you like to come inside for a moment and meet my parents?'*

Bentley smiled. This was something he had been invited to do many times in the past. Not that it was always parents, sometimes other friends and acquaintances, extended family members, employers, party goers and more. So far, and for nearly two hundred years, this was something he had avoided.

Nice of you to suggest that. At the moment I am just eager to see you and see how you are after your procedure. I've been thinking about you a lot. I'm also happy to meet just your friend Crystal for now. Others later – Bentley added a kiss emoji and sent the message.

A minute later, Harmony, wearing a white sweater dress, over-knee-high suede boots, and with a small, long-strapped handbag over her shoulder, was out the door. Behind her an older couple in casual clothes were peering into the street trying to get a glimpse of her man. On the upstairs front verandah, her two brothers were squabbling over who should be using the binoculars to spy on their sister and her date.

'So, you're eager to see me,' she said as she sat and closed the car door. Bentley made eye contact. He nodded and smiled. They leant into each other and kissed warmly and deeply.

On the verandah the youngest brother, watching with the binoculars, fell off a chair.

'And I've been thinking a lot about you too, Bentley,' said Harmony as their mouths parted. 'I seem to have a lot of questions building up in my mind. My parents asked me about you and, outside of telling them what a stunning looking man you are, I had nothing else to say. I have no idea where you work, where you grew up and I know zero about your family.' She clipped up her seat belt and kept chatting as the car moved off. Bentley gave a quick wave to the parents at the top of the stairs. 'I could have told them about your penis,' she continued. 'And your most wonderful and adaptable mouth.' Bentley gave her a quick glance and grinned as he waggled his finger.

Harmony reached across and placed a hand on his thigh. Bentley dropped a warm hand on top of hers. 'You're a pretty quiet guy. Sometimes, Bentley, I get a feeling that you deliberately make me think things... sort of like... you know... almost putting words in my mouth.' Bentley just nodded and smiled.

'Sex with you is amazing. Like magical combined with a sexy sort of mystery. Your dexterity is... beyond my level of comprehension.'

The car slowed as they drove towards the city with the Brisbane River on their left. Bentley pulled into a bus stop, behind a bus that had just come to a halt. He undid his seatbelt and lent across Harmony and kissed her hard on the mouth. As her mouth opened wider his tongue pushed to the back of her throat then upwards behind her nose.

For a split-second Harmony felt a gagging reflex then relaxed back into her car seat. Her eyes closed and the sounds of the traffic on the busy Kingsford Smith Drive faded away, replaced by the sounds of small waves breaking on a shore somewhere.

At first, she was surrounded by a heavy fog which slowly cleared. She found herself sitting on a stool at a bar just off a main street. Next to her was Bentley, still wearing his shiny black jacket with flecks of dark green.

'Where are we?'

'Near a beach in Thailand.'

'Holy shit! I get it. This is a dream, right?' she looked around. There were lots of beach umbrellas and assorted other beach shelters across the road behind a row of palm trees. Just metres away were at least twenty small motorbikes lined up almost touching each other. It was a warm sunny day with a light breeze. Other than the two of them, there were no people anywhere. 'Is this real?'

'It is a real place. It is a memory of mine.'

'I'm inside part of your memory? How does that work?'

'Because I am different to most human beings.'

'Well, duh… I already knew that.'

'I find this is the best way for me to have meaningful dialogue. I normally communicate by making sounds and by psychic connection often through direct eye contact.

'And you have such wonderful blue hypnotic eyes.' Two glasses of iced water materialised on the bar. 'Oh… thank you.' She took a sip. 'This feels so real… way more than a dream. This water is cold.' She stuck a finger in her drink. 'I can even feel the ice cubes… Can we just stay here… you and me.'

'We can stay a while. Perhaps we can take a stroll over the road and down the beach.'

'I'd like that.'

The couple chinked their glasses and drank their water, then crossed the road. The beach, like the paths and streets was deserted, nevertheless there were towels, bags, sun shelters, picnic baskets and children's sand toys along the beach. Harmony could see nearly four hundred metres in every direction, beyond that was hidden by a heavy white cloud. Bentley answered all her questions as they walked. After what seemed like ages, Bentley said, 'I am getting an unusual sense from you today. A mild vibrating feeling.'

'Okay… what's that all about?'

'Something is unclear. There is something you have been told that is both equally disturbing as it is exciting.'

'Sounds strange.'

'Have you had any conversations lately that might explain this?' he asked. As she pondered the question Bentley nodded. 'I see now. It was your friend, Crystal.'

'You're right. She had a fright from some guy called Johnny.'

'She was with Janine.'

'Are you reading my mind?'

'I am. A little faster than you are doing yourself.'

'Weird, but okay… I guess.'

'We need to see Crystal.'

'Yes, I understand… well partly I think.'

'We should return now.'

'I'd rather not, but I remember us pulling up in a bus stop. So, if that's still true we should go. And, as you say, we need to visit Crystal.'

The heavy clouds rolled towards the couple and engulfed them. A moment later Harmony opened her eyes. She was back in her car seat. 'Fuck, Bentley!' she panted loudly. 'That was amazing.' A bus in front of them pulled back out into the traffic. Harmony pointed to it. 'Tell me that's not the same bus we parked behind earlier.'

Bentley opened his big blue eyes and looked at her. He smiled broadly and mouthed the word, *Yes*.

'Oh my God, you must be a fucking timelord too.' Bentley shook his head. 'I best call Crystal. Make sure she's home and get her to hang around until we arrive.'

Chapter 41

Date Night

Thursday 7.30 PM

Richard Davis's home was a modest low-set red brick house, like many others in the Salisbury area that reflected a similar, uninspiring seventies design. The difference though was in the garden. Richard's was a standout, with rows of gardens of flowering plants. Among them tulips, orchids, and roses all surrounded by ferns and blue sea holly. What little grass there was, was short, even and contoured to the garden bed edges. A row of red pavers showed the way to the front door. Even at night it was on display with two spotlights illuminating the area for two hours after dusk.

Constantino parked his motorhome five hundred metres up the road, in a vacant carpark near a construction site, and walked the rest of the way. He had on a backpack and carried a hessian bag with assorted groceries. This evening he dressed casually in a cotton long-sleeved shirt and straight light-blue, draw string trousers. He had spiked his blonde hair a little to impress his date. The main concern Constantino had was if Richard would remember him, after being so intoxicated when they first met.

The two men greeted each other with a smile and a big hug.

'Look at you,' said Richard eyeing him up and down. The two men were similarly attired. The only difference was that Davis had short sleeves.

'Two peas in a pod… well, nearly,' chuckled Constantino.

Richard peered over his date's shoulder. 'I hope you haven't walked too far. I don't see a car.'

'Got an Uber,' lied Con. 'Had the number wrong and got out a hundred metres down the road.'

'A backpack and a carry bag. This must be a feast fit for kings… or at least queens!'

'Show me to your kitchen good sir,' quipped Con.

Richard dropped an arm around his friend's shoulder and walked him inside.

'I was a bit worried you might not recognise me. You being a little under the weather the other night.'

'No amount of grog will ever make me forget a pretty face,' said Richard. Constantino gave him a teethy smile.

The kitchen was small and best only for one cook at a time. 'Looks like my work area.'

'Yeah, it's a bit tiny. Can you make it work?'

'No problems at all. It'll work just fine.'

'Shall we have a beverage before you get underway?'

'I'd like that, thanks.'

'I took the liberty of getting a bubbly. It's in the ice bucket out the back.'

'Sounds nice. Lead the way.' Constantino put the backpack on the floor and the carry bag on the kitchen bench. They moved through the dining and small lounge room, out to the back through the sliding screen doors. The small, cemented area had some comfy padded, outdoor chairs, a matching table and a barbeque on a stand. They both sat. Richard popped out the cork and poured two glasses.

'Cheers. Here's to new friendships and lovely food,' said Richard with a broad smile.

'Cheers.' They chinked glasses and sipped. 'Have you ever had a Black Russian… as in the drink?' asked Con.

'Can't say that I have. That's vodka, right?'

'Yeah, and a coffee liquor. It's my current favourite… and I brought the ingredients. So, if you have ice, and are prepared to give it a shot, I'll prepare one while I cook.'

'Perfect.' They chinked glasses once more.

'What do you do with yourself, Con?' asked Richard.

'Nothing too exciting really. Real estate sales. It pays the bills.'

'Is that something you've done for a long time?'

'About eight years,' lied Constantino. 'I'm a good salesperson. What about you?'

'I'm a detective. Work out of the city.'

Constantino felt a jolt of electricity shoot up his back. He tried not to give away his surprise with his face.

'What's that face for?' smiled Richard.

'Hmm… you guys probably think real estate salesman are tricksters… a bit like used car dealers.'

'I don't think that!'

'Really?'

'It's funny though…' Richard nodded and smiled.

'What's funny?'

'I mentioned I was going on a date to a work colleague. I told him your name… Constantino. He said it sounded like a used car salesman. Don't get conned, he said.' Richard laughed.

'Glad you find it funny.'

'Sorry… but yeah… a bit funny.'

'I suppose,' conceded Con. 'At least I don't sell used cars.'

The pair drank two more glasses of Moët and Chandon before Constantino announced he was off to the kitchen to cook up his surprise. Richard tagged along for a moment. Con put some broccolini, potato and squash on the kitchen bench. 'Off you go,' he said. 'This is a surprise. No peeking. And, just so you know, there's no Brussel sprouts here. I'll get you that drink I promised.'

'You're so nice.' Richard ducked quickly around the bench and kissed him on the cheek.

* * *

It was a struggle to drag Richard from the toilet to the bathroom and Constantino was a little disappointed in himself for not persuading Richard into the shower when the detective declared he was feeling woozy. He undressed Richard on the bathroom floor, then it was another effort to drag him over the edge of the bath.

'Note to self,' said Constantino. 'Stick to hotels and motels that don't have a shower over a bath.' Richard made some guttural noises.

'Yes, I see you agree.'

He sat a floppy naked Davis on the bath's edge and allowed him to fall backwards hitting his head. Constantino pushed Richard's legs over, then reached in and turned the shower on.

'It's an awkward space, Richard. But I think we can manage.'

He left the bathroom and entered the bedroom where he had all his equipment at the ready. Several pillows were mounted at one side of the double bed which was turned down. A blue plastic absorbent sheet was in place. Laid out over the quilt was the yellow daisy dress. On the bedside table all the make-up items were lined up. Near the edge of the bed, alongside a pair of pruning shears, were two syringes filled with a clear liquid.

Constantino methodically undressed himself, folded his clothes and placed them in a neat pile on the floor near the open bedroom door. He picked up the cutting tool.

Back in the bathroom he lay the shears on the sink. He looked in the bath at Richard Davis lying semi-recumbent with his feet against one end of the bath and his head and shoulders at the other. The detective's head was slumped to one side. Constantino's mouth watered. He darted quickly to the adjacent small room and vomited in the toilet.

A minute later Fabian Carver looked over his prey with pruning shears in hand. 'You hurt me. You can never be forgiven for wanting t… t… to penetrate me and do those the ss…sss…same dreadful th… th… things again and again. Well now there will be no m… m… more.' Fabian climbed into the bath and somewhat awkwardly straddled Richard Davis. He lifted the detective's hand…

Right at that moment as the shears began to close around the first joint, a shadow caught Fabian's eye. He looked up. Johnny Randall stood tall looking down at him with a kind smile. Fabian dropped the shears and Richard's hand, but otherwise was not outwardly startled to see the man.

'Have we m… m… met before?' asked Fabian.

Johnny slowly nodded and mouthed an unheard *Yes*. As he stood there, Johnny made some slight movement of his lips. A series of clicks, pops, whistles and gushes of air emanated from him.

'I'm glad you can help me,' said Fabian. He remained in the bath straddling Richard. Johnny squatted near the glass shower screen which extended halfway along the length of the bath. He placed both his hands on the top of Fabian's head. The hands spread out as if made of gel, covering the entire top of the skull. The fingers crept to either side of the naked man's head, just above his ears. Waves of greens and browns waved down Johnny's arms, the tips of his fingers turned inward, becoming shiny, black and sharp.

Simultaneously, all the claws worked like a jigsaw. Blood streamed over the serial killer's forehead, his face and onto his shoulders. It flowed down his chest, over his stomach, and finally down onto Richard's abdomen. In fifteen seconds, the top of the skull was removed. Johnny tilted the head a little towards him. As his mouth enlarged like the mouth of a giant sucker fish, he looked down at the brain of Fabian Carver – the folds of pink tissue, the network of fine capillaries and the few larger blue twisted veins. The Semblant's neck became fatter and longer as the massive mouth descended onto the brain and sucked.

Chapter 42

Johnny's Last Stand

Roderick Ignatius Peabody was in the lounge, relaxing back in the recliner reading a novel, when the sound of a vehicle, and a quick toot of a car horn, grabbed his attention. After three attempts, he managed to flick the footrest back in place, then moved to the window and looked down from the upper level of his cottage.

Parked outside was a small motorhome, and standing at the front door, lit up by the motion sensor floodlight, was Johnny Randall. He was leaning against the side of the house and seemed to be panting.

Rip threw his book on the chair and was down the stairs and to the door in a moment. He turned a key, flipped a bolt and undid a chain to open the door. Johnny had dropped to his knees near the entrance. He was leaning forward with outstretched arms against the house.

'Johnny… Sobo,' said Peabody. 'What has happened?'

Johnny raised his head. Tears cascaded down both cheeks over dry looking skin.

Johnny gagged and gasped before he could speak, and despite how hard it was, the Semblant managed to squeeze out some words through his distress. 'I am filled…' he paused and swallowed. '… I am filled with the essence of a tormented soul.'

'Sobo… are you assimilating?'

He nodded. 'Our search for Kwikal must wait. Please come… with… me.' He stood and staggered back to the motorhome.

Inside on the floor was the body of Fabian Carver. Half his head, above his ears, was missing, and the remaining half was an empty, oozing bloody shell.

'Wow… Oh shit!' said Peabody. 'Oh, apologies for my language. I see you did this the quick way, Sobo. How can I help here?'

Johnny took the undertakers shoulders and looked deep into his eyes, their faces only centimetres apart.

'I see,' said Peabody.

They looked at each other some more.

'Okay, thank you, I have all those details. You do your bit now. Then I'll do mine. And I assure you I will not forget the top of the skull which is on the passenger's seat.'

Johnny knelt over the body. Peabody took a step back. The Semblant held a hand in front of his own face and watched while the fingers transformed back into the razor-sharp claws. He pushed down on Fabian's chest, just left of centre. He sliced up and down through skin, and quickly through some fatty tissue. With another hand movement he was through a layer of muscle. A final three quick slices and he was through the ribs. He reefed them to one side causing a sharp cracking sound, then shoved his cutting hand inside the opened chest. A second later he had Fabian's dead heart in his hand. He dropped the heart in the sink with a splat. A few drops of blood struck the tap and the sides of the sink. The Semblant left the motorhome.

'Oh, my goodness gracious!' said Peabody loudly. He placed a hand to his mouth. Rip watched Johnny disappear into the cottage, then put his attention on the mess in front of him.

*   *   *

The first thing the undertaker had to do was turn on the cremation chamber to allow time to preheat – usually around twenty-five minutes. He switched all the nearby security lighting off before returning to the motorhome with a black leakproof body bag, some disposable gloves, a packet of wet wipes and a heavy-duty plastic bag.

Given the limited space, and the residual blood on the floor, getting the body into the bag was an awkward exercise. Peabody turned the sealed bag over a few times, wiping blood from the outside of the bag and the floor. He placed all the used wipes in the plastic bag, then collected the skull top from the passenger's seat and dropped it in with the rest of the blood-stained rubbish. As instructed, he left the heart in the small sink of the motorhome.

By the time the undertaker had the bagged body and the plastic bag on a trolley just inside the door, the furnace had reached the desired temperature of eight hundred degrees Celsius.

Peabody intentionally had only one dim light on in the spacious room, making the cream walls and two rows of chairs look grey. The seating was for guests wishing to view the full process, but they were rarely used.

Slightly raised on the floor was what looked like a metal fashion parade runway, about four metres long and a metre wide. Set back a little from each side were railings to keep people from getting too close. Rip pushed the trolley to the end of the metal runway, then pushed a button on a remote control. The centre of the runway opened and folded to the side, then a loading bench rose up and stopped level with the cremation chamber.

The body slid easily across rollers, onto the loading bench and up closer to the closed metal door.

Rip took a step back and pushed the remote again. The chamber door slid open, and a bright orange glow filled the room. The top of the bench automatically slid forward into the furnace. The body bag and plastic bag igniting almost immediately before the door slid shut.

It would be around two hours before the ashes could be retrieved.

*   *   *

Peabody waited in the lower level of the cottage, every now and then glancing at the closed bedroom door whenever he heard a sound. There were many – high-pitched whistling, sucking noises, water gurgles and sounds like blasts of steam. After ten minutes without a sound, he nodded to himself and headed upstairs, poured himself a double hit of bourbon over ice and sat back in the recliner.

He knew the process. The Semblant would need rest. This side of things he was becoming more familiar with, but this was the first time he had to assist the Semblant in the disposal of a complete body. Not only did he have more questions, he also had concerns. Could he be guilty of being an accessory after the fact in a murder? Could he be guilty of interfering with a corpse? Could he be charged with aiding and abetting?

Rip decided on a second drink.

Chapter 43

Harmony – Part 9

Bentley and Harmony pulled up outside Crystal's low-set Jindalee home. 'Unfortunately, her place is a little different to a Thailand resort,' said Harmony. 'Hope there's no snakes.'

The couple negotiated their way to the front door which opened before they knocked. Crystal threw her arms around her friend's neck. 'So good to see you.' Harmony squeezed her tightly at the same time. 'Lucky you called. I was almost on my way out.'

'Crystal, this is Bentley, who I've told you about.' She gave a little nod and a knowing smile.

'Oh… right, yeah. Hello Bentley.' She extended her hand. The Semblant took it gently and kissed it. 'Ooh, how lovely. I did see you briefly when we were at the Tribal Moon a while back. Then I fell off my chair and ended up in an ambulance. I was fine though. They just checked me over and let me go.' Bentley gave a quick tilt of his head, a bit of a wink and a tight smile.

'Bentley is a man of few words,' said Harmony. She turned to him. 'Yet he communicates better than any man I have ever met.' His blue eyes widened.

'Huh… I remember you mentioning a few things,' said Crystal coyly. 'And men are normally considered as handsome, but you Bentley, are beautiful.' His eyes and eye sockets were now twice their normal size.

Bentley smiled and mouthed the words *Thank you.* 'Your eyes,' continued Crystal. '… they're… sort of… a lot like someone else's that

I've seen. That's a bit weird, right?' She looked at Harmony then back at Bentley.

'Why don't we go inside,' said Harmony. The three moved down a hallway.

'You're all dressed up and looking lovely. Where were you off to?'

'Just catching up with a couple of friends at the rooftop, at Suzie Wongs, for some cocktails.'

They entered the lounge. There were two young guys sitting on the old leather sofa wearing headsets, and with game controllers in their hands. On the TV they were fighting ghosts in a fantasy style video game.

The carpet was thread bare. The large screen TV was mounted on a plank supported by nine bricks – three at each end and three in the middle.

'Harley! Robbie! Can we have the lounge for half an hour?' shouted Crystal, trying to be noticed above the noise that could even be heard outside of the guy's headsets.

'Fuck off!' yelled Robbie, the redhead. 'Use the dining room. Go to your bedroom. Just fuck off, will you.'

'I have friends here. Come on. You've been playing that shit all fucking day!'

The two continued their on-screen battle. Bentley ambled around in front of them and stood blocking the TV.

'Fuck dude!'

'Piss off.' They both tried to peer around him. He squatted and made eye contact. Firstly, with the redhead. Robbie dropped his controller, stood and left.

'What the fuck? Rob!' bellowed Harley. 'We're on the verge of fucking victory. Get back here!' He glared angrily at Bentley, then his tight mouth eased, and his furrowed brow relaxed. Harley put down his controller, picked up the remote, turned off the TV and left. Bentley stood and waved an open hand at the empty couch inviting the women to take a seat.

Crystal turned to her friend. 'How... what the hell... why did they...'

'I know,' interrupted Harmony. 'Bentley is very influential... as well as being exceedingly dexterous, like I told you.' She raised her eyebrows. 'We should sit. You have no need to worry.'

*   *   *

Bentley was kneeling in front of the two women as they sat next to each other on the sofa, relaxed back with their eyes closed. The Semblant's mouth was wide open. His tongue had bifurcated into two moist, tubular extensions with one part in Harmony's nose and the other in Crystal's.

The two friends opened their eyes at the same time.

'Where are we this time?' asked Harmony. Both she and her friend seemed to be suspended in the air, somehow hovering in an empty space like the inside of a big fluffy cloud. They remained dressed in their evening apparel. Slightly above them was Bentley. Several shafts of light, similar to sun beams, radiated from his shoulders to those of the two women.

'For now, we are in a neutral space,' replied Bentley. His voice had a distant echoing quality. 'Here we can communicate clearly. I am aware you both have questions, but at the same time neither of you are distressed by this process. This is good.'

'How did we get here?' asked Crystal.

'I have created a psychic bridge between the three of us. I can access your thoughts and some past experiences and memories. I can also connect you with some of my own if I choose. Connecting with more than one original human at a time can be difficult, but as Harmony and I have done this several times before, this has made it easier than it has been for me in the past.'

The cloud swirled slowly within itself. Harmony's blonde hair, and the brown ringlets around Crystal's cheeks, floated as if in slow motion and not restricted by gravity.

'Crystal, we are known as the Semblant. We are not alien, as in the sense of beings from outer space, as you are thinking. We are of human origin. I can see you met Johnny. He is also Semblant. For me this is wonderful news.' A trilling whistle filled the air. The high note oscillating up and down the scale for several seconds. All three smiled simultaneously.

'These days one Semblant rarely finds another,' continued Bentley. 'Johnny is known to me as Sobo. I am known to Sobo as Kwikal. We have not seen each other for over a century...'

The two suspended women writhed slightly, their arms and legs moving as if treading water.

'Yes, I am quite old, but from a Semblant point of view still young.' Bentley twisted slightly as he hovered. His gaze focused deeply on Crystal.

'Crystal, I'm very sorry that Johnny frightened you, although I note that you were still wishing to see him and engage in sexual activity. Like me, Johnny detected a loose connection with another Semblant. That was me, on the night I met Harmony at the Tribal Moon. Johnny was overwhelmed, and unfortunately was unable to complete the evening as he had planned and as you desired.... Ah... now I see you had a recent conversation with Janine. Thank you for letting me know that. Johnny greeted her at her place of employment. This is good. Sobo is still in Brisbane. I will find him.'

'I'd love to take Crystal to the Thailand beach,' said Harmony.

'Hmm… I have another place in mind… and I know Crystal's most secret fantasy.'

The three became vertical, the cloud surrounding them began rolling away and the light beams seemed to disintegrate into nothing. They all felt a hard surface under their feet and a cool but pleasant breeze against their skin.

'Oh… we are very high,' said Crystal. She reached over and took Harmony's hand.

'Looking ahead they could see the skyline of Sydney city, and closer to them the sails of the Sydney Opera House. They were standing on the highest point of the Sydney Harbour Bridge.

'We have the best tour guide of all time,' chuckled Harmony.

'I've always wanted to climb this bridge,' said Crystal.

'Yes, I know,' nodded Bentley.

Crystal caught his eye. 'I'm thinking that perhaps …'

'I know too much about you,' interrupted Bentley. 'I know what you were hoping for with Johnny. And you are wondering if I can pick up where he left off.'

'Crystal!' exclaimed Harmony.

'Huh… it seems there are no secrets here. Sorry Harms.'

'Where should we visit next, ladies?' Bentley gazed out across the harbour. 'Neither of you have spent an evening in the Sahara Desert.'

'The Desert? As in Africa?' squawked Crystal.

'How would you wish to be attired there? Evening wear as you are now? A light cotton robe? Naked? Naturally, I already know your answers.' Bentley smiled.

'Hmm…' breathed Harmony. 'Let's just go. See if you're right when we get there, Mister Mind Reader.'

'It's the desert though,' exclaimed Crystal. 'Will we be safe? It seems a long way to travel. It's probably very hot… and what about…' Her words trailed off as the cloud swallowed up the trio.

*   *   *

Both Harmony and Crystal looked up at the canvas shelter that eased gently up and down in the warm breeze. On the underside, it glowed with yellows and oranges from a nearby fire that flamed and crackled. All the sides of the shelter were open, and in the twilight the dunes had assumed a dusky yellow cooler colour and were visible in all directions – at least up to a familiar wall of cloud a long way off. In the gap between the top of the dunes and the edge of the canvas shelter a million stars glistened brightly.

Crystal was naked. Harmony wore a light cotton robe. Both were lying over brightly coloured cushions the size of small beds. The sandy floor below was covered with a red carpet.

'Wow,' breathed Crystal. 'This is amazing. Her hand moved to the side and found Harmony's. She squeezed.

'This is something special,' said Harmony. 'Why did you opt for wearing nothing?'

'Is that a rhetorical question? Are you mad at me?'

'Maybe at another time… another place… under different circumstances I might be. But right now, I'm not.'

Bentley appeared from somewhere. 'Pretty nice here, ladies.' He also wore a pale-yellow cotton robe tied at the front.

'It's wonderful. Feels so real as did Thailand and the Harbour Bridge.'

'It's not as hot as I thought it would be,' said Crystal.

'Gets very cold here at night. Sometimes below zero Celsius. But it won't be doing that while we're here.'

Bentley knelt between the two women, with a knee on each cushion. Lightly, he ran his fingers up Crystal's leg, across a small patch of pubic hair, over her stomach and breasts, and to her mouth which she opened. She sucked and licked his fingers eagerly. Harmony rolled onto her side and watched.

Bentley undid his robe and allowed it to fall from his shoulders. Crystal felt the muscles of his chest and the six-pack of his abdomen while she gazed into his eyes. He moved onto the one cushion and straddled her thighs, his erection now laying across her lower abdomen. He ran his other hand through the brown ringlets hanging at either side of her face, then dragged his nails across her scalp.

'Oh my God,' she breathed. Her body erupted into goosebumps.

As her hand lowered, she felt his penis. Her fingers explored every part of his erection – the shaft, the smooth glans, the urethral opening, the frenulum, and each tortuous vein that ran up, down and around. She briefly fondled his testicles before taking a firmer grip on his penis and gently pulling it towards her. Bentley edged forward with his knees on either side, moving across her abdomen and over her breasts. He pushed his pelvis forward, as she pulled him by his hips to her mouth.

While one hand supported his slightly arched position, his other moved to his back and slid down between Crystal's legs. She drew up her knees and allowed her legs to fall apart.

Two of Bentley's fingers parted her labia while his thumb entered her vagina. His other fingers rolled over and around on her clitoris, applying pressure then easing off. She briefly recalled Harmony telling her how dexterous he was. As this thought entered and left her mind, something down below changed. It was both unusual and thrilling at the same time. As she groaned and moaned, she felt a swelling inside her. The thumb had enlarged to become a digit even larger than his cock. It began moving in and out of her. His penis too seemed to have grown even more and somehow was moving independently of his pelvis.

As Harmony watched the couple her hand slid down to her own groin. A leg moved a little to one side and she began massaging herself through the thin material.

Just moments before Crystal's orgasm, Bentley removed himself from her mouth and took his hand from her groin. His pelvis slid down over her, back to her parted thighs. He sat back up and gave a pelvic push and filled her once more. His fingers tweaked her nipples. Amongst the many mixed sounds of pleasure from all three, Harmony and Crystal orgasmed at the same moment. Bentley lowered himself slowly over Crystal. His hands stroked her hair. Harmony edged closer and threw an arm over his back.

*   *   *

Sometime later, Harmony opened her eyes. It took a moment to regain her orientation, eventually thanks to the nightlight, she realised that she was lying under a sheet on Crystal's double bed. Her arm was draped across her naked best friend. Bentley was nowhere to be seen. Harmony raised the sheet to check herself and was a little surprised to see that she also was naked. There was an object under the sheet at the end of the bed. With her foot she rolled it close enough to grab.

'Fuck. Crystal. Yucky yucky,' she whispered loudly. She grimaced and dropped the double ended dildo then wiped her hands on the sheet. Harmony eased away from her sleeping friend and tiptoed to the door. The push-lock popped out louder than she expected as she turned the round handle. She looked back to the bed, but Crystal hadn't stirred. She eased the door a centimetre open and looked out to the lounge expecting to see Robbie and Harley back playing their video game, but the lounge was empty.

Harmony found her clothes and handbag lying over a wooden rocking chair in the corner of Crystal's bedroom. She checked her phone. 'One-thirty! Jesus!'

As she started to dress, she heard a yawn and noticed Crystal stir. Her naked friend rolled onto her side and looked at her as she clipped up her bra.

'You should come back here,' breathed Crystal.

'Um… no, I think I should be heading home. Where's Bentley?'

'Who?'

'Bentley. Where is he?'

'Well, I don't know, my beautiful. I think you're keeping him all for yourself.'

'I think you're still half asleep.'

'Come back here to me.' Crystal held out her arms. Harmony sighed and moved back and sat on the bed near her friend.

'Are you awake yet? I think Bentley has worn you out.'

'Fuck Bentley. Who needs him. And you're the one that wore me out. Kiss me again.' Crystal pulled on Harmony's arm.

'Are you completely out of your mind. I did no such thing.' She pulled Crystal's grip off her arm.

'Don't be embarrassed. You were beautiful.' Crystal sat up.

'I'm not embarrassed. And I don't know what you're talking about.' Harmony looked her friend up and down. 'I think you should cover up.' The blonde lifted the sheet for Crystal, but she just let it fall.

'Look, it was a special night,' continued Harmony. 'I acknowledge that. You and Bentley... Wow. It was a real turn on for me.'

Crystal stared. 'Huh... are you trying to be funny or something?'

'No. I'm just saying... you know... how it was... very sexy... Bentley with you. Fucking you.'

'I think this must be a dream you had after we went to sleep. There was no Bentley.'

'What about the Sydney Harbour Bridge, the Sahara Desert in Africa?'

'Yeah, you were dreaming Harms. Listen to yourself. Sydney, Africa. We both passed out after we fucked each other senseless. Remember, the double ended dildo. And you pushing yourself over my chest so I could devour your wonderful pussy, and at the same time you were shoving that delightful toy inside me. Holy shit, I'm getting excited just thinking about it all over again.'

Harmony jumped up and was dressing as quickly as she could.

'Don't go.'

She got her long boots on, grabbed her handbag and was out the bedroom door with Crystal shouting her name as she left.

Out the front Harmony looked about for Bentley's white Mercedes. It was gone.

Chapter 44

Sobo & Kwikal

It was Friday, and two in the morning, as Bentley glided into a parking spot near the corner of Adelaide and Edward Streets in Brisbane city. He briefly reflected on the evening and felt well pleased with himself. He had successfully fulfilled Crystal's deepest and most intense desires, and even better, he knew Sobo was still in the city.

The Tribal Moon was just around the corner. Bentley knew it would be closed. Nevertheless, if he left his mark there, that only another Semblant could detect, this would be a good starting point in his search for Sobo.

The city was quiet. A few cars moved around unimpeded by other vehicles. Some homeless individuals were lying in the alcoves of some closed shops. One was on a bench seat at a bus stop completely covered in blankets. It was a cool autumn evening, but at around twelve degrees Celsius, the Semblant felt no need for a coat.

He slowly made his way to the corner and headed up Edward Street. A couple, huddled into each other, scurried past, giving him a fleeting and unsure glance.

Bentley was still a few metres from the entrance to the closed Tribal Moon when he detected a scent. He moved closer and placed an open hand on the cold timber door.

His head arched back, and a high-pitched yelp filled the air. He dropped to his knees and the yelps continued. Across the road a police vehicle stopped, and a bright beam of light lit up the nightclub entrance like daylight. Bentley stood and turned. In the brightness he could see neither the car nor anything else. The flashing lights and siren came on for a second then stopped.

'Hey fella. Best move along now!' Came a shout.

Bentley gave an acknowledging wave and moved off. The police vehicle moved away slowly.

Back in his Mercedes Sports he did a search in the in-car GPS for *Peabody Funerals*.

*   *   *

To be a little less obtrusive, Bentley decided to walk into the Peabody funeral home grounds rather than drive. It was two-thirty in the morning. If Sobo was here the time would be immaterial but startling an original human at this hour could cause problems. He expected a motion sensor to trigger a light, but so far, the only lights he could see were the two dim glows, one from each level of a cottage further down the funeral home roadway. As he neared this building, he sniffed the cool night air. Sobo was here. He felt a tingling vibration run up his back to his head. He approached the cottage door. The scent was even stronger.

Bentley remained standing near the entrance, without knocking, for just thirty seconds. The door opened. Kwikal saw Sobo, who now looked like a fitter and stronger version of Fabian Carver, except that his hair was thicker and longer. Sobo was dressed only in underwear.

The arms of both Semblant met. It started at the wrists. The arms intertwined around themselves like forest vines. Then the arms shortened, and their bodies were pulled into each other. One open mouth met the other and they seemed to join at the lips. A quieter version of the howling sounds from the Tribal Moon doorway began. Bentley's legs wrapped around the back of Sobo who stepped back, closed the door and headed effortlessly through the lounge and to the bedroom carrying the weight of Bentley.

The two let themselves fall onto the mattress on the floor. An almost indiscernible series of rapid pops, clicks, whistles, hisses, and whispers commenced, as the two communicated…

Your arrival here is magnificent,' said Sobo. *'I see you found my message. I missed you, thinking for the past one hundred and seven years you were dead – killed in the Great War.'*

'I was seriously injured by a mortar shell that exploded near me. Our position was overrun. I managed to find shelter in a bunker and avoid capture. Over a few days I was able to heal. I was ultimately listed as killed in action. This was an unexpected convenience. I occupied an alternate persona and worked for years in a French winery.'

'I see you have suffered from the temporary blindness. And after all this time, you still fail to manage it well,' said Sobo.

'Yes, I can become so overwhelmed with passion that I fail to see other matters.'

'You nearly acquired an original human who had but a mild imperfection. I'm glad you realised this in time. This deficit haunts you, Kwikal. Perhaps this is something I can assist you with soon.'

'I would welcome that.'

'As for me. I have a troubled assimilant,' said Sobo.

'I have noticed some anguish. But you have blocked me from full awareness.'

'It is a burden I have acquired. The full details of which are best not shared. His name is Fabian. He is a serial killer.'

'Hello Fabian.'

'I have a plan,' continued Sobo. *'Fabian will achieve closure and peace.*

'I like your plan.'

* * *

In his winter *Where's Wally,* pyjamas, Rip ambled down the stairs after hearing scuffling sounds. He flicked on the light in the lounge. 'Sobo, what's happening?' he mumbled, as he moved towards the bedroom. He waited a moment tilting his head from side to side, before putting an ear against the closed door. The noises got softer and stopped. 'Huh… well let's see your new persona.' He opened the door.

At that instant a head disengaged from the oneness of the two Semblant. It swung around and glared at him with large red eyes, but little else in the way of facial features. Peabody staggered and lunged to a wall with an outstretched hand.

Sobo told Kwikal, *'This is Roderick Ignatius Peabody. He is Semblant friendly and has been my trusty helper for over two years.'* Kwikal's red eyes switched off.

Rip regained his feet. 'Oh, dear. That was most unpleasant.'

A series of louder clicks and pops emanated from somewhere amongst the two Semblant. Then they began untwining and disengaging from each other. Peabody looked on wide-eyed.

'You found Kwikal… or rather Kwikal found you. This is something to behold,' panted the undertaker.

The two Semblant, now fully separated, stood apart and smiled. The pair looked each other up and down, nodding their approval. They stepped a little closer to each other and shook hands strongly and warmly as if meeting for the first time.

Rip gazed on in amazement, then asked the burning question. 'Have you two… you know… done the thing…'

Click, pop, pop, hiss, whistle, whisper, click, click, squeak.

'Oh… well. I see then you have been sharing experiences and understandings. I do not wish to be an intrusion while you complete your necessary copulation.'

Pop, click, hiss, click, pop.

'Oh well, good gentleman... I'm sorry... good Semblant. If you're fine with it then, I will just sit quietly in the corner.' Peabody slid down the wall in the bedroom, drew his knees up and held them somewhat awkwardly with his long arms.

Bentley undressed. Fabian removed his underwear. Peabody diverted his gaze for a moment.

The two naked Semblant moved back together once more. This time, as their skin touched in various places it stuck to the other as if coated with instant glue. Their even wider mouths fused together, followed by their thighs, their chests and abdomens, then their genitals and pelvis. As their bodies moulded, the eight limbs became longer and increasingly flexible, until there were eight tentacles complete with suction pads. The combined bodies twisted and reshaped, forming crevices and holes that the tentacles would dive into, only to resurface elsewhere on the jelly-like mass. Colours were constantly changing with shades of pinks, greys, greens, and blacks, all moving across the moist looking surface.

As the squelching and sucking sounds grew louder, Peabody pushed himself a little harder into the wall.

Suddenly all noise stopped. The tentacles became part of the whole, as the two Semblant morphed into a large pyramid shape with rounded edges and corners. The quivering shape sat upright on the mattress two metres high. For nearly a minute there was silence, then a soft melodic humming began. Inside the pyramid a light glowed and pulsed. Despite the two being joined, there was a fine line within the shape that roughly depicted two people.

Even still unsure what to expect, Peabody was able to relax. He stretched out his legs as he gazed and smiled at the rarest of phenomena. The humming seemed to fill his body with peace and contentment. This was possibly something that no other human had ever witnessed, he thought.

Chapter 45

A Near Miss

Richard woke up shivering and naked in the bath.

'What the fuck?' He looked around trying to get a handle on what was going on. The bathroom light was off, but somewhere else in the house a light was on, and although dim, he was soon able to work out where he was. He pulled himself to a sitting position. His hand slipped on the side of the bath. It felt greasy. He held his hand closer to his face, then squealed. As quickly as he could, and despite his feet also sliding in the tub, he managed to get out and flick the light switch.

'Jesus Christ!' There was blood over his chest, stomach, and hand. The glass shower petition and the bath were bloody, with clumps of clotted blood near the drain, and speckles and spurts over surfaces. The bloody pruning shears lay in the bath. His clothes were shoved untidily into a corner.

He ran to his bedroom. The light was already on.

'Oh fuck!' He ran straight to his wardrobe, flung the sliding door across sending it careering off its rails. He frantically turned a dial this way and that on a wall safe, at the same time looking back over his shoulder. He grabbed his Glock 22 pistol and spun around. 'Constantino!' he shouted. 'Hello. Constantino. Where you?' Shivering, he moved forward over the carpet. He saw the daisy dress laying neatly over the pillows. The makeup sitting on the bedside table. The two loaded syringes on the quilt. And there was something else that looked completely out of place.

After checking every room Richard returned to the bathroom and retrieved his iPhone from his chinos. He called Jan Silverton as he grabbed a beach towel from a cupboard and wrapped it around his shoulders.

'*Richard? It's three-thirty in the morning,*' she answered with a yawn.

'He was here,' yelled Davis.

'*Who was where?*'

'The killer. Daisy. The serial. It's Constantino. He was here.'

'*What?*' *At your place? You sure?*'

'Oh, I'm fucking sure all right. The daisy dress, the makeup, the syringes... the fucking works. Get over here. Bring some forensic guys.'

'*Are you safe?*'

'Yeah. There's no one else here now. There's a lot of blood, but none of it seems to be mine. And there's something else that's pretty weird that I don't quite understand. I'm not touching or cleaning anything for now.'

'*On my way.*' She hung up.

*   *   *

With underpants on, the beach towel now around his waist and a folded blanket wrapped around him, Richard sat at the dining room table. He was still shivering. He had his hands wrapped around a mug of coffee.

The team was taking photos and bagging lots of evidence. Richard Davis had already been photographed and had samples of blood taken from his skin.

Silverton walked in, dragged a chair next to him and gave him a big hug. 'So sorry about all this. Somehow it looks like you've dodged a bullet. How dreadful. You poor thing.'

'Yeah,' he sighed. 'At least I have all my fingers and... all my other bits too. Someone has done me a massive favour.'

'You never saw anyone else?'

'No. Only the Constantino guy.'

'You'll be wanting time off.'

'No, please Jan. No time off. I gotta follow this through.'

'Edwards might insist.'

'He might, but you need to tell him I'm good to go. If I have any issues, you'll be the first to know. I've seen Daisy. I can identify him.'

Jan eased back a little. They looked at each other. Richard was still shaking.

'You should be right to shower soon,' said Silverton. 'They're nearly done with the bathroom. You've still got a few specks...' she pointed at a couple of places on her own face.

'Yeah, blood. I know.'

'The blood has to be Constantino's,' said Jan. 'Not that Constantino Abrahams is his real name. He's left most everything here – the pruning shears, clothes, probably a fake licence, mobile phone. No keys, no wallet though.'

'The license doesn't look like it's his. The picture is similar, but it's not a match. And all his clothes were still folded neatly in my bedroom,' added Davis. 'One way or another I think he's left here naked.'

'Yep, I agree. There's no shortage of evidence this time. And while it looks like a lot of blood, it doesn't look like enough to die from. So wherever he is, he's in bad shape. We'll be checking hospitals, medical centres etcetera.'

'He wrote... or whoever else was here, wrote on the bathroom mirror.'

'Hmm… yeah, *Just one more, Daddy*,' continued Jan. 'At first glance the writing looks similar but to me not an exact match. We'll know more in a few hours.'

'Someone was following Constantino, Daisy, or whatever his name really is. Someone who knows more about him than we do. That other stuff on the bed. What's that all about? I don't get it.'

'I think Anderson might be interested in that little discovery.'

'As in Clive Anderson?'

'Yeah.'

Chapter 46

Two Cases Collide

At ten in the morning on Friday, two teams of detectives, other officers, and several members of the forensic team were milling around in the briefing room waiting for the meeting to be called to order. Both current investigations were represented – the serial killer case and the smaller Tribal Moon team.

Some were sitting while others chatted in small groups. Richard shuffled in. He had his blue police jacket over the top of his civilian clothes. His hands were shoved in the pockets. Clive, who was sitting, stood, and approached him.

'Hey you. You okay?' he asked. Richard grunted and focused on the floor. Clive stood in front of him and placed a hand on both Richard's shoulders. 'This is a tough break. So sorry for you. We gotta catch this guy.'

'Bloody oath,' replied Davis. He raised his head and gave Clive a quick grin. There was a pause as they both weighed each other up.

'You look like shit,' said Clive.

'Inside and out, I can assure you. Precious little sleep.'

'And a fucking near death experience. Fuck it, Richard. This sucks.' Clive stepped closer and embraced him in a firm but brief hug.

'A hug from Clive Anderson,' said Richard. 'Now that's gotta be something special.'

'I made it a quick one. You know, I didn't want you to get the wrong idea.'

'No worries, old man.' They both sat next to each other in the front row and alongside Lachlan Godwin.

Inspector Vince Edwards and Detective Jan Silverton moved out front. 'Seats please,' shouted Edwards.

Clive was sitting upright and a little forward waiting for the show to begin.

'What's with you and this case?' whispered Davis.

'Something big. Something strange. Just wait for it,' replied Anderson.

'It is important that both teams here make themselves familiar with both investigations,' said Edwards. 'We need as many brains as possible working on this. The evidence is presenting us with a puzzle...' He glanced at Clive who smiled back. Anderson's head seemed to have settled into a monotonous nodding, like a bobbing dog toy mounted on a car dash. '... yes, it's confusing, and to put it mildly... it's a bizarre puzzle with pieces that don't seem to fit together. As of last night, these two cases have intersected. I'll let Detective Silverton provide you with the details.'

Silverton swapped places with the inspector. 'Firstly,' she announced. 'I'd like to thank Detective Davis for making it here this morning.' A few of the team who knew what had transpired clapped lightly. Richard waved his hands dismissing the claps as not necessary. 'For those of you that don't know, Detective Davis was attacked last night at his home. Davis has given me the okay to tell you all that it was Daisy – our serial killer.' A mumble of oohs and aahs and general chatter filled the room as various heads turned.

'Thank you all... for your attention,' continued Silverton in a louder voice. The room quietened. 'Be aware that there is still forensic information pending, but some things are now clear and not in dispute. The corpse pulled from the river on Wednesday afternoon is, we believe, victim number one for Daisy. The identity of the deceased is not yet known, but we have a few names of missing persons that we are looking into. There are patches of daisies growing near the sixth hole on the golf course where the body was found.' As she spoke, Silverton stuck more photos onto one of the three whiteboards. 'It appears the victim was killed with a single blow, most likely from a golf club. The body shape and height are consistent with other victims.' Two more graphic images were attached to the board.

'Excuse me Ma'am,' interjected Bryant, who was sitting behind Anderson. 'How does this connect the two cases?'

'We're about to get to that. I'm sure all of you know something about Detective Anderson's past history in regard to the safe house matter some months back.' This time the room erupted into chatter and some laughter. Bryant reached forward and patted Anderson on the shoulder. 'Don't take it too hard. We've all got regrets, mate.'

'Fuck off! And just fucking listen,' retorted Clive in a loud whisper.

'Please!' yelled Silverton. The noise slowly decreased. Jan placed another photo on the wall. It was an enlarged image of a box of KFC with a single playing card stuck on the top with sticky tape – the Ace of Hearts. 'Detective Anderson… the floor is yours for two minutes only.' Clive stood where he was and turned to the group. Over near the wall, Edwards decided he needed to sit.

'I think you all know I have stuck to my guns on my story. As a quick reminder, my partner that day went to get the KFC, yeah everyone knows that part of the story. While he was away, the informant, Jason Galanis, showed me some stupid card trick which turned up my selected card – the ace of hearts. That, my friends, is not common knowledge. Not even disclosed in the hearing. Now here are these two things showing up in Davis's bedroom.' Off went the room again.

Silverton looked at Edwards who shrugged and pushed his hands over his cheeks to the top of his head, momentarily stretching away all his wrinkles. They allowed the room to settle itself.

Clive remained standing looking around the room. 'Now here's the clincher, you lot,' he continued. 'The fingerprints on the card, the ace of hearts, were crystal clear, as if intentionally put there for us to find. They were a perfect match for Johnny Randall, the dead man from the nightclub.' This time the room went off even louder.

'Gotta be a set up,' barked Bryant.

'Is that your handiwork, Clive?' came a yell from somewhere else.

'You been stealing fingerprints from the morgue?' came another.

'No. He's not that clever,' another yelled.

'Happy to accept apologies anytime, you pricks!' shouted Clive above the noise.

Edwards rose, sighed, and walked to the front. 'That'll do!' he bellowed. There was instant quiet. He gave a wave towards the rear windowed door, behind which, three people were waiting. They entered. Nearly every head turned. All three were neatly attired and appeared to be of similar ages, possibly in their early thirties. There were two men and a woman.

'I'd like to introduce, Geraldine Branson, Mark Devine and Alberto Santos.' Each raised a hand as introduced. 'I have called these officers in to assist us in our investigations and with analysis. The seriousness of our findings thus far are suggestive of a potential threat to national security. That being the case, these ASIO officers will be working alongside us. Please afford them all due respect and assistance.'

Mumbling permeated the room. The three Australian Security Intelligence Organisation officers sat in the back row next to each other.

Chapter 47

Daisy Dances

At ten in the morning, on Saturday the second of May, Fabian Carver parked a motorhome over a white line, taking up the last two car parks at the Indooroopilly Police Station. He was dressed smartly in blue chinos, white business shirt and a dark grey bomber jacket. Today Fabian had long brown wavy hair to below his collar. He strode with purpose through the front double swing doors of the brick building.

One older uniformed officer, with three stripes on his sleeve, was attending to a middle-aged woman. Fabian stood behind her. He felt a tingling sensation run up his spine.

'I think someone has kidnapped Horatio,' croaked the woman. She was heavily rugged up. While it was a cool morning, it was not so cold as to demand a heavy coat, scarf, beanie and gloves.

'I hope not,' replied the sergeant. 'He may well turn up in a day or two, Miss Parker.'

'He's never run away before. I let him out the back for a few minutes, just like every other day. Now he's gone… he's gone… left me all alone,' she began to sob. Fabian leaned closer to her and sniffed. Then, while close to her ear, he made a soft hiss followed by two pops and a quick high-pitched whistle.

Miss Parker turned to face him. 'Thank you. I will see my doctor and insist on a brain scan.' Before she left, she briefly turned back to the officer. 'I just remembered. I don't have a cat. Sorry to have bothered you.'

The sergeant stood there puzzled as she turned and walked away. He looked at Fabian. 'Sir, did you just kiss that lady's ear?'

The Semblant shook his head, smiled and leaned forward over the reception desk. The sergeant responded in the same way. Fabian popped, squeaked and whispered. The two men stood back again locked in eye contact.

Without disengaging from the officer, Fabian removed a deck of playing cards from his pocket. He shuffled them, then fanned them out for the sergeant. Without looking down the policeman selected one, turned it over and lay it on the desk. At the bottom of the ace of hearts was a name written in biro – *Daisy*.

'Thank you, sir. I will see that this gets to Detective Clive Anderson, at the city office,' he said. 'Good day.' With a broad smile and a nodding head, he watched Fabian turn and head to the door. 'You have the most gorgeous hair,' he shouted. Carver, kept walking, raising an open hand next to his head as he left. Once outside, he turned and looked up at the camera mounted high on the brickwork. Fabian smiled, held back his hair from his face and gave a thumbs up.

The sergeant slapped his own face. 'What the hell, Scotty. *You have the most gorgeous hair* – Shit, I need a fucking holiday.'

* * *

All armed with a coffee, Anderson, Godwin and Davis sat around an office desk. It was late Saturday morning.

'Davis, you know you shouldn't be here,' said Clive.

'Should be on a few days leave, I know. I managed a few hours' sleep last night even though I'm still pretty shaken. I convinced Jan, who somehow convinced Edwards that I should be here. See this through.'

'You've seen Daisy. So, it makes sense,' added Godwin.

'That's all you're good for.' Clive sipped his drink. 'No driving. No reports. Shit, I don't even know if you could handle a fucking phone call.'

As he said those words the desk phone rang. Richard Davis was closest and reached over. Anderson raised a stop hand and shook his head. Godwin answered the call.

The other two watched as Lachlan nodded and became animated. 'Holy shit!' He shouted then covered the mouthpiece. 'A guy. At the Indooroopilly cop shop. It's him… Daisy… the ace of hearts!'

Clive reached over and took the phone.

'What the hell?' said Davis looking at Godwin for some clarification.

'He just walked in. Gave the Sarge the ace of hearts with the name "Daisy" written at the bottom. Then left.'

Clive hung up. 'They're sending us an image from the CCTV.' Richard Davis moved his chair closer to the monitor. A message with an attachment arrived in Clive's inbox. He double clicked the emailed file and a picture opened. 'Well, Davis?'

Richard was almost out of his chair with his face close to the screen. 'It's a little grainy. The hair is way too long. The face is… sort of familiar. Could be. Not a hundred percent.'

'Really?' said a wide-eyed Anderson.

'Can they send more images?'

'Fuck it guys, we're off to Indooroopilly. The card might have prints and they've got him and his vehicle on CCTV. Davis I just need your eyes, nothing else. Clear? Maybe he's wearing a wig. Fuck knows.'

'Cool,' replied Davis.

Everyone stood. 'You sure you're okay, Davis. Looks like you've just become a whiter shade of pale.'

'Don't worry about me. Let's just go.'

'Godwin, call Silverton. Bring her up to speed. This is his vehicle rego.' He handed Lachlan a post-it note. 'I'll drive. You check that rego out and call in a request to notify all our patrols.'

The three started heading out when Clive stopped. 'A sec guys. One more thing.' He opened the larger bottom desk drawer and pulled out a plastic JB HiFi bag. 'A couple of items I'd like to have at the ready.'

'Like what?' asked Davis.

'Never you mind. It's just in case.'

'It's a headset and a pair of sunglasses,' said Godwin.

'You been prying?'

'Just took a quick peek.'

'Arsehole.'

'If we get bored, are you going to lie in the sun and listen to your old rock songs?' quipped Davis.

'Huh… well it won't be Barbra fucking Streisand, Davis.'

*   *   *

Silverton was at her desk when Godwin called and gave her the message. 'Sounds promising. We're just checking a few things here. If Davis can ID this guy I need to know, and if that motorhome shows up, get back to me ASAP.'

On her desk was the open file of the missing person Logan Bridgeman. Silverton was flicking through a few photos on her computer screen.

'This Carver guy has to be number one on our list,' she said. 'Left his home. Left his job. Gone off the radar, and I reckon he's bought himself a motorhome.'

'Agreed,' replied Henry Bryant. He studied the computer screen. 'That rego is for a Jayco motorhome and registered to a guy in Sydney. If Carver's bought this vehicle recently, he might not have even lodged the paperwork yet. Best call our mates down south to pay this bloke a visit.'

'Okay, put that on the *to do* list. Are you much of a golfer?'

'Never had any real interest.'

'Who around here is?'

'The boss.'

'Edwards?'

'Hell yeah. Plays every week I think.'

'I'll be back.' Jan was up and away.

The inspector had her wait five minutes while he finished a phone call. He poked his head around his door. 'You got the bastard yet?'

'No, but we've got a strong suspect. I need your golfing knowledge.'

'Huh... okay, come in.'

'Can you open the missing person file for Logan Bridgeman?'

Edwards sat at his desk. Silverton rolled a second chair next to him.

'By the way. Did Pendleton call you?' asked Silverton.

'Pendleton is a busy body.' Edwards clicked open a folder.

'He's your friend.'

'Allegedly,' scoffed Edwards. 'What am I looking for?'

'The pics of Bridgeman's golf clubs... zoom up on the one showing the top of his golf bag.'

'Yeah... what now?'

'Is there anything odd about those clubs?'

Edwards zoomed in more and leaned closer to the screen. 'This is a good brand. Callaway. He's got no pitching wedge.'

'There's a few holes empty there... could be missing some clubs.'

'I can see that, Silverton… he has no two, five or eight iron either.'

'Thank you, sir. That's all I needed to know.'

'You thinking that these missing clubs are murder weapons? And that he was hacked up with his own golf clubs? The divers recovered nothing.'

'They could have been washed anywhere in five to eight months. And yes, this points strongly to Fabian Carver being our Daisy killer.'

'Don't call him that. It makes him sound like a pleasant sort of guy, and he's anything but.'

Chapter 48

Identification

In a small side room at the Indooroopilly Police Station, the desk sergeant, Anderson, Godwin and Davis all watched the video footage. They had seen the motorhome arriving, watched the long-haired guy standing behind the woman then talking to the sergeant.

'This was weird here.' The officer pointed at the video. 'I gotta tell you, we don't get many customers showing us fucking card tricks. Then the guy somehow tells me something. You see, his mouth sort of moves, but there's no audio.'

'Yeah… we know,' said Anderson.

'Then off he goes with me making some stupid comment about his lovely hair. I'm losing the plot here guys. Sorry.'

'You're not the first to have such experiences….'

'Woah…' interrupted Davis. 'Wind that back and pause.'

The sergeant obliged. 'You know this guy?'

'Slow forward…' The video slowed as Semblant Fabian looked up at the camera and pulled back his hair. 'There… pause. That's him! That's Constantino Abrahams. He was going to kill me!' Davis swallowed and dropped on a plastic chair. 'Oh fuck.'

Clive's phone played a short burst of an Electric Light Orchestra song – Evil Woman.

He answered. 'Hey boss. What's up?'

Davis lifted his head from his hands and looked at Godwin. Richard gave a little shake of his head. Lachlan raised his eyebrows.

'Yeah. I'll hold.' He looked around at his colleagues and shrugged. 'Send the image through.'

A moment later his text message sounded to a Beatles song – Maxwell's Silver Hammer.' Now the sergeant smiled.

'Got it…' Clive clicked open the image. A picture of Fabian Carver filled his iPhone screen. He showed the others. 'That's him. Same guy that was here at the station. His hair is now longer. He did the mind thing on the poor sarge here. Here's what I'm thinking…'

Just so you know, Clive, said Silverton *We're on speaker phone here, with Vince Edwards, Bryant and the ASIO guys.*

'Well good. You all need to hear this. I know it sounds crazy but you gotta hear me through.'

Knock yourself out, Clive.

'Nicholas Drakos was dead then reappeared, at least he did to me….'

Back at HQ Edwards was already shaking his head and gesticulating. The three ASIO officers just listened not changing their expression.

'… sorry Vince, but that's a fact. Moving on. Medora Hammerstein was dead and came back, sure she was a lot younger. Johnny Randall was definitely dead, and he came back too. Now this Fabian Carver appears here. Someone bled all over Davis. I think that was Carver, who I believe is now also dead, but now he is back, and like the other restored dead people, is doing the mind manipulation. All these come back arseholes have long hair. Why, I don't know, but it's a fact. Carver leaves us his calling card, allows us to see his face, even pulls his hair back so he can be identified. He either wants us to find him, or he's just showing off.'

And where do you think Hammerstein and Randall are now? We have Randall's prints from Richard's place.

'I can't explain that. One thing at a time. Let's find Carver.'

Agreed. He has an aunty, Joanne and a father, George. We'll visit the sister. You check out the father. Given all the Daddy references he might give us some interesting insights. I'll text you his address.

Chapter 49

George Gets a Visit – Part 1

George Carver had lived in the same house at Upper Brookfield, in the outer suburbs of Brisbane, for the past thirty-five years. For the same amount of time, he had worked in the construction industry, the last seven years as a Construction Manager. Since his wife, Maureen, died twenty years ago, he had for the most part, lived alone, sharing just a few years after her death with his only son, Fabian.

The Carver home was an aged, low-set three-bedroom dwelling in need of repair. Despite his construction work, George did little to maintain the premises, which now needed significant exterior and interior painting, new gutters and downpipes and restumping.

The house was on a gently sloping property of two hectares. A furrowed driveway, through overgrown grass, wound its way past some tall eucalypt trees, finishing in front of a standalone garage adjacent to the house. The two wooden garage doors lay to the side rotting away on the ground.

At midday on Saturday a Jayco motor home, with interstate plates, wobbled its way up the driveway.

*　　　*　　　*

The three detectives inched their way towards the pick-up window of the Red Rooster drive-through. Anderson had made the executive decision that they needed lunch before heading out to Upper Brookfield to see George Carver.

As they waited quietly in line, Richard Davis flicked through a few of his handwritten notes. He had notes with all the "Daddy" quotes where he'd try to group them to make sense, tried to make some sort of poetry or song lyric. He also had a few song titles listed that had the word "Daddy" in them. Lachlan sat with his arms crossed, staring at two girls in skimpy denim shorts on bicycles. Clive had his elbow resting on his open window as he gazed up the queue of vehicles trying to determine why they were moving so slow. Richard looked at the page where he had written all the quotes from three known murder scenes. He jotted down the last one that was written in blood on his own bathroom mirror. Then he saw something. 'Fuck! Fuck! Fuck!'

'Davis! What?' retorted Anderson with a jerk as he swung his head round. 'Shit, if Edwards was here, you'd have just fucking killed him!'

Richard leaned forward from the back seat and waved his notes to Clive and Lachlan. 'The last message. On my bathroom window. *Just one more – Daddy*. It's written over two lines. The one more is Daddy. He's going to kill his father!'

'Oh Jesus,' bellowed Clive.

'Damn, I should have seen it sooner.'

'That would have helped.' Anderson flicked on lights and sirens while the car was still in the queue. Those in the cars in front looked around unsurely. They checked rearview mirrors and stuck their heads out the window but didn't move. 'Go tell them to fuck off, Godwin.'

Lachlan was quickly out, shouting and gesticulating at the two cars in front. They ended up moving without collecting their order. He jumped back in, and they screeched away.

'Get on the blower to Silverton,' continued Anderson.

*　　　*　　　*

Semblant Fabian stopped part way along the furrowed tracks in between two large trees. He looked around the property, took a deep breath and shook his head slowly. He applied the handbrake and switched off the motor.

If George's past pattern of behaviour had continued over the past few years, he would still be in bed sleeping off a heavy Friday night of boozing.

Fabian left the motorhome and walked the rest of the way to the house. George's ute was squeezed into the garage. On both sides and at the back of the area were new and rusted garden tools, assorted old drums and tins, some which looked like old, yet unused tins of paint. There were tarps, buckets, old car parts, stacks of timber slats covered in cobwebs and boxes of ceramic tiles where most of the cardboard box had rotted away.

The area in front of the house was reasonably clear. Weed-killer had been used to kill the tall grass and the weeds that had erupted between the cement tiles. All the tall grass was brown. The weeds had fallen over and died. A couple of pot plants seemed to have succumbed to the same fate. The front entrance was double glass sliding doors behind double flyscreened doors, although the screen doors were too damaged to keep out any flies.

Fabian stood under an arched metal frame which was once a part of a walkway covered with bougainvillea. He squatted and picked up several small stones and chipped pieces of cement. One at a time he threw them at the house.

Chapter 50

Rip & Bentley

Saturday Morning

Peabody heard a noise, stirred and rolled to his side, opened his eyes and looked at the digital clock on his bedside table – 10.05. 'Geez!' He checked his watch just to be sure. 'Huh.' He sat up in bed, yawned and stretched.

The undertaker swung out his long legs and stood. His *Where's Wally* pyjamas were not quite long enough to reach his ankles. Suddenly Peabody dropped back to a sitting position on seeing Bentley sitting on the chaise lounge near the bedroom door. The Semblant, was reading a magazine – *Funeral Directors Monthly*.

'Why are you here? Where is Sobo?'

Bentley put down the magazine, stood, smiled and walked over.

'You look... amazing,' stammered Rip with a nervous swallow, as the Semblant approached. Bentley was perfectly groomed, and still wearing his stunning dark jacket with the green fleck that caught the light as he walked.

He sat next to Rip and looked at him with his big blue eyes at very close range.

'Certainly, Mister Bentley,' nodded Rip. His tone relaxed. 'Can I freshen up first and get a coffee? And I do have a service this afternoon at three. From two o'clock you will need to excuse me for three hours, if you wouldn't mind.' The Semblant nodded and left the room. Peabody just sat there a little longer. 'Sobo never came into my room,' he mumbled. 'Not once.' He got up and headed to the bathroom.

*   *   *

Downstairs, Peabody presented himself as requested in the Semblant bedroom. The mattress was on the floor just as it was when he last saw it. The undertaker looked it over, as if expecting to see some sort of stain or wet spot, but there was nothing. He sat cross-legged on the mattress, in front of Semblant Bentley. He knew what to expect. He had done this several times with Sobo.

The Semblant leant forward and opened his mouth. His tongue protruded, extended, and became the familiar tubular shape. It slid into Peabody's nose.

There they were, floating in a neutral place. He noticed, despite having changed into his black clothes, he was once again back in his colourful pyjamas. Bentley remained perfectly neat and tidy in the same clothing.

'I do like those PJs,' said Bentley.

'So it appears. I am thankful you at least dressed me for the occasion.'

'Sobo has left to sort out a troubling matter. A matter you assisted him with on Thursday evening,' said Bentley. His voice had a different quality to that of Sobo, with less nasal sounds and more echo. 'I'm sorry this was disturbing for you, but we both thank you for your help then, for your help in the past, and for your continuing assistance in the future.'

'I have never disposed of an entire body before.'

'I see you are concerned this may lead to apprehension by the authorities. But even more, you feel in some way soiled by it. It has conflicted with your sense of right and wrong. Yet you have disposed of original human heads before, with a lesser impact on your sensibilities.'

'It is one thing to aid those that are dying or enduring immense suffering. It is something else again to take the law into one's own hands.'

'Would you like me to erase your memory of the matter?'

Peabody moved in the space as if in slow motion. His hands floated up and touched his black hair. He stared at Kwikal and told a lie. 'I was unaware such a process was possible.' He sent this thought, and the memory of some past disposals, to Fort Knox.

'I could even alter the memory. I could ensure that you believe the body to be riddled with cancer and was close to death. This may go some way to alleviating your concerns. Ah… but, now I notice that this worries you. And Sobo has not previously instructed you on such matters.'

'I would much prefer if you would not tamper with my memory in any way, despite how I may feel about these and other issues.' Peabody felt thankful to Sobo for Fort Knox, then sent that very thought straight there too.

'Is it that you somehow enjoy these internal discomforts?'

'It's all part of being a complete person. You must promise to leave me with that.'

'Fine then Roderick. I won't interfere.'

'I need to ask…'

'Yes,' interrupted Kwikal. 'Did Sobo and I have a successful encounter. It was a wonderful time. We spent hours locked together in ecstatic entwined somnambulance, moving through each other's bodies. And yes, Roderick, I am generating a new Semblant.'

'Oh, my goodness. I am delighted for you both.'

'You have a little query I see. A man being pregnant. You think I am a man, Roderick?'

'I should have known better. Sobo has been male and female. Apologies, Kwikal.'

'Ah… so many more questions now fill your mind. The birth will be similar in many ways to our copulation… Oh… Sobo has allowed you to see death and now you wish to see birth. We may visit that on Sobo's return. Sobo and I need to interact further.'

The light beams between them and the slow swirling clouds seemed to evaporate. Peabody's eyes closed.

Chapter 51

George Gets a Visit – Part 2

Fabian Carver stopped throwing small stones when the glass and screen doors opened, and his father George, finally emerged. He was dressed in a soiled singlet-shirt, shorts and no footwear. While his hair was still predominantly black it was greyer than Fabian remembered. The short squat man had put on a few kilos and acquired wrinkles around his eyes and flabby skin under his chin.

The sixty-year-old took a couple of tentative steps forward onto the cement pavers and raised a hand to his forehead to block the sunlight.

'Who is that? What do you want?' He stepped forward a little more. As his eyes adjusted, he lowered his hand and with a tilt of his head looked intently at the young man standing a few metres away. 'Jesus! Is that you, Fabian?'

Now, he moved even closer and smiled. 'Shit, look at you.' His eyes wandered up and down over his son.

Fabian's appearance was a stark contrast to that of his father. He was groomed perfectly with his long wavy brown hair to his shoulders. All his clothes, even his shoes, were cream or white, and in the bright sunlight he looked radiant.

'Have you got taller?' continued George. Now he was close enough to touch Fabian. He patted his son's upper arms. 'You look fit and strong. Your hair is… well, a bit too long, son. Looks healthy enough though.'

Semblant Fabian panted as he stared at him. He could feel his own heart pulsating in his mouth. As his eyes widened, he squeezed out a few words. 'Today, will be your last day of existence, daddy.'

George took a step back. 'Is that all you got for me after all these years? You look like you've done well. Grown up. Got nice clothes, and I see a motorhome down there. You had your grandma's inheritance. Not that you deserved it. You were such a special boy once.' He managed one further step back then was stuck.

Fabian's eyes grew even larger.

'What are you doing? What is this? Some of your foolish trickery?' All he could do was flail his arms around and slap his legs to get them moving. Semblant Fabian opened his mouth wider and wider. George trembled. 'Help! Someone help me!' A wavy tongue extended. It curled and whipped through the air in front of George's face as if taunting him. 'Don't be stupid now, Fabian. I am your father. Have respect.'

The tongue tickled and teased his nostril before entering. George's pupils dilated. His arms fell by his side, his head tilted over, yet he remained standing.

*   *   *

Detectives Jan Silverton and Henry Bryant knocked on the door of Joanne Carver's small home. It was number three-hundred and fifteen of nearly five hundred homes at Sunny Banks – a gated community for over fifties at Sunnybank, on the north side of Brisbane.

'Now, we're not here because of unpaid fines, clear?' she looked at Bryant.

'I've already apologised for that,' he replied. 'You do the talking this time.'

They waited. She knocked again. 'You said she was home.'

'That's what I was told.' Bryant shrugged.

'But you rang? Who did you speak to?'

'Well, not me. The ASIO broad, Geraldine, made the call. She said Joanne Carver was here.'

'And where did those three guys end up going?'

'Don't know. They all left together. I just guessed they were following up something else.'

'Fuck!' said Silverton loudly. The door opened. A slim young lady, no more than twenty years of age stood there.

'Can I help you?'

'Is Miss Carver home?'

'Well… yeah. She's always home.'

Jan flashed her ID. 'We need to have a few words with her.'

'Sure… you can. But it may not be very enlightening. I told that to the person who called earlier.'

'Oh… did you? Sorry. Tell me what's wrong with Miss Carver?'

'Like I said on the phone, she has advanced dementia. I'm one of her carers. My name is Emily Mitchell.'

Jan turned and looked at Henry and pushed out a fake smile. 'Emily, do you know, or have you met her nephew, Fabian?'

'I've never met him. I think Julie, the other carer, met him a few years back. He used to visit regularly then, before Joanne declined.'

*   *   *

George Carver hovered in an empty space unable to do little else than move his limbs in the air. There was white and grey cloud in every direction. In front of him he could see his son, also hovering. There were no calming beams of light connecting them.

'Where are we? What have you done?' he yelled.

'We are going on a journey,' said Fabian in a loud whisper. 'Or more correctly, you, Daddy, are going on that journey.'

'Have you drugged me?'

'No drugs.'

'Well, whatever you're doing. Stop! Now!'

Fabian raised a hand and pointed at his father. A large spark shot from his hand to his father's mouth, and he was unable to utter any further sounds. George's eyes were open to their limits. His jaw was tight, and his fists clenched. From both hands of the Semblant, arcs of light left and descended onto George Carver's head. The clouds swirled and rolled in. Wind blew through his black hair. As the mist cleared, he could see himself below on the couch, behind his young son. The daisy dress was lifted over Fabian's back while George pushed himself in and out of his special boy. The song was playing…

You are the one I need
To help me face the day
Being there for me
A tonic that sees me through
My special boy. Lie here with me…

Then the suspended George descended closer to his son. His mouth opened. All he could do was mouth a silent word – *No,* and shake his head. He moved even closer still, until he could nearly touch his young boy. George floated into a position as if on all fours, and his body descended, becoming one with the child. The body of the young boy remained unchanged, yet the face twisted and altered becoming that of George Carver.

Time was in no hurry, as George felt every moment of the excruciating torture, both internal and external – the fear, the powerlessness, the guilt, the shame. Sobo did not allow any escape to a secret place. For George, seeing the clouds roll back in, gave him a brief sense it was ending. Then he found himself bent over in the bathtub with what felt like an entire hand inside him. And the song played…

Love will hold us together
I hear you breathe
I see your sweet shape
So smooth and unique…

*   *   *

Anderson attempted to drive around the motorhome. The car bumped and something grated loudly underneath, then it lunged forward and stopped over a concealed trench. The wheels spun but the car wouldn't move.

'Fuck it,' said Anderson. 'We walk from here. Davis, are you carrying a weapon?'

'Yes. Of course.'

'Leave it in the car.'

'But I may…'

'No fucking way,' interrupted Clive. 'Edwards and Silverton would have my badge. You leave it here in the glove box. Godwin, pass me that JB HiFi bag.'

The three got out. Clive put the reflective sunnies and the headset on. On his phone he connected the blue tooth and had Led Zeppelin's, *Black Dog*, ready to go at max volume. Both he and Godwin had their Glock 22 pistols on display in shoulder holsters.

'Really, Clive?' said Lachlan looking at an image of himself in Anderson's glasses. 'What are you expecting? Aliens?'

'Zip it, Godwin. Let's go. Follow the driveway, it looks the safest.'

*   *   *

Back on the cement pavers, George Carver and Semblant Fabian stood three metres apart. Sobo had finally released George from his firsthand experience of sexual abuse. So far, he had gotten off lightly. The Semblant glared at him with bright red eyes and an open mouth with elongated razor-sharp teeth. Sobo kept him standing with his arms outstretched and feet locked to the ground. George's eyes were not allowed to close. Tears flowed down his cheeks.

A high-pitched squealing started. It seemed to hit the sixty-year-old like a wave and his body began trembling. His skin became flushed, and he started his own screaming which could barely be heard above the Semblant.

The three detectives, stopped in their tracks, gasped and covered their ears at the same time. Clive looked at his phone and fired up *Black Dog…* He nodded to himself as the squealing noise was drowned out.

The trio were still a hundred metres away down the slope.

'Let's hurry along, guys,' shouted Clive, barely able to hear his own voice above the music. He picked up the pace. Davis and Godwin tried to keep up with Anderson while covering their ears.

George Carver's colour had become a much brighter red. While his body shook, his arms remained extended, and his feet continued to be anchored to the pavers. The squealing Semblant's gaze remained locked on to the abuser, and the shrill penetrating noise persisted. The blood vessels in Carver's neck protruded, followed by those on his cheeks and forehead, then his arms, hands, legs and feet. His cheeks shook, and the skin on his neck quivered while he continued screaming.

The three detectives came up to the side of the patio area. Lachlan and Davis were still experiencing discomfort from the noise and were a couple of metres behind Anderson.

Clive looked at the bizarre scene. He saw the monstrous looking face of a man that he thought was probably Fabian Carver. His two colleagues arrived and stared in amazement, still covering their ears.

Semblant Fabian turned his head slowly to the side, and with his glowing red eyes, glared at the three policemen. Immediately, Davis and Godwin fell to the ground. Anderson spun his head left and right, watching as they fell. He pulled out his Glock.

'Stop!' he bellowed, still unable to hear himself. He raised his gun. *Black Dog* continued blaring into his ears.

The Semblant turned back to face George and moved a step closer to him. This seemed to increase the protrusion of blood vessels, intensify the redness, and change the shaking to convulsing.

Clive took aim. 'Stop! I will shoot! Stop!'

George Carver finally felt peace as his body exploded. While his limbs remained more or less intact, his abdomen and thorax were ripped apart, sending blood, bones, and organs in every direction. Clive fired once, striking Semblant Fabian in the left side and causing him to jerk to the right. Three-quarters of George's head flew high and landed on the corrugated iron roof, then rolled down, coming to rest in the gutter next to some tall weeds. Clive fired two more rounds. A shower of blood and tissue fell from the sky, with some intestine getting hooked up on the bare metal frame lining the walkway. Other parts of George splattered here and there, some fragments of organs falling onto the two unconscious detectives. Specks of blood landed on Clive's arms. He fired a fourth shot and hit Semblant Fabian above his left ear – his head jolted to the right, then he dropped to his knees. The squealing stopped. The facial features returned to their human size, and a clearer face of Fabian Carver returned.

'Carver. What are you?' As the detective moved closer, the face altered once more.

Three motorcycles flew at speed across the overgrown property dodging from side to side to avoid large rocks and trees. All the riders had full face helmets with reflective visors.

Clive lowered his Glock and stared, as the Semblant's face went through a rapid series of changes. The bleeding head rocked from side to side as the face morphed through many identities, there were some he recognised – Johnny Randall, Medora Hammerstein, Nicholas Drakos and a missing musician Alastair McCormack. Clive gagged and put a hand on his stomach. A wave of nausea spread over him. On the ground his two companions stirred.

Steam began rising from the kneeling Semblant, increasing every moment like a kettle reaching the boil. The steam gave way to smoke, then the entire body erupted into flames.

The three motorbikes pulled up next to each other. Clive stepped back as the heat from the burning body intensified. He noticed the bikes and once more raised his gun as the riders dismounted. One rider extended a stop hand and removed their helmet. It was Geraldine Branson, from ASIO, she spun her head allowing her long dark hair to straighten and free itself from her jacket. She took a wide birth to avoid the heat, while removing her ear plugs. Anderson pulled his headset off.

'Fuck! We're too late,' she shouted. The other two ASIO officers, remained straddling their motorcycles with their helmets off. 'Anderson, what have you done?'

'Oh, I feel so sick, like I've killed many people all at once. So sorry. I saw faces. Lots of faces.'

'Yes, I know. It's all right,' said Geraldine. 'But you haven't done that. The feeling will pass shortly.'

'I was defending myself and my colleagues…' he gasped and sucked in a few deep breaths. 'Which I did… quite successfully… I might add.'

'We were so close.' She put her helmet on the ground and sat on it.

The intensity of the fire grew. It crackled and spat sparks. For a few seconds it seemed to glow white hot, then the burnt corpse collapsed in on itself. The fire flickered a little more and went out. A few swirls of smoke rose and left the pile of ash, which was all that remained.

Godwin and Davis both moved to a sitting position on the pavers, both panting and grimacing as they noticed bits of flesh on their clothing. Anderson staggered over to them. 'Hey you guys.' He squatted and alternated his attention between both men. 'Come on. You guys with me?'

"Shit. What happened?' said Davis. 'Got some mother of a headache now.'

'Oh… crap. Me too,' moaned Godwin.

'Excuse me.' Clive leant forward and flicked a bit of bloody tissue off Richard's shirt.'

'Fuck, look at me. I think I'm done with having other people's bloody bits on me.'

Clive half smiled. 'At least it seems like you're both okay. George Carver has exploded into thousands of bits. Did either of you see that?'

'I'd have remembered,' said Lachlan.

'What do you remember?'

'Just getting up here to this patio area then nothing,' said Richard. 'Shit my head hurts. Still feel a bit groggy.'

'When you're both up to it. Go down to the motorhome and check it out. Take your time. It's not going anywhere.'

Chapter 52

Grief

In the upstairs dining area, Bentley Hopkin-Jones and Roderick Peabody had been communicating, in a non-direct way, over a cup of tea and some sandwiches.

Bentley put his cup to his mouth then froze, dropped the cup and arched back in his chair, throwing his arms to the side. He squealed and cried at the same time.

Peabody looked at the distraught man. He didn't need to ask any questions. He could feel it too. Tightness in the back of his throat. A knot high in his chest. An unbearable ache behind his eyes. Legs like jelly. They both knew Sobo was dead. 'Oh my God,' gasped Peabody. He pushed his teacup forward and lay his forehead on the edge of the table. He placed an open hand at either side of his head as he panted and overbreathed. 'I'm so sorry, Bentley. This is a tragedy of immense proportions.'

The Semblant stood and moved around to Rip and took his arm, helping him to his feet. He embraced him in a tight hug. Both had their heads on each other's shoulder while they sobbed.

*   *   *

It was ten minutes before they parted and looked at one another. Both men's eyes were red from tears and distress.

'What... what do we do now, Bentley?' The Semblant just stared. 'Is it true that Sobo will have been consumed by fire?' He got a nod.

Bentley took Peabody's shoulders in a similar way that Sobo had done many times before. His deep blue eyes widened, and he squeaked twice, hissed once and clicked three times.

'You're correct,' said Rip. 'You can no longer be Bentley Hopkin-Jones. The police will ultimately connect you from your time at the Tribal Moon. As I understand it, you have several default personas to choose from…' Peabody paused and wiped a tear from his cheek. 'You have been him for so long, Kwikal. This puts even more sadness on top of grief. I feel so deeply for you.'

Click, pop.

'I wish you all the best with your new assimilation.'

Thank you, mouthed Bentley.

Chapter 53

The Mop Up

It was still just the three detectives and the three ASIO officers at the scene. At Anderson's request, Godwin and Davis had moved down the driveway to check out the motorhome. Both continued to complain of a bad headache and feeling woozy.

'We had this, Anderson,' said Geraldine Branson, as she disconnected her last phone call. 'I've called our forensic team. They will sort this mess out.'

'Sort out? What's to sort out? They're coming to gather evidence, right?'

'It's our team. They know what to do,' she replied. 'Our sole purpose for being here was to stop this happening. To detain one of these unusual people.' She walked in slow circles around the paved area, stopping every now and then to look at the ash pile and around at the scattered body parts. Branson unzipped her fitted black leather jacket.

'It would have been nice to have had the heads up,' said Clive as he displayed two open hands.

'This is a highly sensitive matter requiring a good deal of discretion. You're not going to go blabbing about this are you? Your report will need to be significantly modified.'

'Fuck off! A man has been murdered here and someone... or something has been incinerated.'

She moved to the ash pile and kicked it with her biker boots. Ash blew away with the breeze.

What the fuck!' blurted Clive. She kicked it again and again until little more than a scorch mark was left. She knelt and lightly touched four bullets that rested between two pavers. 'Still hot. You'll need to collect these slugs.'

'If you want discretion,' snapped Clive. 'You'll need to tell me what happened here.'

Geraldine moved up to him. 'We don't know exactly who they are. For want of a proper name, we call them the Quirks. Something like a quirk of nature if you like. We do know they can assume another's identity, and that they can psychically influence most anyone. I see you know some of this.' She looked at his headset and tapped her own face near her eyes. 'You came here prepared.'

'As did you.'

'You know, we could use a discreet agent up here. Someone like yourself, Clive. Firsthand experience.' She tipped her head and smiled. 'You know what to look for and you have some idea of how to protect yourself.'

'How would that work?'

'Essentially, you would only respond when you suspected something. You would contact me directly. I'm sure I could get the necessary clearance. You will be remunerated.'

'Hmm…'

'You're already in the bad books here. So, if down the track, you step on a couple more toes, no one would be surprised.' Branson reached over and took Anderson's sunglasses off.

'Best not look at my eyes. I might be one of them.'

'I'll take my chances.'

'Have you seen other cases like this?'

'I only know of one other case where they caused a person to explode. When they die, they burn up, and many faces of past identities are revealed.' She pursed her lips and angled her head. 'That's why, this time, we had high hopes of catching a live one.'

'Are they alien?'

'The jury's out on that one, but we have a leaning to them not being E.T.'

'Are there more?'

'Sure to be. Around here...' Branson glanced up and around. 'Probably not at the moment. It seems they are mostly alone.'

'Are they somehow connected with cephalopods?'

'Wow, you have been busy,' she replied with a tip of her head. 'It is possible there is some DNA connection between Quirks and cephalopods.'

'How many have you encountered?'

'Too many questions, Anderson. I've told you enough. Hopefully enough for you to understand the implications of this for national security.'

'Are they in other countries?'

'That will do... for now. You have a think about my offer.'

'I'll let you know.'

'I don't think your colleagues witnessed the actual explosion or the incineration. That will make it easier for you to write up. My forensic team will distribute some explosive residue. This man...' Branson looked up at a piece of intestine dangling from the metal frame '... has completed suicide.' She passed the sunglasses back to Clive. 'I think you may have even seen the explosives strapped to his body.'

*   *   *

It was early evening on the same day when Clive was summoned to Edwards' office. Vince and Jan both sat in the only two lounge chairs. Both had documents in their hands. Clive rolled over an office chair on castors and sat in front of them on the opposite side of a long coffee table. He looked at both their faces.

'Feels a bit like being back in front of the school principal,' he joked, as he tried to settle into the chair.

'No doubt. You were probably there often enough,' said Edwards sharply. 'Hell of a day, eh?'

'A day like none other.'

'Surprised you have this report completed so promptly. That's very un-Anderson like.'

'It seemed important that we wrap this up quickly.'

'You think we've wrapped it up?' Edwards leaned a little forward.

'The serial killer case. Yes sir. It's over.'

'There's no body. How can it be wrapped up?' The inspector edged forward in his seat. Clive swallowed.

'His heart was found in the sink of the motorhome,' continued Anderson. 'Preliminary pathology has a match. There were five daisy patterned dresses hanging in the van's cupboard. We've saved lives here. Daisy is dead, sir.'

'Don't call him fucking Daisy,' yelled Edwards. His normally pale looking cheeks had become pink. 'Where's the damn body?'

'Apologies, sir. The body is yet to be found.'

'And what about Randall's fingerprints on that playing card?'

'That's still unclear and I'll be looking further into that one.'

Edwards stood and walked around his office, moving around the lounge chairs, then behind his desk and back again. He tapped the pieces of paper in his hand as he read, and eventually stopped his stroll near the seated detective. 'It is clear, Anderson, that you went to the Upper Brookfield address because you believed that George Carver was going to be killed by his son.'

'Correct, sir. Davis is to be thanked for that.'

'You get to the residence. Fabian Carver's motorhome is there. Obviously, the guy is already dead because, as you discover later, his heart is sitting there in the sink. Then the old man walks out strapped with explosives and blows himself into a million pieces. Meanwhile Davis and Godwin have passed out from some... what...' Edwards quickly referred to the paper in his hand '...*unknown toxic gas*. They conveniently have zero recollection of what happened and just woke up to find bits of George Carver on their clothes.'

'That's what I have documented. Explosive residue was detected, and additional explosives were found in George Carver's garage. And, as also noted, there is evidence of blood on the motorhome floor. We believe that is where Fabian was murdered. And as I say in the report, at this stage the only logical suspect is his father. Forensics have recovered some black hairs from the motorhome. I feel confident they will be a match with George Carver. It seems clear to me that Fabian went there with the intention of killing his father, however, it all went horribly wrong.'

'You know that ASIO deliberately sent Silverton and Bryant to the opposite side of town,' continued the inspector. 'Why would they do that?' Jan Silverton rolled her eyes and said nothing.

'You'd have to ask them, sir.'

'I have fucking asked them, you moron!' bellowed Edwards. 'Explain to me how Carver doing this stupid mind trick with the desk sergeant fits in to this entire scenario?'

'I don't believe there was any mind trick, sir. Just a misunderstanding by the sergeant.'

'Bullshit! Bullshit! Bull-fucking-shit!' roared the inspector as he leant closer to Anderson. 'What do you take me for? What fucking game are you… ahh…' Edwards grabbed both sides of his head at the same time, letting the paperwork fall. He staggered backwards and fell heavily to the floor.

'Shit!' yelled Silverton. She was up and over to her boss. He lay there unconscious, but still breathing. 'Call a fucking ambulance. Don't just sit there.'

*　　　*　　　*

Edwards had been taken to hospital. By the time he left he had regained consciousness but was unable to speak. The gathered onlookers had moved away, leaving only Jan Silverton and Clive Anderson standing in the boss's office.

Jan walked to the desk and opened the top drawer. She pulled out two boxes of medication. 'See.' She held up the boxes. 'It's not your fault. Two boxes of his blood pressure meds, both unopened.'

'Okay. I still feel pretty shit about it.' Clive moved to the single lounge chair and dropped heavily into it and sighed.

'That's understandable, but you needn't.' Jan moved over and sat on the edge of the other and angled herself towards him. 'And I know what you're up to, Clive.'

'Huh… I'm glad someone does because I'm not so sure myself.'

'You're helping team ASIO. It's okay. I'm all good with it.' She smiled. 'You fired four shots from your service weapon.'

Clive's hand went into the pocket of his jeans. He felt the four slugs.

'I don't need to see them.' She shook her head and held up a stop hand. 'Happy to go with your story of the rogue kangaroo, as feeble as it sounds. What you have here is essentially, plausible deniability.'

'I know it looks dodgy… sorry,' admitted Clive.

'My take is that you shot and killed Fabian Carver, or at least the re-creation of him, whatever the hell that was. It's my belief that by doing so both Daisy and the mysterious mind controlling person or thing were both killed. That works for me. And while I can't get my head around the whole matter, I don't much care, you've got it and that's good enough.'

'I think the person or whatever I shot was at least one hundred and forty years old…'

'Stop! Don't tell me anything.' She shook her head. 'It's a need-to-know basis and I don't need to know. You're working towards an end with others that have some knowledge. I'm happy to cover you on this. If at any time you need extra support, I'll be here for you.'

'I appreciate that… Jan. Thank you.'

'Hmm… I am sorry you were misjudged, both by me and most others.'

'That's okay. I have cooked the books from time to time, but not with the Drakos / Galanis matter.'

They both sat quietly for a moment. They glanced and smiled at each other.

'If Vince retires, will you be applying for his job?' asked Clive.

'You're a bit ahead of yourself there.'

'Okay, if he dies will you be applying for his job then?'

Jan reached over and slapped his arm. 'Don't go saying that.' She raised her eyebrows. They both laughed.

'Godwin, Davis and Bryant have gone to the pub,' said Clive. 'Somehow Davis has found his second wind. How about we go join them?'

Jan nodded. 'Yeah,' she sighed. 'Why not.'

Chapter 54

Harmony – Part 10

Thanks to a resident entering before them, Harmony and Crystal slipped through the closing door into the South Bank apartment building. They headed to the elevator. Unfortunately, not having a swipe key, it took them longer than anticipated to arrive at level four. They had been up and down and stopped at five other levels before someone on level four was heading down and needed the lift.

'Here we are,' said Crystal. 'Are you really sure he's on level four?'

'We definitely parked in the basement car park. Pretty sure that was number four, four six. We then caught the elevator to level four.'

'Let's just go over what you want to say once more,' said Crystal using her hands and gesturing between herself and Harmony.

'Okay this is our pitch… Hello again Bentley. Crystal and I want to know exactly what happened between us at her place on Thursday night. Please don't try to trick us. We want one hundred percent honesty from you.'

'Really it's *you* that wants to know,' added Crystal. 'I'm sure I already know.'

'Yes, and I know you want that to be true. You and me having wild sex on your bed. That's not what happened… I'm pretty sure.'

'Every day since, you seem a little less sure than the day before. Maybe… if we slept together again it would refresh your memory.'

'Stop it, Crystal. That won't be happening.'

The two had discussed this at length several times. Crystal's take on the event never varied. She insisted she had never even met Bentley, let alone somehow travelled to the Sydney Harbour Bridge and to the

Sahara Desert. Harmony's position had weakened, and every time she went through it, it sounded more farfetched than the time before.

They had both intentionally dressed in casual active wear with long black tights and roomy t-shirts. They didn't wish to give any impression that they were ready to go out anywhere or do anything other than perhaps a walk along the river. They also thought that arriving mid-morning on a Sunday should give them the best chance of him being home.

The two girls stood in front of number 446.

'Well, this is what you wanted. Push that button, girl,' said Crystal.

Harmony took a deep breath and pressed the doorbell. Somewhere inside a pulsating electronic noise sounded. The girls looked at each other.

'That would annoy the shit out of me,' said Crystal. Her friend nodded.

They heard the door unlocking. Harmony was stunned into silence on seeing an attractive lady in her thirties with long blonde hair and dressed in a red kimono.

'Janine!' squawked Crystal looking over her friend's shoulder. 'What the hell?'

'Crystal,' said Janine looking around Harmony. 'What on earth are you doing here?'

'Is this the Janine that Bentley mentioned before we went to Sydney?' asked Harmony turning her head back to her friend.

'Not now, Harms,' she replied looking at her wide-eyed and with a small shake of her head. 'Are you visiting someone here?' she asked Janine.

'Yes. This is Hazel's place.' She turned her head and looked inside. 'Hey, Hazel!' she shouted. A beautiful woman with long wavy auburn hair and wearing a pink kimono appeared further down in the apartment. She waved back to the three at the door.

'Is Bentley home?' asked Harmony.

Janine shook her head. 'You might have the wrong place. Only Hazel lives here.'

'Oh, forgive me,' said Crystal. 'Janine, this is my very good friend Harmony.'

'Hi Harmony. No, I don't know anyone called Bentley. Sorry. Look, if you guys want to come in for a while, I can make you a coffee?'

'Sure. Sounds nice,' said Crystal.

'Okay,' agreed Harmony with a sigh.

*   *   *

They entered the lounge which adjoined the kitchen where Hazel made a start on the coffee.

'This is a stunning room,' said Crystal as she lowered herself slowly to the dark grey modular lounge. 'It's a bit like a show home. You know like you see in prize homes and that.'

In the centre, lying over a lush grey speckled rug, was a large square legless coffee table sitting twenty centimetres high. On top were some decorative, real looking tulips in a vase, a bottle of white wine and a fashion magazine.

Harmony looked around. If she was in this apartment she would have come through this room. Bentley would have been carrying her. She remembered that she only had eyes for him, and as she checked out the room, she was unsure about the furnishings. Then something she remembered occurred to her. 'Can I just have a cold water please, Hazel?' She got a wave and a smile in reply.

In the kitchen, Hazel opened the glasses cupboard. In front of her was six ornate tumblers with carved glass in star shapes. She filled a glass with cold water from the fridge, and for a moment stood there looking at it. She nodded to herself and took it to Harmony.

Harmony drew a sharp breath as Hazel reached forward with the glass. They looked at each other. Their fingers touched lightly as the glass was handed over.

*   *   *

After coffee and water were finished, all four women made their way back to the front door.

'Do you still think this is Bentley's place?' asked Crystal.

'No. I've made a mistake. Maybe it was six, four, four. Who knows. Anyway, it doesn't matter now.'

'See, I told you. You should listen to me more.'

'I should.'

'You and your silly dreams, Harms.' Crystal turned to Janine. 'Lovely to see you,' said Crystal, as she touched her shoulder. 'Can we catch up again sometime?'

'I'd like that. Call me,' she replied.

'Nice to meet you too, Hazel. Sorry about your sore throat. Hope it gets better soon.' Crystal gave her a finger wave.

Harmony reached out to Hazel and took her hand in a light handshake. 'Another time, Hazel.' They smiled warmly at each other.

Chapter 55

Hello Otto

A few weeks later, Peabody decided to pay an overdue visit to his old friend Otto Hammerstein. They greeted each other at the front door.

'Rip, my good friend.' They shook hands firmly. Otto used his other hand to take a grip on the undertaker's forearm. 'This is a pleasant surprise. And look, you're not wearing your deathly colours.'

'And it's good to see you not wearing your pyjamas, Otto.'

'Yes, I've felt somewhat brighter of recent days.'

'Lovely to hear.'

'Come on through. I'll put the kettle on.'

'Always very kind. Thank you.'

The two headed down the hallway of the old home.

'How's the Semblant business going?' chortled Otto.

'Hmm… Let's chat about that with a cuppa in hand.'

'Oh… I see… like that is it?'

'Can I assist you at all?'

'No thanks, Rip. I've got it.'

*   *   *

The two friends sat at the dining table.

'I should use this table more,' said Otto. 'Medora loved it so much. Did her jigsaws here when she was well. Biscuit?' Otto slid over a plate with some Tim Tams and Scotch Finger biscuits.

'Thank you.' Rip took a Scotch finger.

'You were going to say something about the Semblant.' Otto took a sip of his tea.

'You are probably the only person I can really talk to about this,' said Peabody. 'No one else I know has any knowledge of them… well at least to the best of my present understanding. There was a couple of older folks that knew, but they passed away some months ago.'

'Has something happened?'

'The Semblant that acquired Medora has died.'

'Oh shit!' said Hammerstein, a little stunned. 'I'm so sorry, Rip.'

'The thing is… there is another one on the scene.'

'Well… isn't that a good thing?'

'You might think so, but it seems to me that all Semblant are not created equal.' Peabody bit part of his biscuit and used the remaining piece as a pointer as he spoke. 'And this guy… I say guy… a term I use loosely… this guy has more of a focus on himself than others. And I believe he tends to manipulate people's feelings and even their memories if he thinks it's the right thing to do, or if it's something that may give him some pleasure.'

'Changing memories. Wow. You sure they can do that?'

'Positive. Now hold onto your seat Otto because this guy… this person… this Semblant is pregnant.'

'As in a man being pregnant?'

'No. Semblant can be either male or female. Just as Alastair changed when he became Medora.'

'Yes, of course. Silly me.' Otto scratched the top of his head.

'Now this Semblant I knew to be Bentley has become Hazel,' sighed Rip. 'Hazel is sometimes at my place. Sometimes at her own place which was, or still is, Bentley's place… apologies if this sounds confusing.' Rip threw up his hands and raised an eyebrow. 'I have come to learn that this place was gifted to the then Semblant Bentley, along with tens of thousands of dollars, by a wealthy lady. He, who is now she, as in now Hazel, visits this lady periodically, and does whatever he or she needs to do to remain her beneficiary.'

Otto sat more upright at the table. He looked at his friend. 'This sounds serious. We should do something about it.'

'Huh… what are you meaning exactly?'

Otto locked eyes with Peabody. His mouth opened and a tubular tongue darted out into the undertaker's nose.

In a bland neutral space Roderick Ignatius Peabody heard a voice. 'Hello Roderick. I am Schwix, a product of the union of Sobo and Kwikal.'

THE END

ACKNOWLEDGEMENTS

My wife Jenny, for her first read, feedback and identification of the many typos and spelling errors.

My very good friends and writing colleagues - Robin Storey and Ian Laver for their read through and valuable feedback.

A very old ABC TV series called "The Big Pull" which gave me some inspiration for this novel.

The band – Winter Valley, for permission to use the lyrics of their song "Little Crime".

Spiffing Covers – namely Stefan Proudfoot (also an author), for his superb work on the cover, and his continued correspondence on various authoring matters.

ABOUT THE AUTHOR

Bob Goodwin has been writing for many years. He is a registered nurse with psychiatric and counselling qualifications and has a background of over thirty-five years working in mental health settings, and this experience has been a major influence on his work.

He has written novels, screenplays, short stories, short theatrical plays, and one-act plays. Several of his shorter works are available on his website for free, as is a free self-help eBook for managing anxiety and stress.

While Bob writes drama and comedy, most of his work is of the suspense thriller genre. He has written eight novels, the most recent being – "The Semblant." For Bob, this latest book is a switch from his regular genre, and his first venture into Erotic Horror.

There are numerous excellent reviews of his novels on Amazon.com. & on the Readers Favorite site. Bob has managed the website StoriesAndPlays.com and the Facebook group Writers and Readers for over ten years.

Novels by Bob Goodwin:
- Strike Me Dead (2014)
- The 13th Black Candle (2015)
- Max Justice (2016) Book 1 in the Max Judd series
- Max Justice: Turmoil (2017) Book 2 in the Max Judd series
- Max Justice: Vengeance (2019) Book 3 in the Max Judd series
- The Tree of Thorns (2020)
- Ezekiel: Madman, Mastermind or Messiah? (2021)
- The Semblant (2022)

Catch up with Bob at:
http://storiesandplays.com/ ,or
https://www.amazon.com/-/e/B00JC3SHIS
https://www.instagram.com/goodonebob/
https://twitter.com/GoodOneBob
https://www.facebook.com/groups/140516869352008/
https://www.facebook.com/Bob-Goodwin-Author-989354194414457/
https://www.tiktok.com/@bob_goodwin_author?lang=en